Other Voices

Other Voices

stories

Andrew Humphrey

LASTIC
PRESS

ISBN number: 978-0-9553181-4-6

Printed and Bound by Biddles, King's Lynn, Norfolk

Cover design by Nicola L Robinson (www.thesurrealdemon.co.uk)
Cover layout by Dean Harkness
Typeset by Andrew Hook

Published by:
Elastic Press
85 Gertrude Road
Norwich
UK

elasticpress@elasticpress.com
www.elasticpress.com

In memory of mum and dad and my brother, Robin.

Sincere thanks, as always, to Andrew Hook, for his unflagging help and support. Thanks and best wishes also to Andy Cox, Trevor Denyer and Dean Harkness. And a warm thank you to Eric Brown for taking the trouble to write such a thoughtful introduction. It made my day when I first read it. Still does, actually.

Last, but not least, hand shakes, hugs and a cheery wave to all who have helped, encouraged and inspired me. There are many of you and I hope, and trust, that you know who you are.

Table of contents

Truth and Intensity:
An Introduction by Eric Brown

One of the rare delights that visit reviewers from time to time is a book that comes out of the blue, from a writer unknown to the reviewer, which not only succeeds in all the expected categories of a fictional work – good characterisation, rigorous prose, deft narrative and mature handling of theme – but which presents to the jaded palate a unique and startling voice. Andrew Humphrey's first collection, *Open the Box*, 2002, was one such.

His second, *Other Voices*, is even better.

In an age when most large publishers are playing safe with tried and tested products, and writers therefore are compromising by producing formulaic fictions – especially in the genres – it's refreshing to come across a publisher willing to produce that rarity, the single author collection; Elastic Press is that publisher, and in Andrew Humphrey they are showcasing the talents of an author whose work is bound neither by the demands of the market-place nor the safe limitations of genre. His work is hard to define: it fails to fall obligingly into the categories of science fiction, fantasy, crime, mainstream, or even slipstream, though it often comprises elements of all these. The best way to describe it, perhaps, is as gritty, psychological realism written with honesty.

One of the greatest services of fiction is to allow the reader access into realities other than their own; to demonstrate the workings of other minds, to illustrate psychologies that might otherwise remain hidden to us in our singular, locked-in view of the world. The best art and literature does this. At the same time as presenting examples of varied mental states, good fiction should also connect with the reader, giving us glimpses of the familiar, the particular, in the universal. The strength of Humphrey's brilliant short stories is that he shows us a world we would often rather not see, and does so with an unflinchingly honest eye for the seedier, cynical aspects of individual lives wrecked by misfortune and apathy and personal inability to affect circumstance. His characters are tortured by the same self-doubt, insecurity and angst that touch us all from time to time, and often haunted by past events they are powerless to change. While his vision is bleak and sometimes hopeless – and not one all of us would subscribe to – one receives the impression that it is a vision arrived at not merely as a fashionable pose, but as a fully-thought out, or felt, response to the world as perceived by the writer.

Not all of his stories are without hope, however. In two of the finest in this collection, hope is more than hinted at, redemption even suggested. In "Grief Inc", Britain is a war-torn, balkanised wasteland and Carter has the odd ability of being able to absorb the grief of others; he is a brilliantly realised character, the nature of his job and the state of society making him what he is: a man too frightened to trust in others, until the brutal events of the story force him to reassess his life. "Dogfight" has a father haunted by the spectre of his brutal, lying grandfather, while coming to terms with the death of his wife and attempting to forge a relationship with his sullen, grief-stricken son. Humphrey uses the manifestation of World War II fighter planes as a metaphor - something that, together, father and son might face and defeat. The past returning to haunt the present is the also theme of the disturbing title story, "Other Voices"; Troughton is an alcoholic cop in denial of a reality crumbling around him, haunted by the conviction that a murdered prostitute is his sister and living in fear that he is transforming into his hated, alcoholic father; in this story, the bleakness is unremitting, and hope a rare commodity.

It's frequently said, too often and too glibly, that certain works of fiction are unforgettable and will remain with you for ever; in many instances this is the lazy spiel of blurb writers. *Other Voices*, however, contains powerful stories by a writer with an original and unique vision, stories whose truth and intensity ensures they will remain with the reader long after they are read.

Eric Brown,
August, 2007.

Grief Inc

As usual the woman who opened the door was at the wrong end of middle age, mildly unkempt, her eyes shiny and blank with fresh loss. She was, Carter thought, a template for seventy, maybe eighty percent of his customers. He followed her through a shabby hallway into a bleak, bare living room. The house, too, was typical of most of the homes Carter visited these days; clinging to the thinnest thread of respectability, full of the stench of defeat and imminent ruin.

Carter stood by the sofa. The woman motioned for him to sit down. "I'll stand," he said.

She nodded. The collar of her cardigan was frayed and she tugged and fretted at the loose piece of wool. Carter wanted to slap her hand away. Wanted her to look him in the eye for once, to get to the point. Instead he forced a half smile and pointed at a photograph on the table next to her. "Is that your husband?"

She nodded again and looked at the bland, slightly blurred face in the picture, ran a hand across its surface.

"When did he die?"

"A week ago."

Carter waited. Usually the details would come easily now, whether he asked for them or not. But the woman did not elaborate. She seemed lost in the past somewhere. It didn't affect his work, how much, how little he knew. But there were conventions to observe. And Carter was mildly curious.

"How did he die?"

He expected one of the usual answers; maybe he was a conscript, killed on the Welsh border. Or he was shot by a sniper as he walked to work through the city centre. Or perhaps he was simply picked up by the Council and they went a little too far in the soundproofed cells beneath City Hall. She'd have a letter of apology somewhere and a small amount of compensation.

"He was ill for a long time. I nursed him for…two, three years? I don't remember exactly."

"Right," Carter said, surprised. "That must have been…hard."

She didn't bother answering and Carter didn't really blame her. She started to pull at her collar again and said, "How much will this cost me?"

"A hundred and fifty euros."

She looked him in the eye and didn't blink. "The Council would be cheaper."

"I doubt it. I hear they charge nearer two hundred these days."

"But I'd get a guarantee."

"True. You'd probably get a mind probe, too. Do you want them poking around in all your little secrets? They don't need much excuse to stop your benefits, pull you in for questioning."

She thought for a moment, chewing her lip, her eyes turned inward. Carter shivered. He still had his coat on but it seemed colder in this dull little room than it had outside. He pulled a Palmtop from his coat pocket. "Do you want to see some testimonials?"

"You've probably rigged them," she said wearily.

Of course he had. Web-time and live video links were virtually unobtainable these days. "Or I can just go. You can get through this the old fashioned way. I've heard it gets easier with time. A year or two and things will probably seem a whole lot brighter."

She looked at him bleakly. "Do you seriously think any of us has that long?"

"Sure. Why not?"

She shook her head and almost laughed. "How does this work, anyway?"

"Search me. It just does. I need the money up front."

She retrieved her purse from a deep pocket. She did everything slowly. Her face was the colour of weak tea, her eyes wet and accusing.

Before she handed him the cash she said, "I won't…forget him, will I? This feels a little like betrayal."

"You won't forget him. You just remember the good bits better, that's all. I take the sting away. You'll be able to sleep again, without dreaming. You'll appreciate what you had."

She nodded quickly and her eyes gained a little fervour. She gave him the money and glanced at him almost coyly. "What must I do? Should I take off my clothes?"

Jesus. Why did they always think that?

"No need for that. I hug you. That's all."

"You hug me? What good will that do? I want my money back."

He sighed. They never believed it could be so easy. They always expected, even wanted, needles, pain, some degree of suffering. "Just do it," Carter said.

"And if it doesn't work?"

"Then you haven't lost anything."

"Apart from my money."

"Well, yeah, apart from that." He was across the room in two strides and he took her in his arms. She resisted but he pressed himself against her. She was so light, so insubstantial. And she smelt too, but Carter was used to that. He'd worn his own clothes for more than a week. He caught a trace of his odour occasionally and it made his eyes water.

Then she became soft, pliant, folded against him. And he felt the usual slow warmth and tasted something dark and bitter at the back of his throat. She murmured, 'My God, my God,' into his chest and he held her, stroked the top of her head, and felt something tender, something close to love. Even though he charged for this and although he didn't actually give a shit, Carter was suddenly imbued with a tainted, accidental, sense of virtue.

She broke away from him. She looked instantly younger. "My God," she said again. She grabbed the photograph and stroked it. Then she looked at Carter and her eyes were warm and bright. "Thank you."

He gave a little shrug. He didn't take a bow. "No problem," he said. At least she'd been grateful. He hated it when they wouldn't admit it. He'd see in their eyes and face that it had worked and they'd say, 'I feel no different. I want my money back.'

'Fuck you,' he'd say.

Now the woman was still thanking him. "Good," he said. "Now I've got to go."

"Stay," she said. "I have some tea. No milk, though. But still. Stay for a while."

And there it was. The usual invitation. It almost always came. Man, woman, young, old. And he almost always turned it down.

He headed for the door. "Sorry. Lots to do."

"Come again," she said, following him. "Any time." He was at the door, out of it. "You don't even know my name." He was through the gate, onto the empty street. She was calling something to him but he hummed to himself so that he couldn't hear.

Late the next morning he met Josie for coffee. The day was cold and dull. There were more troops on the streets than civilians and Carter nodded at the ones he knew.

She was late as usual. Carter grabbed their usual seat, by the window, with a view of the ruined entrance of St Andrew's Hall. It had been firebombed two years earlier and never re-built. Kieran, the coffee shop's owner and sole employee, tried to make some small talk but Carter wasn't in the mood.

Then Josie bounded in, smiling, short of breath. "What's up with your face?" she said, shrugging off her jacket and hanging it roughly on the back of her chair.

"You're late. Your coffee's cold."

Josie shrugged. She had quick, green eyes with dark smudges under them and curly, tousled hair. She looked too young, too sweet and Carter wanted to touch her face and her small, soft mouth. Which annoyed him. "Grumpy old sod," she said.

"I have an image to live down to. You look like shit. Late night?"

"Something like that. Anyway, did you hear the news? They're going to build a wall around London."

"About time," Carter said.

"To keep out the insurgents, the immigrants. Translates as anyone with a northern accent."

"Midlands too, so I hear."

She sipped her coffee, grimaced. "This is cold. Get us another."

"It tastes just as bad hot." Carter watched a handful of troops pick their way through the rubble outside St Andrew's Hall. They didn't seem to be looking for anything in particular. A couple of them were smoking and laughing at something out of sight. Carter thought suddenly, randomly, of the gangs of teenagers who'd loitered on street corners, bored and vaguely threatening, when he was young. "The world is getting smaller and smaller. Soon it'll be every town, every city, for itself."

"You don't sound that bothered by the prospect."

"What can you do? Anyway, Norwich as an independent state? That would be cool."

"We'd starve."

"That's what they said when the borders first started shrinking. We'll be ok. Most of us."

"Those of you with particular gifts."

"Mine is a humble gift. Which makes it perfect, of course. Now if I were a Healer or a Seer…"

Josie snorted. "If you were a Seer you'd be behind that wall in London. Locked up in a luxury hotel, every whim catered for."

Carter gestured at the streets, the rubble. "Hardly repaying the investment, are they?"

"Maybe it's not their fault. Perhaps they're being misused. Pointed at the wrong targets."

"Almost certainly. Or ridden too hard, burnt out in a week or two. I'm glad my gifts are of less strategic value."

"But ample enough to line your pockets."

Carter gave her a look of mild disapproval. He liked her flashes of anger, though. The way her eyes shone stirred something inside him. "Now, now, my dear," he said, deliberately patronising, provoking. "Isn't that biting the hand that feeds?"

"I can look after myself," she said. Her expression turned sullen and he took a quiet delight in that too, the sulky softness of her mouth.

"I don't doubt it. I'm a mercenary. I'm a cold, self-centred bastard. No argument. But I pay for your accommodation, most of your food. I keep you safe, or as safe as I can, at least. Am I right or am I wrong?"

"I pay you back."

"I can get that anywhere. Without paying for it."

Her head snapped up. "Well, fuck you then. I'll take my chances." She stood suddenly and her chair fell behind her with a clatter. One of the soldiers beyond the window, his rifle at port arms, turned his gaze lazily towards them. Carter's hand pinned Josie's thin wrist to the table.

"Sit down. I'm sorry."

"Are you? Really?"

Carter found that he was. He nodded.

Josie sat again. "You're so cynical, Carter."

He looked out at the ruined street again and laughed. "Really? That's a wonder, isn't it?"

"You don't have to be that way."

He sipped some of the weak, over-priced coffee. "Do you watch TV, Josie?"

"I try not to. Wall to wall news? I'd lose my sunny disposition."

"Not the state stuff." She was right about that. Footage from the wars in Wales and Ireland. Summary executions from the Scottish border. "There's a cable channel that plays overnight. All shows from years and years ago. Most of it crap, of course. Makes me angry, how they always moaned, never appreciated what they had. Pissed it all away. But there's this one show, a cartoon, called *The Simpsons*. I like that. It actually makes me laugh. And it's prescient."

"How?"

"This guy, Homer, he wants his relationships defined. His friend Moe, the bartender, says that he's a well-wisher, in that he wishes Homer no specific harm."

"That's not funny," Josie said. "And how's it prescient?"

"It's the definition of a friend today. Someone who wishes you no specific harm. It's the best we can hope for."

Josie looked at him for a long moment. "I feel sorry for you, Carter."

"I'll accept your pity. I'll accept anything that's offered."

"And you'd better hope that you're wrong. Business will suffer."

"How do you work that out?"

"No friends, no love, no grief."

"Interesting. More death, less grief. It's true that most of my customers are from a generation that indulged in love for its own sake."

"Indulged? Jesus."

"What else would you call it? Everything is currency now. People are what they can do for you."

"Is that all I am? Currency?"

"*Honestly?*" He saw the hurt in her eyes and sighed. "Ok. Let's turn it around. What, exactly, am I to you?"

"Beyond the obvious?"

"Which is?"

"Your money, the fact you have no discernible skin disease."

Carter smiled in spite of himself. "Ah, romance. Yes, beyond that."

"I don't honestly know."

"I know, Josie. I am nothing to you. And that's exactly how it should be. We are what we can do for each other. That's all."

"Well, that's made me feel warm all over. And you're wrong. I just don't think that way. There's got to be more to things, to people. Got to be." Carter could see in her eyes that she meant it and he felt a cold premonition, a warning sweep over him. From a few streets away the tinny clatter of small arms fire grabbed the attention of the troops still patrolling the building opposite.

He leant towards her, lowered his voice. "Just remember this; keep neutral. The Council, the rebels, they're both equally incompetent, equally corrupt. Don't commit to anything, anyone."

"Where did that come from? Do I look as though I need a lecture?"

He studied her face, searched for a trace of calculation, of deceit. Just because he couldn't find it didn't mean it wasn't there.

A little later he said, "I've got to go. Work to do. Some rich bitch out on Newmarket Road."

"Hey, moving up in the world."

"Yeah, it's odd, though."

"What?"

"This girl, she's only twenty…"

"Trying to make me jealous?"

"Right. The thing is, as far as I can see, she hasn't lost anyone. I wonder what, or who, she's grieving for."

"That does sound strange. Be careful."

"I considered cancelling. But the family has money, I can charge more and anyway, I'm curious. Probably just grieving over a pet or something."

"A pet? They've been illegal, what, two, three years?"

"So has alcohol, people still drink. When they can."

"Yeah, lucky bastards."

"Speaking of which," Carter said, "if you come to mine tonight I can offer you shares in a bottle of wine and a large bar of milk chocolate."

"Really?" Her face lit up. Carter was touched by her delight. He turned his face away, irritated.

"You'll come?" he said.

"Try and keep me away," she said.

The gunfire became more persistent. A heavy machine gun joined in, its bass rattle dominating. The door opened and a youngish man entered. He wore a donkey jacket and had dark, unruly hair. His face was pitted with old acne scars. He hesitated, taking in the identity of the coffee shop's occupants. Josie returned his gaze and Carter thought he caught the faintest hint of recognition. The man walked to the counter, ordered a coffee, then said, "They've got a couple of Scousers cornered in the Cathedral." His voice was neutral, wisely accent-less. Carter sensed he was working hard to keep it that way.

"Scousers?" Carter said. "What the hell are they doing here?"

"Dying, I should imagine," the man said.

Carter looked at him. Again something seemed wrong. The answer was too smooth, almost rehearsed.

Although he hadn't requested it the stranger was served his coffee in a takeaway container. He glanced at it, started to say something, then gauged the atmosphere in the room and took the hint.

After he'd gone Carter said, "Do you know him?"

Josie shook her head. "Why do you ask?"

Her green eyes were guileless. "No reason," Carter said.

Carter hadn't been to the outer edges of Newmarket Road for many years. The house was large, detached, set back from the road, bordered on two sides by a thick line of conifers; a chunky, barbed wire-topped wall surrounded the rest of the house.

The girl who answered the door was like a throwback to the ancient television programmes that Carter watched. She was young, pretty, her hair was long and black and glossily clean. She wore make up. Her lips were a shiny red that made Carter swallow involuntarily. She smelled clean. More than clean, actually. The musky scent of her perfume overwhelmed him. Her clothes were immaculate; crisp white blouse, long dark woollen skirt.

She extended a hand toward him. "It's Carter, isn't it? I'm Val. Thanks for coming."

Her grip was cool and firm. Carter drank her in. Then he took a breath, shook himself mentally. "No problem. You've got one minute to tell me why I'm here. Or I'm gone."

"I'm sorry?"

"There's no grief here. I can smell death a mile off. All I can smell is you, Val. Nice as that is, I'm a busy man."

Val smiled briefly. "Things aren't always as they seem."

"Actually, I've found the opposite to be true. Has anyone died here? Yes or no?"

"No."

Carter shrugged, started to turn.

"But I have lost someone. And I'll pay double your usual fee. Give me five minutes? Please?"

Carter faced her again. Her skin was pale and smooth. Carter wanted to stroke it. He thought of Josie and felt a stab of guilt that surprised and worried him.

He closed the front door.

"Five minutes, then."

The living room was large and airy and pleasantly furnished. Val bought him a mug of real coffee and a little jug of cream.

"I wonder if I can guess where your dad works?"

"It's not a secret," Val said. "Loads of people work for the Council."

"He's high up, though, isn't he?"

Val shrugged dismissively, but her tone was defensive. "Not really. And he works hard. For the good of the people. Things are getting better, he says."

"Well, that's ok, then."

"Really. The M11 should be clear soon, then the shops will be full again, you'll see."

"Heard it all before, Val. And anyway, we digress. Who have you lost?"

She sat back on the sofa, pursed her lips with calculated cuteness. "You'll think it's stupid."

"Probably. But I'm not sure that matters. Money talks, after all."

"Right." Her face went blank and all calculation fled. "I've lost my lover. That's all. She is...was...everything to me. And I can't stand it."

"I see. But that's not really..."

"Grief? I think it is. It feels just like it. She has someone else now. She's dead to me." Carter said nothing. "I don't care how stupid I sound. I just want you to help me."

"You loved her, then?"

"Of course. What's so funny?"

"Just reminds me of a conversation I had earlier. What's her name?"

"That doesn't matter. I don't want to talk about her. I just want the pain to go away."

"Do your parents know I'm here?"

"It's just dad. Mum left when I was a kid. And he doesn't even know that I'm a lesbian. It wouldn't...go down well."

"Given the Council's moral stance I can't say I'm surprised. You must have been discreet."

"Very. It was a nightmare. But worth it. Will you help me? I'll give you three hundred."

"It probably won't work."

"Then it's even easier money." Carter hesitated. "Come on, it's just a hug, isn't it?" She fished the money from her bag and handed it to him. "I'm a sceptic, actually. Prove me wrong."

He stuffed the cash into his jacket pocket. They both stood. He held out his arms and she slid into them. He held her tight. It wasn't a chore. "Jesus. Carter," Val said. The same words, almost the same tone that Josie used sometimes when she came. With his face in Val's hair and her warmth seeping into him, Carter felt close to orgasm himself. He composed himself before he pulled away.

"Do you want your money back?" Carter said.

Val still had her hands on his shoulders. She seemed unsteady. Her face shone and her eyes were wide open as she stared into his face. "Shit, no. Jesus Christ. I feel stones lighter. I feel...cured. How does that work, Carter?"

"I don't know. Honestly."

"I almost wish I did men." She shook herself. Carter let his breathing slow. Val's pupils were fully dilated. He found her gaze impossible to hold. "I'm curious, though. When you hold someone, when you screw; is it different?"

Carter sank back into an armchair as he thought about that. Josie's face after the first time; her bewildered delight.

"Jesus, Carter. What the hell did you do to me?" Then, "Do it again."

But days, weeks later…

"Each time we do it you take something from me. I'm becoming less, Carter."

"You like it, though?"

"It blows my fucking mind. But still. There'll be nothing left soon." Then she'd reach for him. "Why do you pay me for this?" He couldn't answer that. Didn't try.

Val was watching him closely. He thought he could see the energy fizz and crackle around her. "No different," he said.

"Really? I might just ask Josie next time I see her."

It took a second to sink in, then he was on his feet, inches from her, close enough to smell the coffee on her breath. "What the fuck does that mean?"

"Easy."

He grabbed her shoulder. "Are you doing a number on me? Remember, if I go to the Council with this dyke stuff then that's you and your dad ruined. Or worse."

She shrugged his hand away. "Jesus. Talk about over reaction. I know your girlfriend, big deal."

"Know her from where?"

"I've trusted you. I heard you were ok. A bit of a bastard, maybe. But ok."

"Why didn't you tell me you knew her? She doesn't mix with people from this side of the city. A little above her, I'm afraid. Probably why I like her. Where did you get her name from?"

"She doesn't know where I live. Or that I look like this. Doesn't know me as Val, either. I live most of my life in disguise, remember? Josie sings in a couple of the clubs that I go to. Used to go to."

"She sings?"

Val's composure was returning now. Her eyes had become normal, her features were flat, neutral, beautiful. "Well, I assumed you knew that. Very good, too. Popular. Everyone loves Josie."

"Do they?" He thought of Josie on a stage, all eyes on her. The image wouldn't hold. "Those bloody clubs. Full of radicals, free thinkers, activists."

"People with minds of their own."

"God, I hate those bastards."

"Then you hate Josie."

"What?"

"She's the original free spirit. Surely, Carter, even you must have noticed that." Carter said nothing. He kept his eyes on the carpet. "You don't know her at all, do you?"

"I've got to go," he said.

Carter drank most of the wine, Josie ate most of the chocolate. Then they went to bed. Afterwards Carter said, "How much of you is there left now, Josie?"

"What?" Her breath was short. She had a hand on her forehead as though checking for a fever.

"A while back you said that I was making you less. Reducing you, something like that."

"I'm still here. Just about."

The wine that Carter had drank earlier tasted sour at the back of his throat. "What do you do when you're not with me?"

"Careful, Carter. It might sound as though you care."

"I just wondered."

"I sit and wait for your call." Her voice was dry, without inflection.

"As I thought."

They were quiet for a while. It was cold in the bedroom and Carter pulled the bedclothes over Josie's breasts, tugged a blanket up to her chin. "Thanks, dad," she said.

"Perhaps later you'll sing for me."

There was a small, taut silence. "Who told you?"

"A mutual friend."

She turned his face towards him. "You don't have any friends."

"Why didn't you tell me?"

"Because I knew you'd be like this. And it's none of your business."

"You've been talking about me."

"So what? Perhaps I tried to put some work your way. You've paid your dues, to the Council and the rebels. Why are you so paranoid?"

"It's what keeps me alive. I think I must be losing it, though."

"Slip through your armour, did I? You're so busy covering your back, keeping everything, everyone at arms length, you've forgotten that you're alive."

Carter put a hand on her bare shoulder. "And why does that matter to you, Josie? I pay you well." He took the hand away and gestured at the bed. "We both enjoy...this. Why try and get close? What's your agenda?"

"My agenda?"

"Those clubs are a breeding ground for..."

"My fucking agenda?" She hurled the bedclothes onto the floor and knelt on the bed, facing him. He loved the sight of her naked, in spite of her bony hips and tiny breasts. Because of them, perhaps. "You think I'm working for someone? Trying to set you up?" She straddled him, opened her legs wide. "Do you want to check for a wire? I mean, you've been pretty thorough over the last half hour or so, but be my guest." Her eyes were wild but he didn't look away from them. Then she flipped onto her front, reached a hand behind her to part her buttocks. "Go on, Carter. Have a good look. I must have something hidden, mustn't I? Some ulterior motive. In your world, everybody has one."

Then she was crying. Carter wanted to hold her, but didn't. "I can't trust anyone. I'm sorry."

"Why not?"

"I don't know. I'm old, you're not."

"And that's it?" She was dressing now.

"It's the best I can do."

"It's crap. I left someone because of you."

Carter tried to hide his surprise. "I didn't ask you to do that."

"I thought..." Josie stopped, put a hand to her mouth. She sat on the bed, next to him.

"You thought what?"

"I thought you might take me to London. Before the wall goes up. A bigger world. We'd be safe. Maybe even happy."

"This city is all I know. London is just…more of everything. More thugs, more death, more grief."

"More business for you, then." Her smile was forced, wrong. "It's not the city. It's the being with you."

The tenderness in her voice shocked him. "I'm sorry."

"Why? No guarantees, no money back." Josie's voice was brisk now, business-like. "I always knew where I stood."

She kissed him and left.

He didn't sleep. That wasn't unusual, but this was harder than he'd thought it would be. The night passed. They always did. But they rarely seemed as long as this.

The following lunchtime Carter visited the coffee shop opposite St Andrew's Hall. The streets were quieter than ever; even the usual gaggle of troops was absent. Carter had heard that a small, futile and utterly doomed uprising had broken out on the outskirts of Taverham. Maybe the troops were there; quelling it with their usual enthusiasm.

The coffee shop was empty except for Kieran. Carter didn't seriously expect Josie to turn up but he kept checking the door anyway.

He and Kieran made guarded, neutral small talk. Then Kieran said, "She's gone, then." Carter nodded. "Pity. That's half my regular custom gone at a stroke."

"Sorry about that."

Kieran washed already clean cups under a stream of warm water and said nothing. His face seemed incapable of holding an expression. His voice too, rarely altered from its dry monotone. Carter had never known Kieran to register surprise, joy, despair. He thought that maybe he was hewn from rock. Next to him, Carter seemed flamboyant.

"Did you know that Josie sang?" Carter said.

"I know nothing," Kieran said. Something tiny flicked across his face. Carter guessed it must have been a smile. "And, of course, everything."

"Of course. What am I thinking. Expecting a straight answer."

"You always were an optimist."

"Compared to you, perhaps."

Kieran dried a white mug carefully, examined it, then lobbed it over his left shoulder. It smashed on the concrete floor. "I've got too many mugs. Far too many. Perhaps I am an optimist."

"Waiting for business to pick up?"

"Something like that."

Carter sipped some coffee, tried not to grimace. "We're roughly the same age, you and I?"

"Probably," Kieran said.

"Do you miss it?"

"Miss what?"

"The old days. Technology. Aircraft. Nuclear weapons. The threat of one big, global war instead of all these stupid, endless, civil ones."

Kieran thought for a moment. "Nah, I don't miss it. I prefer things this way, I think."

"Why, for God's sake?"

A pause. "Dunno. Must be the company." His voice was bone dry.

Carter laughed, Kieran didn't. "It makes no difference, Carter." Carter was mildly shocked by the use of his name. "Whatever path we chose, we'd have fucked it up."

"That's deep," Carter said.

"Coffee and philosophy," Kieran said. "I should put my prices up."

Carter half-smirked. He thought Kieran was joking, but it was so hard to tell. "I'd better go," he said.

"Have you got a message for her, if she comes?"

"She won't come."

Kieran nodded.

"I'll be seeing you," Carter said.

"Watch your back," Kieran said.

"What?" Carter was halfway to the door, but now he turned towards to the counter.

"There's someone coming for you. Tonight. He'll kill you if you let him."

"Tonight?"

"Sorry I can't be more specific. But what time would you reckon? Just before dawn? Between three and four, say. Hardly original, but…"

"Who is it?"

"You'll find that out, won't you? But you'll recognise him."

"Who is he working for?"

"You'll find that out, too. Probably."

"How do you know this?" And at last Kieran's face did register an expression. It was pity. Carter held up a hand. "Sorry. I don't expect an answer."

"Just as well."

"And if I hadn't dropped in today?"

One of Kieran's eyebrows moved a fraction. "Then you'd probably be fucked."

Carter took a deep breath. He didn't doubt Kieran. Information was his currency. Carter felt younger, suddenly. Enervated. "Do I owe you for this?" Kieran shook his head. "Thanks," Carter said, as he turned back towards the door.

"Got to try and keep one customer," Kieran said.

The day was a washed out grey, barely cold enough to count as winter, too bleak and featureless to be anything else. There was no wind to speak of, little cloud, just the sense of things waiting, of nature in abeyance. Carter walked for a while. Past the skeletal ruins of the old library and the handful of shops clinging to life in the city centre. He didn't think much, just let a slow, cold anger build within him.

He was home before dark. He checked the inside of his flat thoroughly then retrieved his father's old revolver from the rear of the underwear drawer. He ate some soup, the gun by his right hand. Then he sat in the armchair in the living room and waited.

Carter was good at not thinking. It was a skill he'd spent most of his adult life trying to perfect. But now, when he needed it most, it deserted him. It was mostly Josie, of course, nagging at the back of his mind. But Val was there, too, and the Council, and Kieran, and the faces of all the people he'd known over the years who'd died, or disappeared, or both. The anger subsided. He let his mind wander. Either the dawn would come for him or it wouldn't. All his paranoia, all the bribes and frantic arse-covering; when it came to it, he found he wasn't that bothered how things turned out.

He nodded off for half an hour at about midnight and woke, terrified and disorientated, his tongue stuck to the roof of his mouth, his familiar room, shot through with darkness and shadow, suddenly alien to him. For a moment he expected his waking to be brief; he imagined the cold muzzle of a pistol pressed against his forehead. Then, with his wits returned and his head clear, Carter waited again.

It happened, pretty much as Kieran had anticipated, just before three-thirty. Carter heard something scrape against his front door. He stood, his mind emptying, hid himself behind the door that led from the small hallway into the living room. He listened as the lock was picked, quietly, but not quite quietly enough. He stilled his own breathing. His eyes were used to the dark and the figure that padded past him into the living room was large and male and walking in an almost comically exaggerated crouch. He waited a moment then shot the man in the back of each leg. The figure crumpled with an oddly emasculated squeal. Carter was at the man's head in an instant, his gun pressed against an eye, his knee pinning the intruder's wrist to the floor, his free hand retrieving the weapon that had spilled from the other man's grasp.

"Who are you? Who sent you? In ten seconds or I blow your head off."

"You shot me," the man said. His teeth were clenched, his voice high, incredulous.

"Well spotted," Carter said. Even in the semi-darkness the features were becoming familiar. A shock of dark, unruly hair. The pockmarks and wide set eyes. "You were in the coffee shop a couple of days ago."

"It hurts like fuck. I'm bleeding to death here. Get out of my face, man, please."

Carter stood and backed up to the light switch and turned it on, blinked down at his handiwork. "That's the carpet ruined. What's your name?"

"Tony."

"Make yourself comfortable."

Tony twisted so that his back leant against an armchair. Below the knee his legs jutted out at odd angles. The bottom half of his faded jeans were black with blood. His face, in contrast, was the colour of skimmed milk and his eyes were wide and without focus. "Just finish it, man."

"Your voice is different. An accent, or a bit of one. Who sent you?"

"What's the point?"

"People trying to kill me, it makes me curious. I'm strange like that."

"I wasn't going to kill you. Just a warning, that's all."

Their eyes met for a moment then Tony grimaced, turned his head to the side and vomited. "That's bollocks," Carter said, without heat. "I hope she paid you well."

"Not well enough, obviously." A ghost of a smile in the death-white face. "Going rate, though, for a first timer."

"Did she call herself Val? Or something else?"

"I'm nearly done, aren't I?" Tony said.

Carter looked at the soaked carpet. Tony tried to stem the flow with his hands but fresh blood pulsed through the fingers. "I think so. I must have nicked an artery."

"Nicked? You fucking shredded it, man."

"I'm sorry."

Tony laughed weakly. His eyes were less wide now and the light was going out of them. "Val. Yeah, fucking dyke."

"I thought I cured her," Carter said.

"What?"

"Nothing."

"I don't know much. Just that you were banging Josie and that pissed Val off."

"Do you know Josie?"

"Just from the clubs. Where I met Val."

"How well do you know her?"

"Just nodding terms, that's all. I saw her sing a couple of times." He closed his eyes. He suddenly looked very tired.

"Is she good?"

"Yeah, she's hot." He swallowed rapidly four, five times. "Too good for you. And Val. Too good for all of us."

Then he stopped talking. His breathing became shallow, irregular, and his head slumped to the side. By the time Carter crouched next to him and placed a hand on his chest he wasn't breathing at all.

It was almost dark by the time Carter reached Newmarket Road. In the half-light it seemed less immune to the rot and ruin that afflicted the rest of the city than it had on the day before. Or maybe he simply noticed more; the boarded up windows, a spray of bullet holes across a gable end, a trail of dried purple vomit, the corpse of a Golden Retriever at the foot of an oak tree. Sink estates bleeding into the suburbs.

He reached Val's house. He'd kept Tony's gun, ditched his own. Tony's was smaller, newer and fully loaded. He was going to kick the front door in, but he tried the handle first and it was unlocked. He pushed it open and the stench of death hit him immediately; physically and mentally. Physically, the smell was similar to one he'd left in his own flat. Cordite, blood, involuntary human functions. Mentally, the sense of fresh loss was like a punch. He reeled from it briefly, then pushed on through the hallway into the neat, ordered living room he'd visited only the day before.

Val's hair was cut brutally short. The make up had gone. Her face was pale, scrubbed far too white, her eyes were liquid, darting, searching for a foothold. She was hugging herself. She wore a sweater and combat trousers.

There was a man half-slumped in the armchair by the fireplace. Most of his face had gone. A pistol similar to the one Carter held in front of him lay on the carpet close to the man's right foot.

"Your father?" Carter said. Val nodded. "Why did you kill him?"

"What?" Her eyes swung up towards Carter's face, achieved some sort of focus. "I didn't. Well, I helped him out at the end, I suppose."

"Helped him out?"

Val shook herself and took a long, shuddering breath. "He shot himself in the mouth. Silly old fucker couldn't even get that right. Bullet went through his cheek. I had to put him out of his misery."

"Am I missing something here? Why did he want to kill himself?"

Val backed up to the leather settee, fell into it. "Carter, I thought you had your finger on the pulse. The Council is all but finished. That thing at Taverham has grown, spread. City Hall will go tomorrow, they say. They've tried to clean up the cells, destroy all the records, but...it won't be pretty."

"The rebels are winning?"

"The Council has always grossly exaggerated the extent of their forces. The rebels finally managed a shred of cohesion and found them out." She looked at her father's corpse. "He knew it was a matter of time before they came for him."

"And you?"

She gave a bitter smile. "I'm reviewing my options."

"You don't seem that surprised to see me."

"You get what you pay for, don't you? Tony was an amateur. I figured it was fifty-fifty."

"Why did you want me dead? I thought I helped you."

"That's partly why. You took something from me. When you hugged me, I mean. I thought that was what I wanted, but I was wrong. It was as though I'd never loved her. I needed the pain to keep Josie real."

"I did my job. You paid me."

"It was spite, too. And jealousy. The fact that you had her and I didn't." She gestured towards her father. "Losing him hasn't touched me. Even the ghost of the feelings I had for Josie, the ersatz grief you left me with, dwarves what I feel for him." She saw the look on Carter's face. "Hey, I never said I was a good person."

"You're lying. I can feel your loss. It's making my head throb."

Val's laugh was harsh, stunted. "You old romantic. It's self-pity you can feel. The imminent loss of myself. The stupid, random unfairness of it."

"I'm not going to kill you."

She looked at him as though he were an imbecile. "I know that. You haven't got it in you." Another nod towards her father's body. "But I'm his daughter. I'm fucked."

"You said you've lived most of your life in disguise. Why not do it again?"

She fingered her stubbled hair. "I thought of that. I've tried to straddle both worlds. But…" She shook her head slowly. "Do you have any idea how bad it's going to be, Carter?"

"Maybe not."

"If they catch me, if they find out who I am."

"I've lived in both worlds, too."

"Better than me." She dropped to the floor and scuttled across to her father's feet. She picked up the pistol.

"Val."

"What are you going to do? Shoot me?" She pressed the muzzle to her forehead. "If I fuck this up…" She closed her eyes, grimaced.

Carter turned away as she pressed the trigger.

He found Josie twenty-four hours later, on a small stage in the crypt of an abandoned church. She was finishing her set in front of a rapt audience. The song that Carter heard was sweet and trippy and incomprehensible. It moved him more than he cared to admit. Her voice, its imperfections somehow adding to its charm, raised the hairs on his arms and neck. She stood in front of a room full of strangers, dressed in a baggy purple sweater and worn leggings, emptied her heart and soul, without pretension or affectation. When she finished she clasped her hands in front of her and bowed her head slightly. Before the applause had finished he was by the side of the stage, waiting for her. When she saw him surprise registered briefly then her eyes became hooded. "You," she said.

"Talk about fiddling while Rome burns."

"What?"

"Can't you hear it? The pitched battle at City Hall. They're fighting hand to hand in the Old Market Place. Some of the Council buildings are burning. The skyline looks quite pretty from a distance."

"What do you want? The keys to your apartment? I'll get them for you."

He grabbed her arm. A young couple had come over to talk to her but they saw the look on Carter's face and moved away again. "The city is imploding. My city."

"And this is my problem, how?" She gestured at the crowded crypt. "We're all taking our chances. Maybe we'll burn. Maybe we'll get to wake up tomorrow. This is your world, Carter. I thought you'd relish it. All that extra business."

"Look, things have changed, I..." He stopped, cursed under his breath. Feelings were bad enough, trying to express them was absurd. "I've got a car. I'm going to London. Come with me if you want."

"You've got a car?" She faced him now. All hostility dropped away, astonishment replacing it.

"I've called in all my favours. Most of my money's gone as well."

"A car? And some petrol?"

"I thought petrol might come in handy. I'm leaving now. I want you to come. But I'm not going to beg."

Her smile was the widest he'd ever seen. "Beg? Shit, Carter, what are we waiting for?"

She grabbed his hand, kissed his mouth. He followed her into the cold night. He heard the low, protracted crump of a building collapsing somewhere to the east. Some gunshots, some screams. He gripped her fingers. His heart sang. He'd never felt happier.

*

It was an old Ford. Nothing special, but Josie stroked the rusted paint work and cooed over the plastic seats. Carter fought his impatience, remembered her age compared to his, all the things that he'd seen that she hadn't.

"We've got to go."

She curled herself into the front seat, almost purred. "I can't believe that you came for me."

He gunned the engine and headed, one last time, for the Newmarket Road. "I don't know if we'll make it, Josie. We'll have to take the back roads, the motorway is too dangerous and probably blocked anyway. And we'll have to walk the last ten miles or so, Christ knows how we'll actually get into London." She was still smiling and hugging herself. "I'm trying to warn you, Josie." He thought of something Val had said. "Our chances are fifty-fifty. At best."

"I like those odds."

"Seriously. I'll drop you somewhere, anywhere. No hard..."

She squeezed his thigh. "Onward and upward, Carter."

He shrugged and drove. Through Colney and Cringleford, then left into a narrow lane he remembered from years before. He let some old, almost forgotten instinct guide him, let the darkness and the country quiet envelop them, found that gradually his breathing approached normality for the first time in two days.

"This is why I could love you," Josie said a little later. Norfolk's flat fields still surrounded them.

"What?"

"You do things. You know stuff. You act."

"Am I supposed to be flattered?"

"The boys I know, the ones from the clubs, they're sweet and kind and totally ineffectual. Most of them will be dead within two years."

"I'm hardly immortal."

"But you're real. In the world. You make me feel safe. These things matter."

"Just currency, Josie. By any other name."

She started to deny that, then settled on a half smile and pursed lips. She'd used the word love, though. That warmed him. He wanted to reciprocate, but didn't know how. Eventually he said, "Back at the crypt I said that things have changed. You didn't ask how."

"Didn't I?"

He approached a crossroads and was pretty sure that a left would take them towards Thetford. He started to speak, then stopped.

"What?" Josie said.

"Do you care?"

"About what?"

"The past."

He watched the road intently, felt her eyes on his face. "Recent past, or years ago?"

"Any of it." He thought of Val and wondered what name Josie knew her by. Then pushed her memory aside. She was gone as utterly as his own parents and grandparents. He thought of Kieran, too, briefly and with an unexpected pang. He'd dropped in on the coffee shop on the way to meet Josie. The front window was shattered, most of the tables and chairs inside strewn across the street. There was no sign of Kieran. Carter noticed that all of Kieran's clean white mugs had been smashed against a wall. He found that sight much sadder than seemed appropriate.

"None of it matters," Josie said at last in an odd, tight little voice. Carter suddenly realised that she was close to tears. "Time starts now."

"I like that," he said. And he believed it to be true.

Strawberry Hill

I recognised him immediately. That's why I turned my head away and tried to usher Vicky from the counter. She'd barely finished paying for her *Guardian* and Diet Coke and she rewarded me with a sudden frown.

"What?"

I shrugged and grinned and kept my face to one side. But it was too late. He'd been standing at the sweet counter, taking his time, deliberating between Twixes and Mars Bars and Snickers. Now his head shot up. "Jeff? It *is* you, isn't it?" Then he was barrelling towards us, chocolate forgotten. "Jeff Derbyshire, as I live and breathe. It must be twenty years."

As I live and breathe? Jesus. I slotted a surprised grin into place and faced him. "Alan. I didn't notice you there. Good to see you. After all this time."

He extended his hand towards me and I shook it. It was less clammy than I'd expected. Vicky watched with amusement. "We'd better go outside," she said. "I think we're in the way."

The three of us stood on the pavement outside the shop. Vicky and I had driven to Blakeney for the day. The coast had been clogged with holidaymakers so we'd parked near the town centre and were going to find somewhere to eat. It was mid-summer, hot, the streets made glossily perfect by the strong sun and flawless sky. Vicky slid her sunglasses on. Alan held a hand out towards her. "And you must be Mrs Derbyshire?" She took his hand and Alan kissed it. "It's a pleasure.

You're far too good for this chump." Chump? "But I expect you know that by now."

"I've had my suspicions," Vicky said, her smile mirroring Alan's. "Jeff? Don't be so rude. Are you going to introduce us?"

"What? Right. This is Alan Thompson. We went to school together."

"Jeff, my dear fellow." He turned to my wife. He really hadn't changed at all. Short, overweight. Streaks of sweat leaking into his fair hair. Small, dark eyes that missed nothing. "He understates things, but then he always did. Your husband and I were friends. Firm friends. I was so sad that we lost touch."

"Me too," I said, fingers crossed. He put an arm around my shoulders. Despite the heat of the day he wore a suit and tie. In our school days he'd smelled of sweat and bad breath. Now he wore a deodorant or cologne that I didn't recognise. It smelled classy, expensive.

"So what have you been up to," Alan said. "Apart from marrying above yourself."

I ran through the handful of jobs I'd had since leaving University. I did it as quickly as I could. I was hungry. I wanted lunch. I wanted Alan Thompson out of my life again. When I'd finished he waited politely for me to ask the same question. He'd still be waiting but Vicky stepped in. "Jeff. Don't be so rude."

I sighed. "So, Alan, what have you been up to?"

His expression became smug. "This and that. I've been in sales since I left school. Got a bit of a flair for it, apparently." He nodded towards a crimson Jaguar parked nearby. "That's my car over there."

"Nice," I said.

"I'm thinking of trading it in. Get something a bit nippier." He looked at me. "No offence, but I thought you'd be some sort of big shot by now. Full of plans when we were at school, as far as I can recall."

"I'm happy," I said. Maybe I sounded defensive. Maybe I was defensive.

Vicky saw the look on my face, changed the subject. "Are you married, Alan?"

His expression changed again. "I was." He glanced away from us. "She died, I'm afraid. A couple of years ago. Cancer."

Vicky put a hand on his arm. "I'm so sorry."

"To be honest, in the end it was a merciful release."

"You poor man," Vicky said.

He patted her hand, absorbed her pity. He'd always been good at that, I remembered. "You're very kind." He looked at me again and I thought I caught a trace of calculation in his smile. "You've every right to be happy, Jeff. You're a lucky man."

"I know," I said. Vicky simpered quietly. "I'm sorry about your wife," I said. "That's hard."

He gave a small, martyred shrug. "Life goes on. Actually you knew her, Jeff."

"I did?"

"I married Sheila Pascoe."

I couldn't keep the shock off my face or out of my voice. "Sheila Pascoe?"

"Is that so odd?"

"No. No, I just hadn't heard, that's all."

"Well, University and all that. You rather lost touch with us plebs."

"Not intentionally," I lied. There was a different atmosphere between us now. "Anyway," I said, "busy, busy. We must be off." Alan and I shook hands again. "It was good to see you."

He produced a business card from somewhere and offered it to me. Vicky took it. "That's my home number, mobile, e-mail address. Don't be strangers. I'd love to take the two of you for dinner somewhere. I don't get out that much these days."

I was about to mutter something suitably vague when Vicky said, "That would be wonderful. Have you a piece of paper, another card? I'll give you our number. You can come to us. Next weekend maybe. I love to cook, but I rarely get the chance." She gave me a dismissive glance. "Beyond spaghetti bolognaise and chilli con carne, that is."

"Mr Cosmopolitan, that's me," I said.

"A home cooked meal? What a rare treat that would be," Alan said. He kissed her cheek.

"Hey, no tongues," I said. They both looked at me and I blushed. Alan walked to his car, opened it with the remote, waved again as he entered it.

We ate in a pub near the town centre. "We weren't friends," I said again.

Vicky extracted an olive from her lasagne and placed it on the side of her plate. "You were just jealous."

"With some justification," I said. We were still smiling more often than not and our voices were light.

"He's sweet. And I felt so sorry for him, losing his wife like that. Imagine how you'd feel if that happened to me."

"Don't say that, Vicky. Don't ever say that. Don't joke about it."

Her brown eyes were all innocence. She tucked a couple of honey-blond hairs behind an ear. "Who's joking? These things happen. He seemed so lonely, that's all. Maybe he needs a friend."

"How many times? He was never…" I stopped, smiled to take the edge off my voice. "Look, Alan was an arsehole when we were at school and, in all probability, he's an arsehole now. He can seem charming. He always could. He'd smarm his way into peoples lives, tag along without asking. He had money then, too. He'd use it. What friends he had, he bought. Not me, though. Nobody liked him. He smelled funny, he behaved…oddly. He was a creep, Vicky. I'm sorry he lost his wife, but it doesn't change anything."

"I see." She looked at her plate, toyed with a chip, put it down again. "Maybe you've changed as well."

"What do you mean?"

"In the last half hour. I've never heard you be unkind about anyone before. Nobody we knew, anyway. If I bitched about my sisters, my friends you'd defend them. You see the good in people, you don't judge. I've always loved that about you."

"I haven't changed."

"It doesn't sound that way."

"Alan always got under my skin. If you get to know him, you'll feel the same."

"I'd rather make my own mind up. I think we should put it to the test. Have him for dinner sometime."

I looked at her face. She looked back without smiling. "You're serious. Why does this matter to you? Maybe I should be jealous."

"Don't be silly." She looked away from me, made a face. "We're in a bit of a rut, aren't we?" I said nothing. "A nice rut," she said quickly. "But some different company wouldn't hurt. And being charming isn't a crime." I drank some wine and still said nothing. "He was bullied, wasn't he?"

"Not by me."

"Because he was fat?"

"He's still fat."

"So?"

"So that makes me slightly less jealous."

"Really?"

"I'm not proud of it, but, yes. And he wasn't bullied because he was fat. He was bullied because he was a wanker."

"Nicely put."

"It's the truth. He deserved it."

"Nobody deserves to be bullied."

"Well, I..." Then I remembered, stupidly, belatedly. "You didn't, Vicky. Shit, I'm sorry, I didn't think."

Her face was angled downwards, her hair shielding her expression. Then she tilted her head upwards and smiled suddenly, from nowhere, all white teeth and deep dimples and a tension that I hadn't realised was there dissipated. "No, I'm sorry, giving you a hard time like this. I'm partly thinking of my sister, actually."

"Mary?" I said, thrown. "What about her?"

"She's been such a pain since David left. Alan's single and lonely and loaded. Couldn't hurt to give them a chance."

Still off balance I said, "Yes it could."

Her smile faltered. "It was just a thought."

"Unthink it," I said. "Really." I shook my head, tried to clear it. "Do you want dessert?"

"No."

"Me neither," I said.

We walked to the beach and talked about other stuff. Things were soon fine again. They usually were. Married ten years we'd survived a seriously bad patch about three years earlier, the reasons for which neither of us could entirely discern. Since then we'd been...happy, to put it simply. No ambitions beyond the straightforward jobs we did and our unpretentious life together.

The day was still bright, hot, the sky squint inducing. It seemed false, somehow. The slick sheen of sunlight, the glossily perfect, blue-green sea. All surface, all charm. Like Alan. Peel the crust away and you'd find something else underneath.

Vicky picked up a pebble, hurled it in the direction of the sea. It fell a long way short.

"You throw like a girl," I said.

"Guilty as charged." She picked up another stone and threw it at me. Missed. "Bugger," she said. Then, "Are you a bit miffed?"

"About what?"

"Alan. Big car. Loadsamoney. Presumably. Him being such a creep and all."

"Compared to me you mean? Five year old Vectra, ex-council house. Swilling around the lower echelons of a local authority."

"Do you know how bitter you sound?" Actually, I didn't. I thought I was joking. "I didn't mean it like that. You said he was a loser at school. It must seem odd that he's done ok for himself."

"I won't lose any sleep over it."

"Fair enough. And Sheila Pascoe?"

"What do you mean?"

"The look on your face when Alan said that he'd married her. Who was she? Did you go out with her or something?"

She was watching me, appraising. Vicky's not complicated. She has no layers, no particular depths. If she thinks something, she says it. If she wants something, she acts. One of the reasons I love her. I kept my expression neutral. "I barely knew her. I suppose I wished that I did. Same as most of the boys in my class. She was two years above us. Different league, that's all. Looks, money, a way of carrying herself. Probably an utter bitch. None of us got close enough to find out. Alan certainly didn't. I wasn't aware that he even spoke to her."

"Well, he did at some point, presumably."

"Presumably. I still find it hard to believe that she married him."

"Perhaps he did change, Jeff. Perhaps she did." She looked at the sea and her expression became wistful. "Perhaps we all do."

Later we walked to Blakeney Quay and caught a ferry to the Point; cooed over the grey seals, watched avocets and plovers strut and feed.

We spoke little. I tried not to think about Alan Thompson and Sheila Pascoe.

As the weeks passed I thought about what Vicky had said about being in a rut and in the autumn I took her to Paris for a surprise long weekend. It stretched my budget a little but it was worth it. I didn't really take to the city but Vicky's obvious enjoyment more than compensated.

Alan Thompson seemed forgotten, by Vicky at least. He lingered at the back of my mind, though, along with Sheila. But then they always had, always would, inextricably linked as they were. Whether they'd married or not.

One day in late November I went home early from work with a headache and spent the afternoon playing Championship Manager on our PC. Vicky came home a little later than usual. "Glad to see dinner's ready," she said.

"Busy," I said. "Norwich are on the verge of winning the Premiership. I'll get us a takeaway."

She looked over my shoulder, knuckled the top of my head. "How old are you? Did you come home from work early?"

"How did you know?"

"Just call me Sherlock. Chocolate biscuits spread decoratively across the kitchen. Three different coffee mugs. It all adds up."

"I had a bit of a headache." I saved the game, turned the PC off. "Job's starting to get on my tits, actually. Thought I might look for something else."

She was in the kitchen again by now but I heard her groan clearly enough. "It's been less than two years. I thought you were going to stick at this one."

I joined her by the sink, slipped an arm around her waist. "You know me. Free spirit."

She shrugged me off. "Translates as lazy sod." She badly wanted to nag, I could tell, but she took a breath and said, "Anyway, I bumped into your friend today."

"You'll have to narrow it down," I said, although I knew who she meant.

"Alan. Saw him in the bank. He said he was going to call but you gave him the impression that you'd rather he didn't."

"Surprisingly perceptive of him."

"I felt awful. He was so sweet. Asking after us both."

"I told you, Vicky. It's all an act."

"I said you'd phone him soon. If you don't, I will."

"Jesus. If it'll make you happy I'll give him a call at the weekend."

"I'll hold you to that. And he said something else. He said ask Jeff if he remembers Strawberry Hill." I was standing by her side at the draining board, drying a mug. It was a Lord of the Rings mug. It had a picture of Frodo on the side of it. Vicky had bought it for me at Easter. I stared at it very hard and said nothing.

"Jeff?"

"What?"

"Did you hear what I said? Strawberry Hill?"

"I heard. Means nothing to me. Fat old bugger must be cracking up."

She studied my face for a long moment. "But you'll phone him at the weekend?"

"Yes. If it means that much to you."

But of course I didn't.

"I left a message on his answerphone," I said. "Not my fault if he hasn't called me back."

It was morning and we were on the verge of being late for work. "I don't believe you, Jeff."

"We're both in a hurry. Can't you just drop it?" She was standing in front of the hall mirror, fiddling with her make up. "You look fine. Do you want a lift or not?"

"I want to know what you're hiding." She still wasn't nagging. Not quite. "And Strawberry Hill. Why so defensive? I'm not totally naïve. I know why people go there. What? Did you double date or something? It was years ago. It makes no difference to me."

I breathed in deeply. I was close to anger now and that was rare for me. Being angry with Vicky was almost unheard of. Perhaps that's why she kept pushing it. It's possible to be too easy going, I suppose. "Told you. I haven't got a clue. I see that printers on St Giles are looking for someone. I might try and get an interview."

Her gaze snapped onto mine. "Printers? What's the point of that? The money'll be crap."

I'd pissed her off, but at least I'd changed the subject. "Might not be. Have to see." I brushed passed her, patted her bum, annoying her a fraction more. "Hurry up or you're walking."

She grabbed her coat and bag as she moaned at me. With Vicky distracted I could slip back into denial again. I felt happier already.

I saw him at lunchtime. I slid out of Logan's deli, my hands full of a brie and salad baguette and a chocolate brownie. He was standing outside Lingards Games with his hands behind his back, gazing at something in the window. For a moment I thought I could slip away without him noticing but he turned his head, a smile already in place, and I knew he'd been waiting for me.

"Are you stalking me, Alan?"

"You don't call, you don't write, what's a boy to do?"

"Yeah. Funny. Did you really think I'd ring you?"

He shrugged hugely, came up alongside me, stuffed his hands in his pockets. "Frankly, no. But you should have done, though."

"Is that a threat."

"A threat?" A stupid false laugh, the pitch of which dragged me back twenty odd years. "My dear chap."

"What do you want, Alan? Stirring Vicky up. All this crap about Strawberry Hill."

"Crap?" Alan said. His tone changed, sharpened. "You haven't faced it all, have you? Ever."

"And you have?"

"Fuck, yes. I married it. I nursed it through two years of cancer. I've paid my dues."

"And I haven't?"

"What do you think? You haven't told Vicky, have you?"

We were on Pottergate now. I had no idea where I was heading. "She doesn't need to know." I shot him a glance, hated the weakness that must have shown in my face. "Is that what all this is about? Blackmail?"

He snorted. "Jeff, you have nothing I want." I hesitated and he glanced at me. "No, not even Vicky. Lovely as she is."

"Jesus. You arrogant bastard. As if that was ever an option."

He started to say something, stopped, satisfied himself with a slow, smug grin. The grin pulled me back, as well. To a warm dusk on an isolated hill, and two fifteen year olds, stifling giggles, stinking of sweat, huddled behind a cluster of bushes, each pushing the other in an attempt to get a better view. "You've got to pay your dues, Jeff. Draw a line."

"And if I don't?"

"It's got to happen. For your own good."

"Like you give a shit about me."

"Fair enough. For Sheila, then. It's about doing the right thing."

"Spare me, Alan. How does telling Vicky help Sheila, you, or anyone?"

"If she loves you it won't make any difference." He nudged my shoulder and headed for St Andrews. "I'll be seeing you," he said.

"I don't think so," I said. I stood and watched him go. On the way back to the office I dumped my food in a bin.

I thought maybe the dreams would start again, but they didn't. The general, low-grade guilt that I always felt hummed along in the background, undisturbed. I slept well. I knew he'd be back at some point, somehow. I didn't pretend to face it. I took life second by second, minute by minute and congratulated myself on my maturity.

Vicky saw him next. One Friday evening she'd been vague, distracted, quieter than usual.

"Do you want to tell me what's up?" I said when friends had finished.

She stared at the screen for a moment, chewing her lip. "I feel bad, Jeff. Guilty."

I sat forward. Something in her tone made me. "Come on, love. It can't be that bad."

"Well, no. It's not really." She puffed her cheeks out. "I saw Alan today. For lunch."

"Ok."

"I called him. Arranged it behind your back. I'm sorry."

"It was only lunch, after all." I looked hard at her. "It was only lunch?"

"Yes." Almost a shout. "Shit, Jeff. But you're angry, aren't you?"

I thought about it. "As it happens, yes. I mean, why did you want to see him, Vick?"

"Hazard a guess."

Her gaze was cool, appraising. "You've lost me," I said.

"Strawberry Hill. You. Him. Whatever the hell it is you're hiding from me."

"Jesus. I don't know what you're talking about."

"Right. Mr Easy-going. Tossing and turning all night."

"I sleep like a log."

"Well, I bloody don't. And you're not eating. We don't...and you're so distracted. Your head's not here half the time."

"I'm fine. Same as I ever was."

"No, Jeff. You're not."

I closed my eyes, took a long breath. "So, did he help? Mr Charm?"

"Yes, actually." Her voice, her confidence, faltered. "Not how I expected, though. I ended up talking about my past, not yours. School. You know. Bad times."

"You talked about that stuff with him?"

"He's a nice man. He's kind, he listens, seems to care."

"Seems being the operative word."

"And don't look like that. I'm not attracted to him at all..."

"I didn't think for a minute you were."

"Right. And it helped. Talking to him. It was therapeutic."

"But you can talk to me." I tried to nudge the whine out of my voice, failed. "Those things are between us. At least I thought they were."

She shrugged. "It helped. I'm sorry if that hurts you."

"I'm not hurt," I lied. "Just bewildered."

"Me too." Her voice became even, the defensiveness fled. "You were friends, weren't you? Despite what you said."

"Of sorts."

"You were both misfits. Friends by default."

"That's stretching it a bit." I stared at the television. Graham Norton was on. Christ knows what he was talking about. He seemed to find it funny, though. "Although maybe not that much. He was a creep. Maybe I was too. It was a long time ago. As you said, we all change. Thank God."

"So why lie about it?"

"Why not? It's ancient history. No use to anyone." I felt her eyes on me. I hesitated then went on, "And I didn't want you to know what I was. Jeff the creep. I've kind of airbrushed it out of my history. It was my mum's fault, actually. She made me wear shorts on my first day at the Comprehensive." I closed my eyes, remembering. "God, I was crucified. And that was all it took. After that I was a joke. So I worked hard, kept myself to myself."

"And Strawberry Hill?"

"What about it?"

"Alan wouldn't tell me. He said that was up to you." Her voice was gentle now. Showing me a sympathy I didn't want or deserve. "What did you do, Jeff?"

"I didn't do anything." Which was kind of the point, actually. "I was fifteen. *We* were fifteen."

Vicky waited for me to continue. I didn't. A little later we went to bed and made love. It felt as though a sheet of glass had been slid between us.

Sunday, just after lunch. I help Vicky wash up. I can't stand the strained politeness, the miniscule differences, the inability to look each other in the eye. I toss the tea towel onto the draining board and make a phone call.

"Who was that?" Vicky says. Her hands are still wet, the sleeves of her blouse rolled up to the elbow.

I point at the kitchen. "Leave that. We're going out."

"Why?" she says. "Where?"

"You'll see. Just humour me, Vicky. Afterwards…well, I haven't got a clue about afterwards. If there will even be one."

"You're scaring me," she says. But she doesn't sound scared.

We drive to Alan's house in silence. He's waiting for us at the corner of his road. He's wearing a lemon roll-neck and a burgundy fleece and stands out against the drabness of the day.

He slides onto our cramped back seat with surprising agility. "Hi, kids," he says. The smell of him washes over us. Something warm, spicy, a hint of sandalwood in it. "How's tricks?"

I say nothing. Vicky nods slightly then says to me. "You could just tell me. There's no need for this."

I know that she's right so I keep my mouth shut and drive.

Alan tries to make small talk. It's trite, predictable, but Vicky thaws a little anyway and I add this to my resentment. Then Vicky says, "Who was Sheila Pascoe? Really?"

"My wife," Alan says.

"Before that," Vicky says.

There's a pause. I glance in the rear view mirror but Alan's eyes are fixed on the roadside as the city gives way to hedgerows and fields. "She was the school bike," I say at last.

"Nice," Alan says.

"Jeff."

"It's true," I say.

Eventually Alan nods and says, "It's true. She worked her way through most of her year. Most of ours as well, actually. Except me and handsome, here. Wouldn't touch us, would she?"

I said nothing. I felt my cheeks burn. Vicky says, "But you tried?"

"Of course we did. A couple of horny fifteen year olds? And God knows she encouraged us. Flirted. Teased."

"She was good at that," I say.

Vicky twists in her seat. "You did something to her, didn't you? The pair of you..."

Alan says softly, "We didn't rape her, Vicky." Then, to me, "See, this will be easier than you thought."

Vicky looks at me. I study the road. "Nearly there," I say.

Strawberry Hill. Five miles from the city outskirts. A shallow hill coated with brief wooded areas, odd shaped meadows, secluded grassy banks shielded by shrubs and bushes. It attracted what you'd expect it to attract. Lovers, prostitutes and their charges, dog walkers, peeping toms.

I park the car and we walk up a mild incline. The day is cold, still, neutral. I remember Sheila at break time, leant over me, a hand on my shoulder, her mouth next to my ear. The smell of Juicy Fruit chewing gum and my eyes widening at her warm, wet breath as she described what she'd been up to the evening before. I didn't understand most of the words she used, but I didn't need to. The tone, the timbre of her voice did it, and the proximity of her lips, her tongue. She did the same to Alan. We'd talk about it, discuss what we'd like to do to her.

The going gets slightly harder now as the hill steepens. The path narrows. "Did you take her here?" Vicky says. Her eyes are wide.

"Someone took her here," Alan says. "We followed."

"Why?" Vicky says. She looks at me, but it's Alan who speaks again, his voice even, unconcerned.

"She told us she had a hot date. With a real man. Someone older. She taunted us with it, as usual. Said they were coming out here, she'd tell us all about it later." He looks at Vicky. "She was a real bitch." Vicky looks away. "Yeah, we followed. We wanted to watch."

"We got a lift with my dad," I say. "He was on his way to Easton, for cricket practice. Told him it was something to do with a school project."

Alan stops. "We're close," he says. He points at a copse. "There."

We walk up to the copse. It hides a cluster of bushes, some trees, a small hollow.

"We followed them here and hid behind those bushes," Alan says.

"And you watched them?" Vicky says. She looks puzzled. "That's a bit sick. But...well, I thought it would be worse, somehow." She almost smiles. I close my eyes.

When I open them Alan is looking at me. He looks younger, sad, vulnerable. For a moment I almost feel something for him. Almost. I remember the weather that day; the sky, a cloudless, static blue. The glossy perfection of it. I don't trust days like that. Scratch at the seams a little, peer beneath the surface, see what you find underneath.

"She was raped," Alan says.

"What?" Vicky says. I look away.

"They were arguing when we first saw them. He was shouting, pushing her, she was close to tears." He points to a large oak at the edge of the hollow. "He shoved her against that tree, slapped her face, pinned her against it. The first time was very quick and I don't think we knew what was going on. But..."

"The first time?" Vicky says. "How many..."

"How many times?" Alan shrugs and looks at me nonchalantly and I hate him again. "Jeff? Want to come up with a figure? Ballpark?"

"Jesus, Alan."

"Lost count, to be honest, Vicky. He was persistent and inventive and he had considerable stamina. It must have gone on for almost an hour."

"And you just watched? Both of you?"

"We were fifteen," I said, "he was..."

"Late thirties, forties maybe. But he wasn't a big guy. And we weren't small for our age. Don't make excuses, Jeff." He looks into my face but his eyes drop quickly from mine and I know that there's something he won't admit, despite his apparent frankness. It's something that I'll never say either; that we enjoyed it. The rawness of it, at least for a while, after the initial shock and until Sheila's first screams had subsided to a series of low, racking, sobs that touched even me. Not enough that I actually did anything, though. But I had an erection most of the time we hid there and that night I masturbated repeatedly. I'd bet anything that Alan did the same.

"We could have gone for help, at the very least," Alan goes on. He takes a long breath. "But we didn't. We crouched behind that bush and watched Sheila struggle and listened to her scream. And just before the end she saw us, looked us both in the eye. And gave up. A little later he left her there. So did we."

"My dad picked us up. Bought us fish and chips on the way home. We didn't report it and neither did Sheila. She was off school for a bit, the rumour was that she'd got herself pregnant."

Vicky has her hands in front of her face, maybe she's crying. I make no effort to comfort her and neither does Alan. She rallies a little, stares at Alan's face. I wonder if she finds him quite as charming now. "And yet she married you?" she says.

He makes a face, looks down into the hollow one last time then turns away. "She was ill when I met her. Bumped into her in a pub a few years back. She tried to ignore me at first." He nods in my direction. "Much like you did when I saw you in that newsagents. It turned out she needed me. Maybe we needed each other. After school she..." He winces as he searches for the right words. "She had a hard life. She looked so old, worn, half dead already. She had no one. She needed my help. I was glad to give it, I found I came to terms with what I did. Rather, what I didn't do. In the end we almost loved each other. I think."

Vicky and I say nothing. She hasn't looked at me for a long while now. Eventually she says, "Are we done?"

"Yes," I say slowly.

"Can we go, then? I'm cold."

"Go home?"

"Where else?" she says. Our eyes meet. Beneath the shock and the thin sheen of hurt I see reams of calculations unfolding. Vicky, who I'd thought had no depths, no hidden layers, is working out the cost of things, sifting through the implications.

She turns and walks ahead. Alan comes alongside me and says, "See. I told you. If she loves you it'll be ok." His voice is at once warm and bitter. Quite a trick.

Vicky drives back to Norwich and none of us speak. We drop Alan near his home and Vicky accelerates away almost before he's shut the car door. The last I see of him is his back and that shrinks quickly as Vicky slides through the gears.

Other Voices

The telephone woke him. He pulled his watch off the bedside table and peered at it as he waited for the fluorescent dial, the numbers, to mean anything. The phone kept ringing and his wife slept on. "It's the phone, Helen," he said, his voice thick with sleep. She didn't stir. Why should she? It would be for him, obviously, but he resented it. Not the call so much, merely that she could sleep on and he had to think about work at a quarter to five in the morning.

He picked up the receiver. A torrent of words hit him before he could speak and he understood most of them.

"Where?" he said during a pause. Then, redundantly, "What, now?"

He put the phone down, lay on his back and stared at the ceiling. He hadn't had a drink for the best part of a month, yet his head throbbed and his mouth tasted of stale whisky. "Fuck," he said, then kicked Helen under the covers, feeling her fleshy buttocks against his bare foot, and then a sudden, unexpected stab of arousal. He resented that as well. She stirred, but didn't wake. "Bitch," he said and stumbled out of bed.

The body had been found in an alley close to the city centre. It was a fifteen-minute drive from the outskirts through deserted streets. The dawn was blue-grey. The air, fetid through over-use, felt as though it belonged to the previous day. It was late-summer and the season was ready to change. Troughton would welcome autumn, its fresher air and muted light.

He parked on a double yellow and walked towards a PC who was taping off the crime scene. Troughton flashed his card. "Is Fisher here yet?"

The PC, who Troughton knew but couldn't place, glanced up at him, met his eyes then let his gaze drift past Troughton's left shoulder. He turned.

"You took your time," DS Fisher said. He was immaculate in a charcoal suit. His freshly shaved jowls shined pinkly and he smelled of cologne that was too expensive for Troughton to recognise.

"Good to see you, Frank. Have you been here all night? Perhaps you're a suspect."

"Funny," Fisher said. His nose wrinkled. "Have you heard about that stuff they have these days, Steve? Deodorant, they call it. And toothpaste. You should give them a try, mate, you really should."

"My sides are splitting." Troughton was suddenly aware that he was wearing the same clothes that he'd worn the day before.

"Who says I'm joking?" Fisher said. "Actually, you look a wreck. Rough night?"

"I haven't had a drink for weeks."

"Who mentioned drink? I just..."

"Where is she?" Troughton said. He turned away from his colleague and looked across at the old market place. It was brighter now and new sunlight was picking out colours on the multitude of awnings. There was no breeze. A solitary refuse lorry pulled into The Walk, its engine sounding abnormally loud in the silence.

"This way," Fisher said. They were standing outside a restaurant. An Italian place. Troughton had taken Helen there for one of their anniversaries. He couldn't remember which one.

He followed Fisher into the gap between the restaurant and a Building Society. Another, wider alleyway ran across the back of the buildings. Two bright orange industrial wheelie-bins stood against the restaurant's rear wall. A pair of small bare feet jutted from between the bins. Fisher stood over them and pointed. Troughton stood where he was for a moment and stuck his hands in his pockets.

"Squeamish?" Fisher said.

"You know I'm not." He searched his pockets for some chewing gum but couldn't find any. "Is she naked?"

"Yep."

"Hooker?"

"What are the odds? Not that I'm jumping to any conclusions."

"As if you would. Who found her?"

"Homeless guy. This is his pitch, apparently."

"Cosy."

"He called it in on his mobile."

"His mobile?"

"Everyone's got one these days, Steve."

"I haven't." Fisher didn't say anything. He just stood by the body and waited. He was tall and good-looking in a corpulent kind of way. Troughton didn't like him. The feeling was mutual. This wasn't unusual amongst people that Troughton knew. "Where's the tramp?"

"Puking up around the corner. Collins is taking his details."

"Pretty public spirited, calling it in."

"I suppose. He's still a suspect, though."

"Of course," Troughton said. He walked towards the body. As he grew closer he noticed a tattoo of a bluebird on the girl's left ankle. He stopped.

"What?" Fisher said.

"Give me a minute, will you, Frank?"

"Why?"

"Just give me a fucking minute."

Fisher shrugged and searched in his jacket pocket for his cigarettes as he wandered towards the mouth of the alley.

Troughton swallowed hard and stepped forward. She was lying on her front, wedged tightly between the wheelie-bins, her face buried in a pile of black plastic rubbish bags. Her arms were tucked underneath her. Her hair was blond with dark streaks, matted against her skull. The skin on her back and legs was pale and unblemished.

Troughton pushed the bins apart and she sagged forward, freeing an arm. He manoeuvred her onto her side then bent forward and cradled her face in his hands. Her mouth and eyes were open.

He heard Fisher's quick footsteps. "What the fuck are you doing? SOCO will be here in…"

"I know her."

"What?" Fisher said.

"She's my sister," Troughton said.

*

He was in Detective Inspector Dryden's office. It was late morning and through the tinted window he could see the bland, cloudless sky and the hands of the clock on City Hall, stuck on 11.50, just like they always were.

Dryden was looking at him. Troughton was aware that the older man had spoken a moment ago but he had no idea what he'd said. Dryden coughed. He was expressionless, his greying hair neatly cut, his shirt and tie immaculate.

"I understand this must be difficult for you." He didn't sound as though he understood or as though he particularly wanted to make the effort to. This was fair enough, Troughton thought. If the situation were reversed, he wouldn't pretend to give a shit.

"Yes," Troughton said. He felt hung-over. This was unfair, but he was used to it. Troughton had never been drunk in his life, but he often woke stinking of booze. By mid-morning some days he'd be running with sweat; swollen, amber-coloured drops, they'd ooze between the hairs on his arms and smell and taste of whisky.

"There's no record of you having a sister," Dryden said.

"I haven't now, have I? She's dead."

Dryden puffed out his cheeks and glanced at the computer screen in front of him. He made a couple of rapid mouse strokes. Troughton wondered what he was doing. Selling some shares? Downloading some porn? Who could tell.

"You've been given considerable leeway here, haven't you, Steve? All things considered. Given your appearance sometimes, your unpopularity and tendency towards violence. Not to mention your drinking." Troughton closed his eyes. "If it wasn't for your father's memory, I doubt you'd still be here."

There it was again. His father. The shambling drunk who'd become an accidental hero when he'd fallen in front of a robber's shotgun during a bungled bank raid.

"I worked with him for twelve years. I consider it a privilege," Dryden said. Troughton said nothing. There was a photograph on the wall behind the older man that showed Dryden shaking hands with a former Norwich City manager. Troughton stared at that. His dad had taken him to the football once with some of his colleagues. His father had made a fuss of him during the game, ruffled his hair, showed him off to his friends. When they got home he'd beaten him with a coat hanger.

"In all those years he never mentioned a daughter. Don't you think that's strange, Steve?"

"Not really," Troughton said. "She left home when she was very young. The old fucker was probably fiddling with her."

Dryden's face went white. "I won't have talk like that. Your father was a hero. He was decorated, for God's sake..."

"For stupidity."

"That's enough." Dryden stood. "What would your mother say?"

That was a good question. Troughton had once watched his father pin her to the wall and punch her methodically in the face until she'd dropped to her knees in front of him, weeping and spitting out teeth. Now her house was a shrine to him. Go figure, as the Americans say.

"I just want to find my sister's killer."

"You never had a sister. Take a holiday."

"I don't want a..."

"Take a fucking holiday." Dryden closed his eyes, composed himself. "You don't look...well."

"I'm fine."

"You're quite obviously not. You stink of booze, for Christ's sake. Again."

"That's not..." Troughton's voice faltered.

"Not, what? Fair?" Dryden stared at him. His eyes were very blue and Troughton could see tiny brown flecks circling in their depths. He hoped they were the precursor to some unpleasant disease. "Holiday, Steve. Four week minimum. Do you understand?" Troughton nodded slowly. "Good. Now, fuck off."

He did.

When he got home the house was empty. He called his wife's name a couple of times then ran upstairs. Helen's clothes had gone. He stared into the empty wardrobe for several minutes as though he didn't understand what it meant.

Downstairs he dry swallowed a couple of aspirin and dialled Helen's sister's number. The line was engaged. He drank some water and took some more tablets. He tried the telephone again, with the same result. He threw the receiver against the wall. Then he sat in the kitchen and waited.

He was asleep when Angela called. His head throbbed. He thought the noise he could hear was the telephone but when he went to it he saw that the receiver was on the floor. The front doorbell sounded insistently. He opened the door and let his sister-in-law in.

"What's the time?" Troughton said.

"Just gone eight. I tried to phone but the line was dead." Angela was taller and prettier than her sister. Troughton was pretty sure he'd had an affair with her several years ago. "Helen was worried."

"Really?"

Angela shrugged. "A little. She thought you might have done something stupid. Didn't want you bleeding over the carpet."

"I think she's flattering herself a little."

"I said you weren't the type."

"Why did she leave?"

"How long have you got, Steve?"

"Why now?"

"That's a good question. Do you remember kicking her as she slept, calling her a bitch?"

"That? I always do that. It's just a joke."

"You're a funny man, Steve."

"So I'm told."

They looked at each other for a moment. "You can't be surprised," Angela said, her voice a fraction softer. "This has been coming for years. Look at the state of you."

He stood and peered in the kitchen mirror. His face and hair were slick with sweat. "I think I've got a virus."

"A virus? Right."

"I don't drink, Angela. Helen has never seen me drink."

"No, she's just seen the results. I'm a counsellor, remember? I know how secretive addicts can be. Get some help, Steve."

He sat again, heavily, remembering. "I saw my sister's body today."

"Sister? What sister?"

"Her name was Carol. She left home when she was twelve. We

never mentioned her again. She got in touch six months ago. We met for coffee a couple of times. I gave her some money. She didn't say she was on the game but it wasn't hard to work out. I recognised the tattoo on her ankle."

"Tattoo? What the hell are you talking about, Steve?"

"She said she couldn't understand why I didn't go after her. I didn't know what to say. I just gave her some more money. She said she still loved me, though. Just me. No one else. Poor little bugger."

"Get that help, Steve. Soon."

Troughton looked up and tried to blink Angela's face into focus. "Is Helen coming back?"

"I don't think so."

"Whatever."

"That's all you've got to say?"

"I don't want her getting the idea that I actually care."

Angela held his gaze for almost a minute. "Do you remember when you beat that guy up?"

"You'll have to narrow it down."

"The one in the sports car, years ago, beeped at Helen as you walked together in the city. He leered at her and she smiled back. You memorised his registration number, found out where he lived, went round there after dark and beat the shit out of him."

"I remember."

"She loved that. She gave you hell, didn't she? But I remember her face as she told me about it. She got off on it. This isn't all your fault, Steve."

"What are you trying to say?"

"I've got no idea."

He nodded, then looked into Angela's face and his eyes narrowed. "We did fuck once, didn't we?"

Angela smiled briefly. "You sure know how to make a girl feel good about herself." Troughton didn't say anything. "Anyway, there's some stuff that Helen wants. It's in the cupboard under the stairs, she says. Pictures of mum and dad, cards, letters. Can I get them?"

"They'll need sorting out. I'll do it, you can fetch them tomorrow, the day after."

"Ok. Thanks."

"No problem."

"I'm off now. Any message for Helen?"

"No."

Angela waited for him to continue but he didn't. She nodded slowly, turned and left.

After a while Troughton retrieved a box from the cupboard, tipped its contents into a black plastic bag, took them into the garden and burnt them.

Just after ten he drove to a pub that he knew was Fisher's local. He found him sitting in a dark corner, speaking to a blond girl who looked to be about half his age. He tapped Fisher on the shoulder. "Have you got a minute, Frank?"

The girl glanced up into Troughton's face, her expression startled, guilty. Whatever she saw there, she didn't seem to like it much. She stood quickly, banging her knee on the table, gathered her cigarettes and lighter, touched Fisher's arm and said, "Call me. Ok?" She didn't wait for an answer.

Troughton took her place. "Good timing," Fisher said.

"I've probably saved you from a world of pain. She's a bit young, isn't she? Even for you."

"And that's your business, how?"

"Just looking out for a mate."

Fisher snorted. "We don't even like each other."

Troughton fiddled with a battered beer mat. The pain in his head was continuous now, his vision tinged with red. "You're the closest thing to a friend that I've got."

"Jesus, Steve. You're in more trouble than you thought."

"Have you ID'd the girl yet?"

"I'm not supposed to be talking to you."

"Have you?"

"No."

"I told you who it is."

"Don't start..." Troughton slid a piece of paper across the table. "What's this?" Fisher said.

"All I can remember about Carol. Date of birth, her first couple of schools, stuff like that. I'm going to see mum tomorrow, see if she's got her birth certificate. Just check it out, will you?" Fisher looked at him blankly. "What have you got to lose? Just humour me. Please."

After a moment Fisher shrugged and slipped the piece of paper into a jacket pocket. "I'll see what I can do."

"Thanks," Troughton said. Then, "What? What are you looking at?"

Fisher was leant forward, staring at him. "Your eyes."

"What about them?" Troughton put a hand to his face.

"Are you wearing lenses?"

"No." Troughton blinked rapidly, involuntarily.

"It's just that they've changed colour. Not that I've ever looked that closely. But they were blue, right? Or green. Something pale, anyway."

"So?"

Fisher shrugged. "Go to the bathroom, look in the mirror. It's weird, that's all."

Troughton stumbled to the bathroom. Every bit of him hurt. The sight of his reflection made him flinch. The pinched, white cheeks and bloodless lips. He looked into his own eyes and his breathing stopped. They were a rich, chocolate brown. The same colour as his father's eyes.

His mother seemed smaller than ever and far too old.

"It's early, Steven," she said when she finally opened the door.

"I couldn't sleep," he said.

She peered at him myopically. "It's funny, when the doorbell woke me I thought your father had come back."

"God forbid," Troughton said. "Can I come in? I've got something to tell you."

His mother stood aside and he squeezed past her. It was a small hallway in a small house. "It's four-thirty in the morning, boy."

"I know. I'm sorry." He headed for the kitchen, avoiding the living room. He wasn't sure he could stand it, the dozens of photographs of his father, the walls crammed with newspaper cuttings from the week or two following his death.

Happy days, Troughton thought. The sudden, exhilarating freedom. He'd expected to see his own happiness mirrored in his mother, but it wasn't to be. She'd turned inward, re-invented the past, himself, his father.

"You'll have some tea?" she said, joining him. She moved so slowly he thought he could feel time thicken, solidify, allowing the past to rush up and join them.

"It's Carol, mum. She's dead." He spoke quickly, trying to break the spell.

His mother filled the kettle, plucked a teapot from the depths of a cupboard. "That's sad, dear. Who's Carol?"

"Come on, mum. Your daughter, my sister."

She turned to face him. Her eyes, behind the pebble glasses, were milky and indistinct. "Do you still take sugar, Steven?"

"I've never taken sugar."

"You had a very sweet tooth as a boy."

"You're not senile, mum. Stop pretending to be."

She switched the kettle off before it came to the boil. "I think you should probably leave now."

"Why?"

"Because I expect in a minute we'll get to the bit where you badmouth your father. I don't want to hear it." She was quiet for a moment. She smelled of hand-cream and lavender. "I'm sorry about your friend."

"My friend?"

"I'm old and tired and I don't..." She stopped abruptly, her head cocked as though listening for something.

"What?" Troughton said. They stood in a silence that wasn't silence. He was aware of whispers, traces of other voices, echoes of people, lingering. He felt a tug at his shirtsleeve and turned and stared at empty air. "I'll go then," he said.

"It's for the best." Then, in a voice that was suddenly younger and quicker, she said, "You look awful. You should take more water with it, as your dad used to say."

He almost ran. Time was different here, he thought. He could feel it distort, fold in on itself. He imagined himself caught in its creases.

He slept until midday and it was Angela who woke him. He let her in then ran to the bathroom and washed without looking in the mirror. When he joined Angela in the kitchen she'd made them both coffee.

"The rumpled look suits you, Steve," she said.

"What colour are my eyes?" Troughton said.

"What?"

"Just humour me. Please."

She moved a little closer. "The usual insipid blue. Why?"

"Just wondered. I went to see my mother this morning. At least I think I did."

"You think you did?"

"Maybe I just slipped into the twilight zone."

"You're not making much sense, Steve."

"How's Helen?"

"Fine. I came to pick up her stuff."

"I couldn't find the box."

"I'll look for it."

"In a minute." He drank some coffee and looked at her. She was wearing a thin floral blouse, tight jeans, just the right amount of make up. The smell of her perfume seeped into his coffee and he imagined that as he tasted it he was tasting her. "I feel a little better. My head seems clearer, at least."

"Good," Angela said.

"Perhaps it was a virus."

Angela's head tilted to one side and her expression changed. "Helen told me about the doctor's, the tests you had."

"So?"

"He said you had the liver of a man twice your age, that if you didn't stop drinking you'd be dead inside ten years."

"He was wrong." Troughton's voice was flat. "I don't drink. I've never had more than the occasional pint or glass of wine. I grew up with a drunk. I learnt my lessons."

"You told the doctor that?"

"I told him I'm being haunted by the ghost of my father's addiction."

"What did he say to that?"

"Nothing. He just looked at me for a long time."

Angela finished her coffee and stared into the empty mug as though it could tell her something. "I think Helen's going to want a divorce."

"Ok."

"As easy as that?"

"No. I'll fight it."

"Why?"

"Why not?"

Angela took a breath and seemed to shake herself mentally. "I'll look for that box."

"No need. I burnt it."

"Why, Steve?"

"Because I'm a bastard."

"There's got to be more to it than that." There was a kind of empathy in her voice that he hadn't expected and he turned away from it.

"No there hasn't," he said.

After Angela had gone he slept for six hours. Then he showered, shaved and dressed in clean clothes. He ate some soup and drank two pints of water. He felt lighter, younger. The pains in his kidneys and chest and head had gone. He walked for two hours through cooling air and soft, dying light. He read a little, then watched TV without his attention sliding from the screen. He went to bed at eleven and his sleep was unbroken and dreamless.

He woke at eight, refreshed. He sat up, stretched, yawned. Carol sat on Helen's side of the bed. She was naked with her back to him, looking into his face over her right shoulder. Her head shook. Her eyes were wide, her mouth locked open in a scream that he couldn't hear. He blinked and she was gone.

He ran to the bathroom, washed his face and looked in the mirror. His hair was slicked back with sweat and his eyes were brown.

He called Fisher from the telephone in the living room.

"What?" Fisher said.

"I thought you'd be in touch."

"You don't read the papers?"

"What are you talking about?"

"It was the lead story in last nights Evening News. We identified the girl. Dawn Thomas. She's from Glamorgan, ran away six months ago. She's been living rough. Her mum identified her yesterday."

"This is wrong."

"Tell her mum that. And we don't think she was murdered. It was a heroin overdose, but probably not deliberate. Someone panicked and dumped her. We've got a few leads."

"It's Carol."

"Carol who?" Fisher's voice had been toneless throughout and it didn't waver now. "I did some checks. You've never had a sister, Steve."

"That's not true."

"Yes it is. It's what we call on the Force, a fact." Now his voice did soften. "You've still got some credit here, Steve. Or at least your father has. You can still get some help here, when you come back."

Troughton broke the connection.

He stared at the telephone for some time. When it rang he almost screamed. The tone seemed different somehow, deeper maybe, and the handset seemed to yearn towards him, vibrating with need, begging him to pick it up. He didn't touch it. He knew whose voice he would hear.

He heard a door close in the room above him. The footsteps on the stairs were soft and quick; bare feet, probably a woman. He turned towards the door. It didn't open. Someone sighed. It was daylight outside but the room was dark and rich with shadow. Beyond the window, inches and miles away, rain fell so softly it was almost subliminal.

Old Wounds

Five years ago

It was snowing when we reached the hotel. It wasn't yet settling, but the air and the dying light had an odd ethereal quality and the flakes that gathered in our hair and on our shoulders were getting bigger by the minute.

"It's kind of romantic, isn't it?" Ellen said. I searched her face for a trace of irony, but found none. I pressed a button on my key ring and our BMW sealed itself with a squawk.

"I hope it doesn't lay," I said. "It'll be a bastard driving back tomorrow."

"Jesus," Ellen said. She closed her eyes, bit her lip. The failing, lemony light suited her; accentuated the positives in her even features, hid the lines that lurked in the shadows. I suppose she was entitled to the lines, had earned them, even. She was in her late-forties, same as me. "We don't have to be here. But we all agreed. All. That means you too, Jack."

"I know, I know." Something akin to excitement bubbled in the pit of my stomach. I scanned the car park for Danny's Volvo, couldn't find it. "We're early, though. I said we'd be early."

I heard the sigh before it came, sensed the timbre of it. I wondered how many thousands of times I'd heard it before. "We'll go in then, shall we? Unpack, have a drink. Relax. You know that word, do you,

Jack? You're familiar with the concept?" And that smile, too; the one with her head half-tilted, just a hint of sharp white teeth. How well I knew her. Far too well.

The hotel was The Hart Inn, on the edge of the Peak District. We visited a different hotel every year. Mostly in England, although we tried Scotland a couple of times, Wales once. We had never considered going abroad, although the first week in February would be a pretty good time for a weekend somewhere warm. It was never even discussed, though. Didn't seem right somehow, I suppose.

The hotel's lounge was all burgundy leather and flock wallpaper, oil paintings depicting hunting scenes, muted light and long, thick, velvet curtains. There was an open fire. Ellen and I sat next to it. We sipped malt whisky from cut glass tumblers and didn't look at each other.

It was almost four when the large oak door opened. Danny came in and closed it behind him. It was a year since I'd seen him and he looked no older. His thick, dark hair was longer than it should have been but, being Danny, he got away with it. He wore an ankle-length black leather coat that only he and Gary Oldman could carry off. My hair was greying and cut scrupulously short. I wore Cashmere coats and, in my wardrobe, charcoal was considered daring. I'd never possessed an iota of Danny's style or flamboyance or confidence. The difference between us. One of the differences.

But that confidence seemed a long way off now. As he approached us I saw the wildness in his eyes and the spots of colour high on his cheeks. Ellen and I stood.

"Where's Carol?" I said. I heard the petulance in my voice. The tone of a child denied a favourite toy.

He stopped, looked at the fire. It took a moment but I realised he was trying to smile. "We've got a problem," he said. I heard the tremor as he spoke and I knew things were bad. Danny did voice-overs for commercials. His voice was chocolate-smooth and just listening to it softened Ellen's features and made her pupils dilate.

"Is she ok?" Ellen said.

Danny ran a hand through the full extent of his hair. It took a while. "Well, no. She's dead."

Then Ellen surprised me. She found an expression I hadn't seen before.

Now

I watch Luke across the breakfast table. He sips coffee and scans the Telegraph's front page and drags a hand through his hair in a way that reminds me of Danny. Our son's final year at the University of Manchester is a couple of weeks away. He's spent the summer in Norwich, keeping his parents from each other's throats. I often watch him as he eats, reads, sleeps. He's beautiful, actually. Twenty-one years old and never a moment's trouble. That's probably an exaggeration, but that's how it seems. He's bright, kind, funny. And stable. His mother is a mass of neuroses. I consider myself the epitome of self-loathing. Genetically speaking, Luke is a miracle.

"Any chance of a look at the paper?" I say. "I mean, before it's out of date." I try to stick to my usual persona. Grumpy old bastard. But Luke smiles at me and my cover is blown.

"Sorry, mate," he says and tosses the Telegraph in my direction. "I'm off anyway."

"Hot date?"

"Something like that," Luke says. "Great breakfast, Mum."

"Cornflakes and toast," I grunt. "Very cordon bleu."

Ellen's applying make-up whilst pulling a smart navy jacket over her crisp white blouse. Multi-tasking. She darts over to Luke, kisses his cheek, mutters something I don't quite catch.

At the door Luke says, "Dad. Norwich play West Ham Saturday. Pre-season friendly. Steve got me a couple of tickets. Want to come?"

I mumble something about how busy I am and Luke looks at me pityingly. He knows I'll say yes.

"Yes," I say.

"Good stuff," Luke says. He nods at us and is gone. The room seems darker.

Ellen starts to clear the dishes from the table. "I'll be late for work," she says.

"Leave it. I'll do it in a minute. I'm not going in until ten."

"I'll do it," she says. I lift the newspaper so she can reach my bowl and coffee cup. I can smell her perfume. I remember that we made love last night. An odd, separate little universe that has nothing to do with normal life.

Ellen earns more than I do. She's an account manager at a brokers in the city centre. I run an ailing engineering company that I set up thirty years ago. Perhaps 'run' is an overstatement. My fellow directors have me cornered now and are eyeing me warily. I'm no longer the majority shareholder. I'm slowly being eased out. Not that it matters. We own the house outright. It's a detached on the Newmarket Road, complete with real oak beams in the living room and a conservatory and a water feature in the back lawn. Classy. We have more than enough for ourselves and plenty to leave to Luke when we're gone.

Later I drive to work. I sit in my office all day and try to look as though I give a fuck.

*

We sat in my BMW. I was in the driver's seat, Danny next to me, Ellen in the back, leant towards us, her face the colour of the increasingly vast snowflakes that circled and settled beyond the tinted windscreen.

I looked at Danny. "Talk," I said.

"Give me a break. I've just lost my wife."

I nodded. "Talk," I said again. Ellen's eyes darted between us. She seemed incapable of speech. Her expression was slack and empty.

Three times Danny started to speak, then stopped. Then he threw his arms in the air, did the thing with his hair again, both hands this time, raking back across his head. "Look, we're grown ups here, right?" I said nothing. He sighed, said, "Ok. We played games. If you know what I mean."

"You and Carol?"

"No. Me and Anne Widdecombe. Of course, me and Carol."

"What sort of games?"

"Come on, Jack. Do I have to spell it out?" He nodded minutely in Ellen's direction.

"Apparently," I said.

"Right. Have it your way. The thing is, Carol liked to be dominated."

Something large and sickly did a backflip in my stomach. I thought of the Carol that I'd known. The one I'd dated back at our old school, at the same time that Danny was dating Ellen. I thought of the Carol that yielded to me once a year in an anonymous hotel room. Soft, sweet, warm. "You like to dominate her, you mean."

A shrug. "Whatever. A little from column a, a little from column b. The thing is, I used to tie her up." A pause.

"And?"

"And then I'd leave her."

"Leave her?"

"For an hour or two. Maybe an afternoon, an evening."

I looked at him for a moment. "And this turned you on?"

"It was all part of the game. It's hard to explain, Jack."

"Really? You amaze me."

"So yesterday lunchtime I tied her up. The usual. Handcuffed her hands behind her back, fixed her ankles together with a silk scarf. Gagged her."

"And they say romance is dead."

"I didn't speak. She begged a little."

I tried to keep my voice even. "Part of the game?"

"Now you're getting it. I went out. Had some lunch. Played a little golf."

I put a hand on his arm. "You played golf? What are we talking here? Eighteen holes?"

"Something like that." He tried to shrug my hand away. "Look…"

"How long did you leave her?"

"The thing is…"

"How long, Danny?"

He chewed his lip. I released his arm. "About six hours." I mouthed the words back at him. "When I got back I thought she was asleep. Then I touched her and she was cold. I mean, I'd left the heating on, drawn the curtains."

"What a prince."

"What can I say? She was dead. Heart attack, maybe. I don't know."

"You didn't call anyone?"

More lip chewing. "Look. Jack. I panicked, ok? I…"

"Where is she, Danny? What did you do with Carol?"

"Nothing. Nothing, man." He closed his eyes. "She's still on the bed."

I swore. "You just left her there? Tied up and…I assume she's naked, Danny. Have I got that one right?" A faint nod. "Trussed up and naked."

"It's not as though she can feel it."

We sat there for a while. I stared at him, he kept his eyes on his hands. When my nails drew blood I realised how tightly my fists were clenched. "And you don't care, do you? Not at all."

"Don't give me that. We were married over twenty years. I'll miss her. I can't believe she's gone." There was no heat in his voice, though. He might as well have been talking about a pet.

I leant towards him. "I loved her, though. I always loved her. You didn't."

"Yeah, well. It was a one-way street. These yearly trysts? They bored her. She closed her eyes and thought of me."

"You fucker. I…"

Then Ellen sat forward, thrust her head between us. "You bastard," she said. Her voice was even and she stared at the windscreen directly in front of her. Danny and I looked at each other and tried to work out which one of us she was talking to.

*

It's too hot for football. Norwich and West Ham seem to agree. They stroll their way through a sunny afternoon. Cole and Defoe pick Norwich off eventually, when they can be bothered. No one cares too much. It's only a friendly, after all. It matters to me, though. An afternoon with my son. I first took Luke to see Norwich when he was nine. He loved it and we had season tickets together for the next five years. Then we stopped. I'm not sure why. I was busy maybe or Luke had friends he'd rather see. A bit of both, perhaps. A little from column a, a little from column b, as Danny and Abe Simpson might have said. *The Simpsons* were something else that Luke and I shared. He'd tape it and we'd watch it together at the weekend. I pretended to like it at first, then, like most adults, I was hooked. Thinking of those days makes my throat tighten and I blink twice and sit back so that Luke can't see me.

Norwich lose 3-1. Luke and I stop for a drink at The Coach and Horses on the way home.

"We used to go to McDonalds. After the football."

"I know, Dad. It wasn't that long ago."

It seems like a lifetime, I nearly say, but don't. "I bloody hate McDonalds."

Luke grunts a half-laugh, sips some lager. "Me too. I never said anything. Didn't want to hurt your feelings."

"Jesus. The bloody quarter-pounders we forced down. And those awful chips. Sorry, fries."

"Yep. I can almost feel my arteries clogging."

I put my pint glass on the table. I fiddle with it for a moment, try to place it in the exact centre of the circular beer mat. "When Uni's over maybe we can catch the odd game. If you're around this way."

Luke hesitates only for a moment. His smile seems genuine. Luke's smiles always seem genuine. "Don't see why not. That'd be great, Dad." His smile falters. He starts to say something, stops.

"What?"

"Nothing. Nothing much, anyway. I'm seeing someone, that's all. I thought you should know. I'll tell mum later."

"You've had girlfriends before, Luke. What's the big deal?"

He opens a bag of cheese and onion crisps and offers them to me. I shake my head and he looks at the bag and puts it on the table. For a moment I think he's going to tell me that he's gay. Another moment and I realise that the thought horrifies me. Then the shame kicks in. Then the consolation that at least there is some shame. Luke still doesn't speak. The pub is warm and full of sunlight and young men wearing Norwich City shirts and the stink of testosterone, sweat and cheap deodorant. The silence could be awkward, but Luke seems to have forgotten that I'm here.

"Well, I'm pleased, boy. You've met someone nice. I'm sure your mum will be pleased too. Happy for you."

"What?" Luke comes out of his reverie slowly. "Right. Thanks, Dad. Look, you and mum. The way you...are. Was it always like that?"

I look into my drink. Luke's not a shy boy, he's never afraid to say what's on his mind, but this surprises me a little. "Not entirely," I say slowly.

"But..." he says, meeting my gaze, holding it, leaving a tight little silence between us.

"But," I say with a big, empty smile, "we had you, loved you to bits. We've stuck at it, done our best."

"But you've never loved each other?"

The smile fades. "Not entirely," I say again. Luke says nothing. I sigh, "We were both engaged to other people. Our first loves, I suppose. The four of us were friends. Our fiancées cheated on us with each other. To wax poetical for a moment, your mother and I sought solace in each others arms."

Luke grunted. "Seamus Heaney eat your heart out. So, you were each others consolation prize?"

"I suppose so."

"I'm sorry."

"Don't be. Long time ago and all that."

"Some friends, though. What happened to them?"

"They got married."

"Did you keep in touch?"

"For a while." I drank some beer and felt my cheeks redden. "Anyway, neat change of subject. About this girl?"

"Girl. Mmm," Luke said. He ate a crisp slowly.

"Come on, boy. What's up with her?"

He drains his glass. "As you said, I've had girlfriends before. You've met most of them. Nice girls. I don't remember a damn thing about them, though."

"That's not very gallant, Luke."

"Well, no," he says, raising an eyebrow. "It's different with Claire, that's all. It's hard to study, hard to think of anything but her. I haven't felt like this before."

"It's a bastard, isn't it?"

"Yes. It is a bit. I mean it's wonderful too, but…yeah, it can be a bastard. She lives in Manchester. She's undecided about us." He tries to smile but it doesn't work. The fear of loss, the uncharacteristic lack of certainty in my son's face shakes me for a moment. "I don't know what I'd do without her. And I know how pathetic that sounds."

"It doesn't sound pathetic. Anyway, what's wrong with the girl? You're nearly as charming and handsome as your father. What's to decide?"

He doesn't smile. "She's forty-five, Dad."

"What?"

"She's the same age as mum. Almost exactly, actually. That's the problem. Well, it is to her. It wouldn't bother me if she was sixteen or sixty."

"Forty-five?"

"She's from around this way originally. She was married. No kids. Her husband died in a car crash five years ago." Luke looks into my face. I realise my mouth is open and I close it. "I knew I shouldn't say anything. You've gone as white as a sheet."

"I'm sorry. I'm fine. Really. Everything'll work out, you'll see." I stand. "We'd better go. What did you say her name was again?"

"Claire. Claire Hunter. I don't know what her married name was." I nod. "What does she look like?"

"What?"

"I'm curious, that's all. Humour your old man."

He shrugs. "I've got a photo." He pulls his wallet from a back pocket and hunts through it. "Bollocks. Maybe it's in my other jacket. Or back at Uni." He sees me looking at him. "She's mum's height, ok. She's blond. She's got blue eyes. She looks a lot younger than forty-five. And she's soft and warm and sweet and I love her to bits, Dad. Do you know what I mean?"

I nod slowly and turn away so that he can't see my face.

*

"I need your help," Danny said.

"You've lost me," I said. We were standing by the car now. Ellen was still in the back seat, crying. I could just about make out her blurred, white face through the side window.

"It looks bad. I've got my career to think of."

My hands were buried deep in my pockets. It was snowing hard but it didn't feel especially cold. The air around us seemed muffled, self-contained. "Your career? You do voice-overs. Nobody knows who the hell you are. And Carol's dead. At least, I assume she is."

"What does that mean?"

"I'm not sure I believe you. Maybe you're fed up with sharing her once a year. This is all a fabrication, an excuse."

"Yeah, you cling to that. Me and Carol, we're not like you and Ellen. I share her more than once a year, Jack. We have an understanding." He blinked and a fresh snowflake slid down his cheek and lingered on his chin. "*Had* an understanding."

"Right."

"She's dead. Believe it, Jack. We've got a problem here."

"We?"

He shrugged and snow fell from his shoulders. "Come on. We're friends, right? We go back a long way. I need your help."

"Friends? Well, we were. Now we see each other once a year and screw each other's wives. Pretty loose definition of friendship, don't you think?"

"Don't be a cunt. Look, I've got an audition next week. New animated series, cross between *The Simpsons* and *South Park*. English, though. It could be my big break. This thing with Carol? It could be construed as being my fault. I'll be fucked."

My face burnt, snowflakes melted on contact. "Could be construed as being your fault? Let's think. You tie up your wife, leave her naked on a bed for six hours, she begs you not to, she dies. I can see where some people might hold you partially responsible. So what shall we do? Go back to yours, stick her in the boot, bury her somewhere?"

"It's a thought," he said.

Danny was bigger and stronger than me but I stepped forward and pushed him hard. He staggered back and his legs and rump hit the car with a muffled thump. I heard Ellen scream and saw her eyes, bright and wide, peering out through the window. "Do you know what you're going to do, Danny?" I was on him quickly, I had the lapels of his leather coat bunched in my fists. "You're going home. You'll cover Carol's body. Then you'll ring the police. And you'll face whatever you have coming to you, you conceited, heartless, piece of shit."

His face was close to mine and he looked into my eyes. His body seemed boneless. Eventually he said, "You won't help me, then?"

I let go of him and he slumped against the BMW.

"Jealousy, Jack. Not a pretty emotion." Memories of Carol gathered at the back of my mind. I fought to keep them there. A few crept forward and I stamped on them quickly. Not quickly enough, though. Her smell. The way she murmured my name over and over when she came. Her laugh. "She loved me, not you. Not my fault. You got her once a year. More than you deserved, if you ask me."

"You still here?"

He rubbed his face, started to walk towards his car. "I'll work this out. You'll see." He walked a little further, stopped, half-turned back towards me. "Give Ellen my love. I used to make her scream, you know? Did she tell you that?" He grinned at me and waited for a response. I said nothing and eventually he shook snow from his hair and turned and got into his Volvo. I turned away from him as he drove off. He put the headlights on full beam and they picked out Ellen's white, gaunt features and her eyes as they followed Danny's car as it disappeared from sight.

*

It's Sunday. I've washed the car, cut the lawn and now I'm standing by the open French windows, arms folded, smelling my own sweat, watching Ellen fret and fuss between the kitchen and the dining room. She folds the tablecloth neatly, slides it into a dresser draw. She stacks the place mats carefully, then stops and stares at the back of her hands. She's wearing a caramel-coloured sweat shirt and old jeans. She looks good, though. She's kept her figure better than I have. Talk about damning with faint praise. "Claire Hunter. Carol Hoggard," she says.

"And? Carol's dead."

"Is she?" I close my eyes. Ellen's face is pinched, drawn. She looks younger, prettier when she smiles. At least I think she does. My memory isn't that good. "And the description?"

"Loads of blond, blue-eyed women about. So I'm told." There's wine left over from dinner. I pour myself some and tilt the bottle towards Ellen. She shakes her head. I say, "I'm worried about Luke, though. How he'll take it if this woman dumps him. He's got an important year coming up."

"I'm sure he can handle a little rejection. We all have to, after all."

"It's not as though there's a future in it. Forty-five. When Luke's her age she'll be…"

"Seventy. Yes. Luke's doing a degree in mathematical science. He's probably worked that out. You've spoilt him, Jack. That sound you hear is chickens coming home to roost."

I slip Nick Drake's *Five Leaves Left* into the CD player and turn the volume up as the first track comes on. I see Ellen's expression. "What? You like Nick Drake."

"Twenty years ago maybe. And don't change the subject."

I could argue, but what's the point? I look at her face, her hands, her breasts. I feel nothing at all. I think of Danny and Carol. I imagine stripping Ellen naked and tying her to our bed. Leaving her there for a week, a fortnight.

*

Ellen and I went back to the hotel. We cancelled Danny's booking and spent the night in a four-poster bed in a richly decorated, too-warm room. We didn't sleep or speak or touch each other. The next morning we drove home in silence.

*

"She left a message on my mobile," Luke says. "Waited until three in the morning, just to make sure it was turned off."

"I'm sorry," I say.

"I haven't told you what she said yet."

"The expression on your face, Luke." It's Monday evening. We're in the garden watching the sky turn an odd shade of purple. Ellen's in the kitchen.

"She says she loves me. But…" My son turns towards me and tries to smile, his head tilted at an angle that reminds me of his mother. The hurt in his eyes tears at my heart. "There's always a 'but', isn't there? She's going away. Won't tell me where. I mustn't contact her. I mean, I can't anyway; I haven't a clue where she is. But I wouldn't anyway. She said not to. It's important to respect people's wishes, I think."

"Did she say why?"

"Yes. And you can probably guess it. The age difference. Doesn't want to ruin my life. All bollocks, of course."

"I'm sure it isn't."

"Yes it is. She doesn't want me. That's all. People do what they want to do. The rest is just words. Something to hide behind." His voice is flat and precise. I try to think of something to say that isn't a platitude.

"And don't, Dad, ok?"

"What?"

"Say it's for the best. Or there's plenty more fish in the sea. You don't have to say anything, actually. I just wanted to let you know, that's all." His hands are tucked into his pockets and his shoulders are slumped. The air is warm and sweet and smells of jasmine.

"I worry. That is, we worry. Your mother and I."

"No need. I'm fine."

"It's a big year, isn't it? Your finals. Important stuff."

There's a tiny pause. "My degree. Don't worry about that, Dad. Really. Look, I'm meeting Steve. We're going for a drink. Tell mum for me, will you? About Claire."

"Of course." We turn and walk slowly towards the house. "Did that photo turn up?"

"What?"

"That photo of Claire." Luke shakes his head. The light is fading and shadows gather on his face and neck and he looks older, weary, too much like me. I shrug. "Just wondered, that's all."

*

When we got home I called my parents to see if Luke was ok and to tell them they could bring him home early if they wanted to. There was a message from Danny's brother, Peter, asking me to call him back. I did. I let Peter speak without interruption. Then I asked a couple of questions and muttered something appropriate, put the receiver down and turned to face Ellen. She saw the expression on my face and stood.

"It's Danny," I said.

"What?"

"He had an accident on the way home. His car skidded and hit a tree. He's dead."

"I see." No obvious emotion. A slight widening of her eyes, perhaps. "And Carol?"

"I don't know."

"What do you mean?"

"The police went to the house first. To tell Carol. They got no reply."

"Understandably."

"So they contacted Peter. He has a key. He tried her mobile then let himself in. The house was empty."

"Empty?"

"No Carol, I mean. Nothing else missing that Peter could see. Wardrobes, drawers, all full. Her car was in the garage, her mobile in the kitchen. Everything was neat, clean, tidy."

"So…" Ellen began.

"Danny lied."

"No."

"You knew him that well?"

"Yes. He wasn't lying, Jack." She tilted her face towards me. Her eyes were dry and remarkably clear. "How about you? Were you lying?"

"When?"

"When you said you loved Carol. Always had, always will."

"I was in shock."

"Of course."

"You know how I felt. Don't tell me you didn't feel the same way about Danny."

"Love? That's such a stupid word, don't you think? It's easy to love someone you screw once a year and don't see in between. It's easy to be romantic and soppy and drop off to sleep with a stupid grin on your face and murmur her name in your dreams. Someone you've shared twenty years with, though. Raised a child with, stood by her side and watched her bury her parents. Love comes a little harder then, doesn't it?"

"You didn't love Danny, then?"

"Of course I bloody did."

"Right." I hesitated. "That stuff he talked about. What he did with Carol. Tying her up and that. Did he ever try that with you?"

Ellen's voice was soft. I couldn't look at her. "We agreed. Years ago, Jack. We'd never ask each other about…that." I nodded. "And do you really care?" I said nothing. Eventually she said, "So what do we do?"

"About what?"

"Carol. Danny."

I stared at the fire in her eyes and the set of her jaw and the way her breasts thrust against her blouse. I wanted to take her to bed. "What can we do? Nothing. Forget them. Get on with…things."

"Just like that?"

"What difference does it make? We save on a hotel bill once a year. We'll take Luke somewhere instead. They've both gone, one way or another. We should have put them behind us years ago. Now we can."

I expected an argument. I thought she'd say what a callous bastard I was. Instead she said, "OK. Works for me."

Five years passed before we mentioned Danny or Carol again.

*

Two days before the new term starts I drive Luke to the railway station. The day is dull and warm, the traffic minimal, and I find myself driving more slowly than usual. Luke will be gone soon enough as it is, and all that lies ahead of me is the house, Ellen, and a job that's rejecting me just as unequivocally as I'm rejecting it.

Luke fiddles with the radio tuner, dismissing each option in turn. He turns the set off and says, "Anyway, thanks, Dad."

"For what?"

"For not patronising me. I had the speech from Mum. The pep talk. You know how it goes."

"I'm sorry, boy. I did ask her not to."

"She means well. I think. It goes back to what I said before. About respecting people's wishes. Accepting what they want."

I have no idea what he's talking about, but I nod anyway and indicate left as I ease into St Stephens.

A little later I park outside the station entrance and release my seat belt.

"You stay here, Dad. I'll be fine."

"I thought I'd give you a hand."

"I've got two suitcases. I think I can manage."

We sit in silence for a moment then Luke fishes something from the pocket of his jeans. "Look what I found."

He hands me a small photograph. The woman in it is blond, pretty, with a wry angled smile. She must have been moving when the picture was taken because her features are blurred slightly. I look at it briefly, nod and hand it back to him. Luke shakes his head. "Keep it. Burn it. Whatever. It's no longer of any use to me."

"Luke."

"What? I'm fine."

Then he shocks me. He leans forward and grips my shoulders and kisses my cheek. I hug him back awkwardly. My eyes feel hot and I blink a couple of times and try to laugh. He eases away from me and opens the car door. "See you, Dad," he says. I rub my face as he fetches his bags from the boot. He turns and waves as he approaches the station entrance and I wave back. When he's gone I look at the photo again and place it gently on the still-warm passenger seat.

"It's all my fault as usual, is it?" Ellen says. "Luke's upset and it's down to me."

"That's not what I said."

"What you meant, though." We're in the kitchen. Ellen's making sandwiches. "Someone had to tell him like it is. I knew you wouldn't."

"He didn't need it, that's all."

She opens the fridge door, looks at me. "Pickle?" I shake my head. "It's Friday, isn't it? I assume he's ringing you?"

"He always does."

"You can have your usual little bonding session, can't you? Gang up on me. For a change."

"It's not like that, Ellen. He's a better son than either of us deserve."

"My, Jack. That's deep." Then she stops buttering the bread for a moment and says, in a different voice, "Give him my love, though. Tell him I'm sorry."

"Of course." I hesitate then take the photo from my shirt pocket and slide it onto the work surface in front of her. It dislodges some breadcrumbs, a piece of cheese. Ellen pushes a stray hair away from her forehead and looks at the picture. "That's that, then," she says and butters some more bread. I pick the photo up, fold it in half, tear it into small pieces, and put them in the bin.

About nine-thirty we make some hot chocolate and wait for Luke to ring.

It's three hours later and we're still waiting.

War Stories

I stood at my bedroom window, looking out at the frost-stricken street. It was three in the morning. I'd lain awake for almost an hour, breathing in the cold dark air, trying to will myself asleep. The previous afternoon and evening I'd attended our office Christmas party. I drank too much beer too quickly then switched to cokes and now I was slightly dehydrated, mildly wired. I was fairly sure I hadn't made a fool of myself. Even when I was drunk, early on, I'd kept a lid on things, watched other people giggle and kiss and puke and laugh too loudly.

I wore a white vest and boxer shorts. The central heating had switched itself off hours ago and I thought I should feel colder than I did. Condensation kept forming on the inside of the window and I kept wiping it away with the back of my hand. I'd pulled the net curtain to one side. I was surprised how dirty it was close up, how strongly it smelled of dust. The street I gazed at was narrow with cars parked nose to tail on either side. Frost sparkled on the car windscreens and the small hedges and walls that fronted the terraced houses. The bed behind me was empty. Julie had left a week ago.

I suppose I was thinking of Julie when the man appeared. She occupied most of my thoughts at that time. All through the party, surrounded by attractive, drunken women, I'd thought about Julie.

I say the man appeared and that's how it seemed to me. Maybe I dozed for a second, but from my perspective, one moment the street was empty and the next he was standing there, tall, well-built with long dark

Other Voices

hair, naked. He was just standing, looking. He seemed completely at ease. He didn't shiver with cold and his breath didn't mist in front of him. His penis was large and flaccid. He approached the nearest car, a mud-brown Sierra, laid a hand on the frozen windscreen and looked directly up into my face. I jumped backwards. His eyes seemed very dark and his face held no expression. Then drunken laughter echoed from the nearby main road and the man's head snapped to one side and he started to run, away to my left, effortlessly, and within seconds he was out of my sight.

Now the bedroom seemed cold. I rearranged the curtains then went to the kitchen and drank a pint of water and swallowed a couple of aspirin. Back in the bedroom I pulled an extra blanket over the bed. It smelt strongly of Julie and I remembered a fortnight or so ago: Julie, flu-ridden, huddled on our sofa with this blanket pretty much spot-welded to her. I climbed beneath the covers and after a moment's thought I snapped the light off and surprised myself by sleeping for five hours solid.

The next day, at lunchtime, I found Mick in his usual corner table at The York. He had a half-pint of mild in front of him and when he saw me he drained it quickly and waggled the empty glass in my direction. "John. Long time no see."

He was alone. He was always alone. I think I was his only friend. He was in the army once, apparently, and now he lived off benefits. He'd beg sometimes, sat on an old blanket in an empty storefront on Gentleman's Walk. I'd walked past him once and tried to catch his gaze but his eyes had slid away from mine and he'd stared at the pavement until I was half a road away. I'm not sure where he lived, whether he slept rough or in a hostel. He never smelled unwashed in my company. I handed him his pint of mild and sat opposite him. "I don't know how you drink that muck," I said.

He nodded at the glass of orange juice in front of me. "Ditto."

"How have you been?" It had been almost a month since I'd seen him and I felt an irritating, unwarranted surge of guilt.

"Good." His eyes narrowed. They were his best feature; a clear, intelligent grey. His complexion was another matter. His skin was coarse; his face peppered with sprays of tiny blackheads, his nose and

72

cheeks a mass of broken capillaries. I never knew his age; some days I'd put him in his late thirties, others, two decades older. "How about you? You look like shit warmed up."

"Cheers, Mick."

"Just stating a fact. I take it she left."

"That obvious, is it?"

"Yep. And you said you were expecting it." He made a face. "As I recall you also said you'd be better off without her, that you wouldn't miss her at all."

"No fool like an old fool."

"You're not that old. Where has she gone?"

"I've got no idea."

"Are you going to try and find her?"

"No."

"Would you take her back?"

"I don't think so. Not this time."

He nodded. We both glanced at the door as it opened and a young couple entered and then Mick shivered as a gust of cold air swept in from the street. "I could do with a whisky," he said.

I got him one and he sipped it slowly. I told him about the figure I'd seen in my road the night before. He started to laugh, then stopped. He looked at me for a while, drank some more whisky, chased it down with a little beer. "That was a dream, mate."

"No it wasn't."

"How much had you had to drink?" I started to say something but he interrupted me. "I mean, did you have to mention his cock? Dream or not, I'd keep that little story to yourself, John."

"Right," I said. I felt my cheeks redden. "I can't help what I saw."

He nodded slowly, gazing over my left shoulder. "Did I ever tell you about that taxi driver in Belfast? He…"

"Yes, Mick," I said quickly. I was in no mood for third hand tales of knee-cappings and beatings and summary executions. "Many times. Anyway, I've got to go."

"Fine," he said. I got him another pint of mild and left a five pound note next to it on the table. He looked at the bar and said nothing and I left.

*

I was glad to get back to work after the Christmas holiday and the dull routine was an odd, disturbing comfort. I'd lived alone before I met Julie and she'd left me three times previously. The last time was early spring, just under a year ago and it was mid-summer before she returned. I remember the relief and resentment I felt when I saw her. I stood on the doorstep with my hands in my pockets as she hesitated at our front gate. She wore a flimsy cotton dress and her thin legs were bare, her shoulders hunched, her arms angled out in front of her. "You didn't come after me," she said.

"You knew I wouldn't. I told you I wouldn't."

"Do you want to know where I've been?"

"No."

"Good." Her expression was empty. I felt a brief, bitter hatred flare inside me. I looked at her hard and tried to identify what it was that I'd missed, what exactly I loved. "You've been waiting for me, haven't you? All this time."

"I've been getting on with my life."

"Right."

When she brushed past me to enter the house she laid a hand on my cheek and her expression changed. Something moved inside me then, although I have no idea what it was.

I was in Sainsbury's on a grey cold January Saturday, shopping mindlessly, when I saw the man who ran naked past my house just before Christmas. He was at the till opposite mine. He was shovelling some toiletries and fresh vegetables and a couple of packets of pasta into a plastic bag and chatting easily to the cheery red-haired girl who was serving him. He wore a black leather jacket over a navy roll-neck sweater. His black hair was still long and he was clean shaven.

"I said, have you got a Reward card?"

"What?" I said. The woman at my till was looking at me impatiently. She was middle-aged with a tight perm and a mottled complexion. "No. Sorry." She mumbled something about keeping my receipt but I ignored her and grabbed my change and shopping and followed the dark haired man towards the automatic doors that led to the car park. He hesitated, fished in his jacket pocket for car keys and I moved alongside him and touched his arm. "I know you," I said.

He looked into my face and although for a moment he seemed less familiar I was still sure it was the same man. "I beg your pardon?" His bemusement seemed genuine. He smiled pleasantly.

"I saw you. Just before Christmas. You looked right into my face. You know what I'm talking about."

He kept smiling. He leant towards me and his voice dropped a little. "Are you hitting on me?"

I took a step back. "What? No. Shit, no. I'm sorry…"

"No big deal. I'm spoken for, but, hey, I'm flattered."

"Really, I…"

His expression changed. "Are you ok? You look like you're going to puke. Do you want some water or something?"

"I'm fine. I've got to go. I've made a mistake, I'm sorry."

He started to say something else and I think he reached for me but I stumbled away from him, face burning. I heard shrill laughter from the girls at the cigarette kiosk. It seemed to take an age to reach the next exit. I stood in the cold air and watched the man put his shopping bag in the boot of his maroon Renault. Now he seemed shorter than I previously thought. His hair was shorter too, and lighter than I remembered. He glanced at me and I looked away quickly. I started to walk in the opposite direction then something twisted in the pit of my stomach and I bent double and vomited briefly and violently onto the car park's damp tarmac. I think a child laughed. An elderly woman said, "Whoops-a-daisy, dear. Better out than in."

"She'll bleed you dry," Julie's father once told me, years ago, just before Julie and I first moved in together. He was a withered, mean-spirited old man who had seemed on the brink of death for the five years that I knew him. Yet when Julie told me, dry eyed, emotionless, that he had died, of a heart attack, in the bath, I didn't believe her. Eventually I went to comfort her and she pushed me away, laughing.

"It's not as though we're married or anything," I told him. We were in his council flat. It stank of cats. He had two of them and they were as desiccated and devoid of warmth as their master.

"Just warning you, boy. She'll take you for all she can and then she'll dump you." He sat heavily in his armchair and dust exploded around him. "She's not a bad girl, it's just her way, that's all."

"I love her." I felt stupid saying it and Julie's father duly chuckled wetly and his cats watched me with dead eyes from their permanent positions on the sofa.

Eventually he shrugged and said, "You do what you've got to do. Don't mistake me for someone who gives a shit. Just giving you a friendly warning, that's all."

"I'm touched by your concern," I said. He chuckled again and I left him. Both cats' eyes followed me all the way to the door.

The first weekend in April I packed Julie's dresses and underwear carefully into a large cardboard box. Her clothes felt damp, slick to the touch. I remembered doing something similar with my mothers' clothes. Emptying our old house after she died, years ago. That must have been worse than this. Must have been. I gathered Julie's books and CD's together as well, stored them in another box. I decided to give her a fortnight then it could all go to charity.

In May I had a couple of dates with a girl from work. Her name was Sue and she was petite and pretty, several years younger than me. After our second date we walked towards the city centre from the cinema. Sue had her arm in mine and the air was still and warm. As we passed the entrance to the car park on St Giles I saw a figure move in the shadows to my left. I stopped suddenly and peered into the gloom. It was a man, dark-haired, naked.

"What?" Sue said.

I put my arm around her shoulder and pointed. "Look."

"I can't see anything."

"Look harder," I said, but I followed her gaze and saw that she was right.

"You're hurting my arm."

"He's gone."

"I said, you're hurting me. Let go of me, John." She was looking up into my face. Her eyes were very blue and her breath smelled of chewing gum.

"I'm sorry," I said. A little later she caught a taxi home. We didn't go out again.

*

I saw Mick once more before he died. It was in the usual place on a baking hot August afternoon. It was cool and dark in the bar and my eyes took a few moments to adjust after the harsh brightness of the street.

"I thought you'd been avoiding me," Mick said. I squinted and his features became clear. He looked older, thinner. His glass was empty, though, so some things hadn't changed.

"I've been busy," I said.

"Right. Busy waiting for Julie."

"She might be back for all you know."

"Is she?" After a moment I shook my head. "It's written all over your face."

"I'm seeing someone else," I lied.

"That's nice."

I was still standing. I blinked sweat out of my eyes. "It's not as though I loved her. Not really. It was more of an obsession. She wasn't even much to look at. Was she?" I looked into his face. His eyes were sunken, his skin grey.

"I never saw her, John. As far as I know, she's a figment of your imagination."

"I wish."

I kept looking at him until he said, "Hey, John?"

"Yeah?"

"Are you getting me a drink or what?"

I sat opposite him. "You don't look so good," I said.

"I've had the flu. I feel better than I look. At least, I hope I do." He looked at his hands. His fingernails were clean, but dirt seemed ingrained in the skin around his knuckles. "I had a job interview. Dogsbody in a warehouse. I was ill so I couldn't make it."

"Wouldn't they re-schedule?"

"I don't know. I didn't call them." He drank some beer. "It doesn't matter. I put my life on the line for Queen and country, I don't think I can handle shifting boxes in a warehouse."

"Right."

He knuckled his eyes and sat back slowly. I heard his joints creak. "I was in Bosnia. Did I tell you that?"

"Yes. Mick, look…"

"In the early nineties. Summer. The weather was like this, I remember. Stupidly hot. The sky was the clearest blue. And the air stank of rotting flesh. Bodies lay at the sides of country roads. People, animals, as though there was no distinction between the two."

"Mick, I don't really..."

"John, do me a favour? Shut up, please? Just for a minute." He smiled and spoke softly. I shrugged and looked away from his face. "We went into this tiny village two days after the Chechens had cleansed it. At first we thought they'd killed everyone but after a while I found this one guy, huddled in the corner of what was left of his kitchen. I thought he was maybe seventy, eighty years old. I found out later he was barely fifty. His face was grey and he couldn't stop shaking. After a bit he started to talk. He had a little English. More than enough, anyway."

"Do you want another drink?"

"Not yet. He was a baker. He said when the Chechens came he was just firing up his oven. He had two daughters. Twins. Eight years old. Pretty, blonde things. He showed me the photos." He paused. Slabs of rich, yellow light fell in triangles across tables and chairs. Dust spun slowly in the shadows between. "He told me that when his wife died of cancer five years earlier he couldn't imagine a greater grief." He looked into my face. "He said he should have tried harder. He hid the girls but one of them cried too loudly and they found the pair of them. Our baker knew what was going on, he could hear the screams and the gunshots. The Chechen who found the girls told the baker he had to make a choice. He had five minutes to decide which of the twins could live. The girls huddled together and screamed and wet themselves. The baker knelt at the man's feet and begged him to let them go. He said the guy stank of stale whisky and filth and something else he couldn't place. He ignored his pleas and counted five minutes exactly and asked the baker if he'd made his choice. He said he couldn't choose, no man could. So the Chechen shot both of the girls. In the head. One after the other. And left the baker alive."

"Jesus Christ."

"That evening, when it was dark, the man ran into a wooded area and hanged himself from a tree. The only wonder was that it took him so long."

My mouth was dry. I drank some coke but it was too cold and too sweet. "Do you like me, Mick?"

He threw his shoulders back, laughed a little. "What sort of question is that? Of course I like you. What's not to like?"

"Then why do you tell me this stuff? I have a hard enough time sleeping as it is."

"It rots inside me. It's made me the way I am. I have to get these things off my chest."

"Have you heard of the Samaritans? Why do you always unload on me, Mick?"

His face went still. "Because you keep coming back." His voice dropped a fraction. "Why do you think that is, John?"

I started to say something then realised I had no answer for him.

A week later Julie phoned. It was a Sunday and I was dozing in an armchair.

"It's me," she said.

"Right."

She started to say something but the line was bad and I couldn't make out the words. Then the line cleared and she said, "John? You still there?"

"Where else would I be?"

"I thought you should know. I'm not coming back."

"I think I'd gathered that."

"Really? I wonder." She sounded distant, tired, lost. Whether that was her or the quality of the line, I had no way of knowing.

"Where are you, Julie?"

"A long way away. No point trying to find me."

"Where have you been? Who have you been with? What's his name, their names? Tell me, Julie."

"John."

"What? Were they better than me? Must have been, I suppose." I paused but she didn't say anything. I heard her breathing. It seemed ragged. I thought I could smell her. "Your dad was right, after all."

A moment, then, "No. I never took your money. Not a penny."

"Right."

"Well, not much anyway. Look, I don't need this shit. I'm just telling you, I'm not coming back. Forget me, meet someone else. Do what the fuck you want. It's night-time here and I'm tired."

"I think someone's after me."

"Don't flatter yourself."

"Not like that."

"Like what, then?"

"I...don't know. Come back to me, Julie."

"That's not going to happen."

She broke the connection. I tried 1471 but the number was withheld. I went into my front garden and watched a mediocre sunset.

The air smelled of the sea although I was miles inland.

It was autumn before I went back to The York. Mick's seat was empty. It was lunchtime and the only other occupants were a couple of middle-aged men who stood by the fruit machine. Keith was behind the bar. He was built like a bouncer; broad shoulders, muscles distorting the sleeves of his black t-shirt. His head was shaved and he had a neat ginger beard. He saw me and nodded and came over to my side of the bar. "What can I get you, John?" His voice, soft, educated, always surprised me.

"Just looking for Mick."

Keith was quiet for a moment. "You obviously haven't heard."

"Heard what?"

"Mick's dead." He made a face. "Shit, must be three, four weeks ago now."

"Bloody hell. Last time I saw him he didn't look so good, but..."

"That wasn't it, John. He was stabbed. On the corner of Magdalen Street. Opposite that pizza place."

"That's next to where I live. I didn't hear about it."

"It was in the local papers for a couple of days. Inside page. It's not that big a deal. Mick never amounted to much. They haven't caught whoever did it. I don't suppose they're busting a gut trying."

"Still, I..."

"He gave you all that army shit, didn't he? Same as he gave the rest of us. Mick's war stories."

"Army shit?"

"He was never in the army, John. His brother was. Paul. Now he was a tough little bastard. He used to box. Pretty good too, by all accounts. My cousin sparred with him years ago. Paul was in the marines. Career soldier."

"Where is he now?"

"Dead, like his brother. Died of exposure during a training exercise in the Antarctic."

"Mick never mentioned him to me."

"Nor to me. It was my cousin that found out. Through a friend of a friend."

"So those stories of his, he made them all up?"

"Presumably. You haven't been around much recently. He asked after you from time to time."

"Perhaps I was a good audience."

"Perhaps. I work here, I had no choice but to listen to him." He gave me an odd look. "But you..."

"Yes, I know," I said. "I kept coming back."

Julie came back a week before Christmas. There was a knock at the front door and I answered it and there she stood. I felt genuine shock for one of the few times in my life. She wore a fake-fur jacket that reached to just below her waist, and blue jeans that looked too big for her. She had her hair cut short. Her eyes were huge and luminous in her tanned face.

"Things didn't work out," she said.

"Obviously."

"Can I come in? I'm freezing."

"Where's your luggage?"

"Somewhere. Let me in. We need to talk."

"No we don't."

"Don't be like that."

"Like what? You can't come in. I don't even know you."

"Grow up, John."

"I'm just stating a fact. I don't know you. I don't want to know you. You can go now."

She nodded towards the hallway behind me. "Have you got someone in there? Is that it?"

"I'm alone," I said.

"I'm not sure I believe you."

"I don't care if you believe me or not."

She started to say something, then stopped. Her expression changed and she said, "You're different."

"I hope so."

"Don't you want to know where I'm staying? Who I'm with?"

"No."

"Good for you." She turned and headed for the gate. Just before she got there she stopped and half-faced me. "On the phone you said something that stayed with me. You said someone was after you. Did they get you, John?"

I looked at her and she held my eyes and my throat ached. "Yes," I said, "I think they did."

Another summer. Another night, too, with dawn hours away and the air warm and thick and difficult to breathe.

The house is empty except for me and the occasional, familiar ghost. Julie's smell, part sweat, part perfume, in the morning mostly. My mother's face in the shaving mirror. Mick's figure bent over me when I wake. He has a pint of mild in one hand, a half-smile on his face. Ghosts or dreams, I no longer bother to distinguish between the two.

I'm by the window. I'm wearing only boxer shorts and sweat coats my legs and back. The street is empty, almost. A figure lingers at the edge of my vision, its shadow flicking in and out of my sight. And then the road is frozen, the windows of the houses, the glass in front of me, crusted with frost. The sweat freezes on my body and I shudder. My breath turns to smoke, my skin is ridged with goose-pimples.

Something moves, but it is still, and will always be, just beyond my sight. I close my eyes and concentrate. I'm sure I can hear the sound of Julie breathing.

Butter Wouldn't Melt

The air stank of creosote. Adam had about half the fence covered. He wore builder's gloves and his sleeves were rolled up and his bare arms and cotton-check shirt were dotted with dark brown splashes. Sweat dripped from the end of his nose and from his thick black moustache. He grinned when he saw me.

"Nice job," I said.

"Thanks."

"I'm being sarcastic. You stink, by the way."

"Good. That's for Claire's benefit."

"Claire?"

"She loves the smell of this stuff." He kicked the tin by his feet. "Turns her on, apparently."

"Well, now. Takes all sorts, I suppose."

"You can give me a hand if you like."

"Most generous." It was a golden October afternoon and I had better things to do. "And I'd love to, of course. Too busy."

"Right. Thanks, mate." He dropped the brush onto the grass, peeled his gloves off, rubbed his face with both hands.

"You wanted to see me," I said.

"I did?"

"That's what you said on the phone last night. I said you didn't sound yourself and you said you weren't. Reckoned you needed a chat."

"Oh, that." He took a breath. "On second thoughts, maybe denial's the better option."

I waited. The air, creosote apart, was warm and sweet. I could hear a mower from a few doors down.

"It's not easy, Tom. It's Claire."

"Claire?" I said, and waited some more.

He took a breath and looked at the ground. "She's seeing someone."

"Yes?"

"Well, fucking someone, to be precise. Seeing them first, then fucking them. I should imagine that's the order of things." His voice became clipped, his eyes distant.

"Are you sure of this?"

"Pretty sure. She doesn't even bother showering now. She comes to bed stinking of him."

"Bloody hell, Adam."

"I've made love to her with the smell of him in my nostrils. I think I've tasted him, even." I didn't say anything. He saw the look on my face. "I'm sorry, Tom."

"What?"

"I've embarrassed you."

"As you said, not easy. I mean, Claire of all people. Butter wouldn't melt."

"But we don't talk about this stuff, do we? How long have we been friends?"

"Since we were in nappies?"

"Near enough. But you can't look at me now, can you? We talk about football. And cars. Or computers. Then maybe football again."

"Actually, I don't like cars much."

"You know what I mean."

"I know what you mean. But look, we're men, aren't we?"

"I always thought so."

"What do you expect, then? Feelings? Fuck 'em. Roll them up into a tight little ball and swallow them down."

He looked at me. The sky was still a rich blue and there was no breeze. "Do you believe that?"

I shrugged. "Works for me."

"Does it?"

I said nothing.

"Still, I'm sorry," he said. "That I brought it up."

"No need to be."

"I had to talk to someone."

"I understand. So what'll you do?"

"Do?" He thought for a moment. "No idea. What would you do? If it was Sarah?"

"If it was Sarah? I'd kill her in her sleep."

A pause, then, "You are joking?"

"No idea. If it happened we'd find out, wouldn't we? You could confront her?"

"God, no. What if she loves him, or something? What would I do then? This is bad enough, but if she left me?" He sighed and looked down at the tin of creosote. He kicked it over suddenly and the contents glistened briefly like brown blood then soaked into his front lawn.

"Bit of a waste," I said.

"Yes. Fucked that bit of grass up as well."

We stood in silence and stared at the brown patch. I put my hands in my pockets. "Where's Claire now?" It was an empty question. I knew exactly where she was.

"Out. She didn't say where. And I didn't ask."

"Just leave it. It'll sort itself out."

He looked at me sharply. I had to look away from the hope in his eyes. "Do you really think so?"

"Yes. Are you playing football tomorrow?"

"Of course."

"See you then, then. We'll have a drink after."

"We always have a drink after."

I nodded.

"Again, I'm sorry," he said. "This is awkward, isn't it? I feel as though I've burdened you."

I grinned brightly, emptily. "No worries. I'm a big boy. I can handle it."

"Thanks, anyway."

"Anytime," I said.

"You're late," Claire said. She was leant back against a tree with her arms folded. We were in a glade, in a hollow, in an isolated spot near Ringland Hills. We'd used it before. The leaves were turning various shades of brown and they sliced the sunlight into bite-sized pieces and scattered them over Claire's hair and shoulders.

"Late? You're lucky I'm here at all."

"Lucky?" She wore a thin, strappy summer dress and, I suspected, not a lot else.

"Just been speaking to hubby. Shall we take a few Polaroid's? Rub his face in it a little more?"

"It's a bit late for a conscience to suddenly appear." She was small, the plain side of pretty. She looked prim. As I said, butter wouldn't melt.

"We've been friends a long time."

"Friends?" she said, feigning a puzzled expression. Her eyes, a dark green, were often dull and flat, but now they shone with an odd light. "Didn't seem to bother you much the other night. You remember. I had your cock in my mouth at the time."

"Claire."

"What? You'll be blushing next. After the things we've done? What's that all about?"

I shook my head. She'd laid a blanket between two trees. I looked at it. "Do you want me to go?"

"You'd bloody better not. I'm as wet as anything."

She knelt on the blanket and I sat beside her. A hint of perfume, a little sweat. The sense of something on her breath, but I wasn't sure what. She put her hand on my stomach. Her fingers were slender, the nails neatly trimmed and unpainted.

"I like pushing you both. Especially Adam. See how far I can go."

"It's just a game, then?"

She leant over and bit my shoulder lightly. "What else is it, Tom? What is it to you?" Then, "Don't answer that. I don't want to know."

"Just as well. I haven't the first idea."

She started to laugh and I reached for her. I might have thought of Adam then. But only for a moment.

"Your dinner is in the oven," Sarah said. "I expect it's ruined. It's pasta. Probably gone all hard."

"Sorry," I said.

"Well, we both know that's bollocks."

"Sarah."

We were in our house. She stood in the doorway between the kitchen and living room. Her eyes were hard. She wore old jeans and a t-shirt that didn't cover her navel. "Nearly made a mistake there," she said. "Nearly asked who she is. Silly me."

"You know better than that."

"Of course I do. But you don't even bother trying to hide it anymore. How do you think that makes me feel?" She wore no make-up. Her dark hair was tied back in a loose bun. She looked more beautiful than ever.

"Don't look at me like that. It was you that wanted an open relationship, remember?"

She came into the living room. She carried a tea towel, which she slung over the back of a chair. "That was ten years ago. We weren't even married. You didn't have to take me so literally."

I looked at her and her expression changed and she couldn't hold my gaze. I laughed. "You bitch. How does this make you feel?" I thought of Claire. "Wet. Doesn't it? We both know it does."

"Bastard."

"Well, of course. That's why you love me."

"How about if I told you I was screwing around?"

"Are you?"

A pause and a pout. "What do you think?"

"Funny you should say that. Someone asked me recently what I'd do if you were unfaithful."

"Who on earth asked you that?"

"It doesn't matter. Somebody at work."

"What did you say?"

"I said I love you. I'd forgive you anything."

"Anything?"

"That's what I said." She was standing by me now, holding my gaze. She moved against me and I put my hand on her bare, flat stomach.

"Tom?"

"What?"

"What the fuck are we doing to each other?"

"Don't ask me," I said. I kissed her fiercely, briefly. "I only live here."

*

Sunday morning Adam picked me up as usual and we drove to Earlham Park to play football for our local pub. It was something we'd been doing for years. Too many years perhaps. We were both in our late thirties now and the rest of the team was about fifteen to twenty years younger. Adam and I usually changed on our own, in the corner of the dressing room. The other blokes were all right, in their way, but they seemed to have their own clothes, their own music, their own language, even. Adam and I were the butt of several jokes. We took them well enough, but I saw the irritation I felt reflected in Adam's face.

I sat in the passenger seat of Adam's Volvo. The weather had changed. Clouds had gathered and there was an erratic breeze with a hint of winter in it.

"You're quiet," I said.

He waited for the lights at the Colman Road junction to change then pulled forward carefully. "She was at it again yesterday."

"Right."

"She threw herself at me last night. There were scratches on her back and on her thighs. She must have known I'd see them."

"Did you say anything?"

"No."

"Perhaps she wants you to."

"I can't."

"Have you any idea who it is?"

He eased past a moped then slowed as he approached Earlham Road. "Someone she works with, I suppose. I don't want to know."

"I'm not sure I believe you."

"Some days I want to know. Some days I want to kill the bastard with my bare hands."

"And other days?"

"Other days I'd be happy if he died of natural causes."

"Fair enough," I said.

The game didn't go well. We scored early; a glorious volley by our central midfielder, a goal several levels above our usual standard of play. Things soon returned to normal. Thanks to me. Their right-winger cut inside and scuffed a shot straight at me from outside the area. It slipped between my fingers and then my legs and just had enough energy left to creep over the line. There were hoots of derision from the opposing supporters on the touchline and an utter silence from my team-mates. When I turned after retrieving the ball they all had their back to me. Even Adam couldn't look at me. Maybe the ball was wet, maybe the sun was in my eyes. Maybe I'm just a crap goalkeeper.

Five minutes later it was Adam's turn. Their centre forward, a tricky little sod with a bad perm, beat him once, then went back for another go. Adam lunged at him, took his legs away and the ref gave a penalty. I dived the wrong way, naturally, and we were behind.

"You fucking muppet," Danny said. He was our best player, a hard, compact little bastard of a right back. I wasn't sure if he was talking to Adam or to me. I got the feeling we could take our pick.

They scored again near the end, a goal that was neither my fault nor Adam's. Which made it something of a novelty.

Afterwards the atmosphere in the changing room was a little tense. "If it wasn't for bloody Laurel and Hardy over there," someone said.

"Out of the way, granddad," Danny said, as he pushed past me on the way to the shower. I actually apologised, something that made me wince with embarrassment later.

Adam and I went to a pub on our own. We sat in a corner, nursing pints of bitter. A line of froth from his beer ran across Adam's moustache. I pointed at it. "Lose the foam, mate. You look a right twat." He wiped his mouth absently. "Don't take it so hard. There's always next week."

He looked up and his eyes came into focus. "Do you think I give a fuck about the football?"

I started to say something, then thought better of it

After a while Adam said, "How's Sarah?"

"Fine. Why?"

"Haven't seen her for a while, that's all. We haven't been out as a foursome since, when? Claire's birthday?"

"Something like that," I said. Sarah had said something similar a couple of days earlier. "Time goes so quick, doesn't it? And work's awkward. You know, shifts and everything. And Sarah's always tired. Lots of PTA meetings."

He nodded slowly. "Still, maybe we can do something soon. A meal. Somewhere nice."

"Sure. I'll have a word with Sarah. We'll sort something out."

"How about a fortnight from now. Sunday evening."

"Yeah, probably. I'll check my rota."

"I thought your weekends were free until November? That's what you said."

"Is it? I just wanted to check, that's all."

"I'll book a table. How about the Thirty Nine Steps?"

"Bit posh."

"It'll make a change. What's up? You don't seem keen."

"That's fine."

I felt his eyes on me. "It's Claire, isn't it?"

"What?"

"You think it might be awkward. Knowing what she's been up to. I'm sorry, mate. But I need it. Something to look forward to."

I nodded. We left shortly afterwards. Adam dropped me off and I checked my mobile for messages. There weren't any. Claire had been sending me four or five text messages a day, so it seemed odd. I frowned. It actually hurt a little. I stuffed my phone back in my pocket and went and had dinner with my wife.

Later that day we spent a couple of surreal hours at Sarah's parents house, drinking tea and eating crab paste and cucumber sandwiches and chatting politely about things of no consequence. As usual I watched Sarah regress to the prim teenager she had presumably once been. She simpered and giggled. It was hard to stomach. Both my parents were dead and I constantly looked forward to when the same could be said of Sarah's.

I was glancing at my watch when her father cornered me by a potted plant. He smiled affably. He smelled of Old Spice and stale tobacco.

"All right then, Tom?"

"Oh, yes."

"Work?"

"Yes, indeed."

"Going well, is it?"

"Wonderful."

"Prospects?"

"What?"

"Promotion, that sort of thing."

"Promotion? God, yes. Imminent, I'd say."

"Excellent. Well done." He slapped me on the back and started to wander off.

"Unless that thing goes to court, of course."

"Court?"

"Well, yes. Casts a bit of a shadow, I suppose." He didn't say anything. I saw the look of gentle bemusement on his face and almost felt sorry for him. "But, as I said, I was nowhere near that park. Not on that particular night, at least."

"Right." His brow furrowed briefly, then cleared again. "Oh, well. All come out in the wash, I expect."

"That's the spirit," I said.

"More tea, Tom?"

"Please," I said.

Sarah drove home. The sun was low and the sky was crammed with odd colours and slabs of muscular cloud.

"Tell me," I said, "what was the score?"

Sarah tapped the steering wheel and squinted. "Nine, ten maybe."

"Bloody hell, she's getting worse." Nine or ten was the number of times Sarah's mother had referred to the possibility of grandchildren. Which was close to a personal best.

"Were you teasing dad again?" Sarah said.

"Teasing? Hardly. What's the point? I could say anything, do anything, it simply wouldn't register. I could stand there all evening with my cock out and they wouldn't bat an eyelid. Although they might offer me another sandwich."

"My parents, eh? Got to love 'em."

After a moment I said, "Or not, as the case may be."

Later, as we were getting ready for bed, I told her about the meal that Adam had arranged.

"Thirty Nine Steps. I know," she said.

"You know?"

"Adam called me earlier, to make sure it was ok."

"Right."

"It'll be good. I haven't seen them for ages. Is Adam ok, though? He sounds odd."

"He's fine. Played like a wanker this morning, though. At fault for all their goals. Probably upset him a bit."

We were in the bathroom. I watched her as she brushed her teeth. She swilled and spat. "Adam doesn't seem the type to let a game of football get to him."

"You'd be surprised."

"Be good to see Claire again."

"Claire. Yes. Nice girl."

"Girl? She's the same age as me. You never call me a girl."

"She's so small, isn't she? Nothing to her. Not really a woman, if you know what I mean."

"I don't, actually."

I squeezed past her to get to the wash basin. "You smell all minty," I said. I touched her cheek.

"Not tonight, Tom. I'm tired."

"Right," I said.

We went to bed and I stared at the ceiling while Sarah lay with her back to me and slept, or pretended to.

I'd checked my mobile frequently during the day, but there were no messages.

By Wednesday I'd left more than a dozen messages on Claire's mobile phone but she hadn't answered any of them.

On Thursday, at work, I grabbed a patient by the throat, pinned him in a corner and told him to fuck off.

A little later I was in Colin's office. Colin was my boss. He sat behind a cluttered desk. He wore a white shirt and his tie was askew. He had fair, thinning hair and a florid expression. He looked tired.

"You can't do that, Tom."

"He tried to hit me."

He waited a moment, chewed his lip, didn't quite look at me. "Derek barely knows who he is, Tom. You know that."

"He's younger than me. Stronger. And he tried to hit me."

"From what I hear, you were looking for it."

"You know Derek. Always causing trouble. Nobody likes him."

He steepled his fingers in front of him and rested his chin on them. "Nobody likes you much either, do they? Ever think about that?"

"Frequently."

"Will you sit down, please?"

"I'd rather stand."

Colin sighed. He did that a lot, I noticed.

"Are going to sack me, then? Suspend me? What?"

"I can't, can I? Too bloody short staffed. Won't matter much in six months or so. This place will be history."

"That's the sign of a good boss. Always thinking of staff morale."

He sat back and straightened his tie. "Fuck off, Tom," he said, "just get out of my sight."

So I did.

On Sunday Adam and I gave away a goal each as usual, but our opponents were somehow even worse than us, and by some distance, so we managed to score five in reply. The atmosphere in the dressing room afterwards was better than usual and Adam and I tagged along to our local with the rest of the team, where we were benevolently ignored until we slipped off to another, quieter, pub a little way away.

"You've still got a job, then?" Adam said. We'd settled ourselves in white plastic chairs at a table in the pub's garden. The sunlight was watery and there was little breeze.

"Just about. Not that I actually give a shit, either way."

"Why not look for something else. Something you'll enjoy."

"Enjoyable work? Interesting concept."

"Got to do something, haven't you? To keep Sarah in the style to which she's accustomed."

I grunted. Adam's face was the colour of wet cement. "What's up with you?" I said.

"Hazard a guess."

"Claire."

He rubbed his face. His moustache needed a trim. "Last night. Again."

Something twisted inside me. "Last night?"

"Fresh scratches. She's so subtle. I think I'll kill her."

"I think I'll help."

"What?"

"Nothing. You've got to confront her. She's just taking the piss."

"I know."

"What must she think of you? Just lying there, taking it."

"Thanks, mate. That makes me feel a lot better."

I drank some beer.

"Are you ok?" he said.

"Me? I'm fine. Just worried about you, that's all."

Adam nodded slowly.

"You look nice," Sarah said. It was Sunday evening and I was straightening my tie in front of the hall mirror. "Don't often see you in a suit."

"Don't like them. But thanks. You don't look so bad yourself."

She wore a simple black dress with a low cut V-neck. And she wore the jade necklace that I'd bought her for Christmas a couple of years earlier. Her hair was loose and fell to her shoulders. "Thanks. I think." Then, with her head tilted to the side and her eyes hidden, "You've been a good boy recently, haven't you?"

"Yes," I said. "Sorry about that."

"Don't be," she said. She fingered the necklace. "I like it."

"Right."

"Perhaps it's time we grew up. We can't live like this for ever, can we?"

"I suppose not." My tie was straight enough but I kept fiddling with it anyway. "I've not thought about it." Then, "I don't know, Sarah."

"I do." She said it gently and she put her hand on my shoulder.

We took a taxi to the Thirty Nine Steps and Claire and Adam were waiting for us in the bar. My heart almost stopped when I saw Claire. I have no idea why. She looked like a child compared to Sarah. When I leant forward to kiss her cheek I smelled her perfume and had to fight the urge to curl an arm around her waist and pull her to me. Adam and Sarah were embracing at the same time and I tried, and failed, to catch Claire's eye as she withdrew from me.

Adam's cheeks were red and he was talking too much and laughing too loudly. "Bit pissed, aren't you, love?" Claire said, patting his arm.

"Not at all," Adam said. Then he laughed again and his eyes slid out of focus.

Later, Sarah assured me the food was superb. I had no idea. I didn't taste a thing. I spent the meal trying not to look at Claire. Claire and Sarah ate slowly and gossiped frantically. Adam drank far too much red wine. He spoke less and less as the evening progressed and his face went slack. I watched him. I watched them all and I drank little.

After the meal we went to the Ten Bells. Claire made her way to the bar and I followed her. I saw Sarah take Adam's arm and guide him towards a corner table.

"You're pretty slick," I said.

"Am I?" Claire said. It was busy at the bar and we waited to be served.

"Who's the lucky man?"

"Does it matter?" she said.

"I expect it matters to Adam."

She laughed. I wanted to hit her. I wanted to stroke her face. She leant forward to try and catch the barman's eye and her hip pressed against me. After she ordered our drinks she said, "You're a sanctimonious bastard, Tom." I couldn't argue with that so I didn't try.

"You don't care about Adam."

"Well, no."

"You still want me though, don't you?"

"Yes."

She paid for the drinks. "That's not going to happen."

She turned away from the bar and I put a hand on her arm. "Bitch," I said.

She shrugged and lager spilled onto her fingers. She licked it off. "And your point is?" she said.

"What did he do to you?"

"Who?"

"Adam. To make you like this?"

"Nothing. This is nothing to do with him. Or you. Or Sarah. You don't know me at all. None of you do. You never did. It's about me, that's all. What I want. What I need."

"And that boils down to a good shag, does it? You must be very proud."

She smiled. "It's no good, Tom. You can't get under my skin. You never could."

We took our drinks to our table. Adam had one of Sarah's hands between both of his. He dropped it and sat back suddenly as we approached. "Well, well," Claire said.

"What was that all about?" I said. We'd caught a taxi home. It was late and I was tired. Sarah stretched and yawned.

"What?"

"You and Adam. Very cosy."

"Oh. That."

"Well?"

"Jealous?"

"I just want to know, that's all."

"I'm going to bed," she said. I followed her upstairs. She undressed quickly and slipped into her dressing gown. I watched her. "He told me about Claire."

"What about her?"

"Her screwing around. Don't pretend you didn't know."

There's a mirror on the wall next to our wardrobe and she stood in front of it, combing her hair. "Right," I said. She combed and combed and stared at her reflection. I reached for her.

"Don't," she said.

"What have I done?"

"I'm not entirely stupid." She stopped combing. Then she turned and threw her comb at me. It whistled past my head and buried itself in the curtains behind me. "You bastard. I knew it was her. Deep down. I could smell her bloody perfume on you."

I shrugged. "So what? The games we've played, what difference does it make?"

"Not Claire, Tom. Not our friends. That wasn't in the contract."

"Terms and conditions apply," I said.

"What?"

"Nothing. Nothing at all."

"What about Adam?"

"Adam? No, I don't fancy him at all. Never have."

"Oh, fuck you, you smug bastard."

"Nicely put."

"Adam doesn't deserve it."

"What's that got to do with anything? Don't look like that. You know what I am. You've always known." She bowed her head. I remembered the taste of Claire's kisses. "Anyway, whoever she's screwing now, it isn't me."

"And that hurts, doesn't it?"

I hesitated. "No."

"Liar. Good. I hope it hurts like fuck."

"And how about Claire's part in all this? Your mate. How do you feel about her?"

"I feel sorry for her. I don't think she's well."

"Maybe it's Adam's fault. Maybe he beat her up or something."

"Not Adam. He's a sweetheart."

"Of course. Adam's a sweetheart, Claire's ill. It's all down to me."

"Yes, that's about it. And it's no use looking at the bed. You're not sleeping with me tonight."

So I spent the night on the sofa, dozing fitfully, dreaming thin, ragged dreams. And then I'd wake and sit, and wait for the first signs of dawn to peer around the edges of the thick living room curtains. And I thought of Adam. And Sarah. And quite a bit about Claire. But mostly I thought about me.

We struggled through the next week. Sarah and I barely spoke. Each shift at work seemed to take a month to pass and yet when it finally ended there was nothing I particularly wanted to do. I was too distracted to read or watch TV. I tried not to think about Claire. I didn't always succeed. And when I did think of her I felt a pang of something I didn't recognise. On Tuesday I called her mobile but the line was dead.

Thursday night Sarah told me to come to bed. I did and I made love to her and when we'd finished she told me to go back to the sofa.

"What was that all about?" I said.

"The batteries in my vibrator are flat," she said.

I almost laughed.

*

Other Voices

On Saturday night Adam left a message saying that he was ill and that he wouldn't be playing football the next morning. It was odd, a match without Adam. Still, we lost and I played like a twat, so some things didn't change.

Sunday evening Sarah visited her parents alone and I was dozing in an armchair when Adam knocked at the door.

"You look like shit," he said, when I let him in.

"Half asleep. Feeling better?"

"Better?"

"You were ill, weren't you? That's why you missed the football."

He followed me into the living room. Neither of us sat. There was an odd, unfocussed energy about him. Something had changed and I had a pretty good idea what it was. "I'm fine. Let's just say I've retired. I know, Tom."

"Know what?"

"Don't fuck about. Sarah told me."

"And you believe her, of course."

"Yes."

"What a fine judge of character you are."

He took a breath, started to say something, stopped, then, "It's all a game, then, is it? Our friendship. All those years, Tom. And Sarah. Just thrown away, for what? A couple of quick shags?"

Suddenly, I was bored. It was almost dark outside and I pulled the curtains across and flicked on the standard lamp in the corner. Its warm light made the room seem cosy. Inappropriately so, perhaps. "What do you want me to say?"

"Something. Anything."

"Do you want me to say that I'm sorry? That I give a shit? Because I'm not and I don't. Look, hit me. Beat the crap out of me if you want, if it'll make you feel better. You're a big guy, I couldn't stop you."

"I know that. You're not worth it."

"Whatever," I said. I started to turn away from him and he punched me in the stomach. I tensed at the last moment but it made little difference. I doubled over and felt the breath rush out of me. I coughed, almost vomited and braced myself as I tried to breathe. But he didn't hit me again. I straightened slowly, grimacing. "Feel better?" I said eventually.

"No."

"Good," I said. "How's Claire, by the way? Still screwing this other guy?"

His face changed, and I flinched away from him. But then I saw that his features had gone slack and his eyes were dull, turned inward, almost. "She's gone," he said.

"Gone?" I said. Stupidly.

He looked into my face and for a moment I think he was weighing something up. Making a choice. "She's gone to her parents'. In Ireland. She won't be back."

"Ireland? What part of Ireland? She doesn't sound Irish."

He seemed lost for a moment, then he said, "The Republic. Somewhere near Dublin, I think. And she never had an accent. Her folks came to England when she was very young."

"And then moved back again?"

"Yes."

"Well, I'm sorry," I said. And I was, but not for him.

"Of course you are."

"There's no point giving a shit, you know. About anything. Ever."

"You keep believing that."

"I will."

"You're such a wanker, Tom." I thought for a moment that he was going to say something else, but he didn't. Instead he left.

My stomach hurt. That was ok. It was the other ache that bothered me, the one I could never quite trace. Suddenly I tried to retrieve a single memory from my childhood. But I couldn't remember my parents' faces, their voices, their names, even. But that wasn't unusual. It was the fact that I'd even tried that surprised me.

Sarah didn't come home. I waited until midnight then called her mobile, which was switched off. Reluctantly, I tried her parents' number but it was constantly engaged. I shrugged and told myself I didn't give a shit. I took a couple of aspirin and dozed in a hot bath until the water became too cold to bear. I went to bed. I slept well. In the morning I took all of Sarah's clothes into the garden and burnt them.

She called for her stuff the next day while I was at work. She left a note saying she hoped I was pleased with myself and that she'd send me a bill for the clothes.

The next time I saw her was a Wednesday afternoon just over a fortnight later. I was standing in the living room with my hands in my pockets listening to *Closer* by Joy Division. It was halfway through *Passover* when she burst in. Her hair was loose and she wore a lemon cheese-cloth blouse and tight jeans. She came up to me and linked her arms around my neck and kissed me, pushing her tongue deep into my mouth. Just as I started to respond she pulled away from me. "Joy Division?" she said. "This is mine, isn't it?" She ejected the CD and slipped it into the case.

"What was that all about?" I said.

"Are you sure you want to know?" I stared at her and she said, "You remember Adam? Your best friend? Well, your ex-best friend. He's in the car outside." She glanced at her watch, pursed her lips. "Ten, fifteen minutes ago? We were on the sofa in his living room. I was giving him a blow job." She smiled. I rubbed my mouth. I went into the kitchen and drank some water and spat into the sink. "He's waiting for me. He's taking me home in a minute."

"Home?"

"Try to keep up. I've got myself a solicitor. You'll be hearing from him soon."

"You and Adam. He doesn't love you. He's just getting back at me."

"We'll see." She stood by the door. Her eyes narrowed. "You said you'd kill me in my sleep."

"Did I?"

"Adam told me."

"It was a joke."

"Ha ha."

"This isn't fair. You knew what I was like."

"Yes. But I've changed. You haven't."

She opened the door.

"My parents aren't dead," I said.

"What?"

"I lied about that. I was molested when I was a kid. By my father. When I was a teenager I tried to take him to court but there wasn't enough evidence. They live in Peterborough somewhere. They have no idea where I am."

"What are you doing?"

"Trying to explain."

"God, I despise you. You'll do anything, say anything." She started to leave.

"Where are you going?"

"I told you. With Adam."

"You're living in his house?"

"Yes."

"All those memories of Claire. Must be difficult."

"Adam doesn't want to move. That's fine with me."

"Right. You knew about Claire's folks in Ireland, did you?"

Her face changed minutely. "Of course I did. So did you, I think."

"Odd that. I don't remember. In fact, I thought they were dead. I'm sure she said that once. She never talked about them, upset her too much, but we were all pissed one night. Still, I must be mistaken."

"Yes, you must. Can I go now?"

"I wish you would," I said. "That stuff about my parents? All bollocks, of course."

"Well, d'uh," she said, and left. I went to the window and watched her get into Adam's Volvo. She didn't look up. I could see Adam but his face was in shadow. They drove off. That was two years ago and I haven't seen either of them since.

I didn't contest the divorce and it went through in less than four months. I quit my job and sold the house and moved into a little flat in Cromer. I got a job in a run down old people's home near the sea front. The inmates there seem to like me. I'm kind and attentive and I do them favours sometimes, when they least expect it.

I don't sleep well. And when I do I dream of Claire. Not Sarah or Adam, they could be dead for all I care. Just Claire. The usual stuff. Her taste. Her smell. The way her breath felt on my neck. Perhaps she wants to know why I haven't looked for her. Perhaps she doesn't. And what's the point in searching for a ghost?

Another night shift. I'm at the window of Mr Hennessey's room. It's a clear night and the sea and the sky seem to run together and there's a blue-grey, metallic sheen to everything.

Mr Hennessey's breathing is so soft I can hardly hear it. How old is he? Mid, late eighties? No visitors. I like him, though. But he's recently had that look in his eyes. I saw it when I wiped tomato soup from his chin earlier this evening. Loss. Distance. Yearning. I tried to tell him, it's not worth giving a shit. About anything. Ever.

I'm not sure what I'm feeling when I ease one of the pillows from behind his head and press it over his face.

Three Days

Ginny had just turned eight when she was taken. We'd held her birthday party at home on the Saturday afternoon. I'd hated it. I wanted to watch England play France in the rugby international on TV. Instead I served endless glasses of coke and bowls of ice cream to a never-ending cast of interchangeably shrill eight-year-old girls. I played my part, though. I smiled at the right times and cooed at the presents Ginny showed me every five minutes or so and I only checked the score on Teletext on a couple of occasions at most. Beth was a star, of course. Baking mini pizzas and helping Heidi or Caitlin or Bonnie with their make up. Jesus. The thing I remember most about the day is that England won 21-13. It was a dull match by all accounts, I didn't miss much. Wilkinson kicked all our points from penalties. My daughter's birthday, a week before she disappeared.

*

It was shaping up to be a crap Monday even before I got the telephone call. The car was in for a service so I caught the bus, which was late and over-crowded and the woman I sat next to stank of garlic. It was a fifteen minute walk from the bus stop to the office and the day was dark and November-cold with a low, mean wind that nipped at my ankles and cut through a coat that was a little too thin. As I walked I thought that something had to change. I couldn't stand this any longer; the routine, the job, the marriage, even. The feeling of rotting, slowly, from the inside out. The faces of the people I passed told me they felt the same. Or maybe, like me, they'd overdone the red wine the previous night and then been rejected by their partner in bed. A hand on a warm hip, a sigh and a sharp shrug. Shorthand for another night spent back to back.

I was ten minutes early but Tim was already in. Surprise, surprise.

"Hi, Martin. Good weekend?"

"Great," I said. "You?" Obviously I didn't want an answer and I was heading for the coffee room as I spoke. But Tim was quick.

"Yeah, thanks. Work, mostly. Unpaid, of course. But..." He gave a small, martyred shrug. "You know what Robert's like." I nodded. "I expect you've been working on the Bishopgate report." He looked up at me expectantly, his smile bland, his eyes brighter than they had any right to be at that time in the morning.

"Hardly," I said. "I only did the site visit Friday."

"Still," Tim said. "Meeting this afternoon, at the clients. I expect it's in your diary." This time I think the smile was meant to be sympathetic but I caught only the smugness and I had to turn away from him before the disgust showed on my face.

"Great," I said. "Do you want a coffee, Tim?"

"Please. De-caff."

"Of course," I said.

I spent the next half-hour desperately trying to sort my notes from Friday into some sort of order. Robert was late, but not late enough. He breezed past my desk, then stopped at his office door, turned on his heel and pointed at me. "Martin. We're at Coleman's this afternoon. Two-thirty. That's not a problem, is it?"

I tried to look as nonchalant as I could. "Of course not."

"Good man," he said with a wink, then disappeared into his office.

"Fuck," I said.

Cheryl put the call through to me at about ten-thirty. It was a welcome distraction.

"Martin?" Cheryl said. "It's Beth. I think."

"You think?" No alarm bells sounded. I had no inkling that my life was a telephone call away from changing forever. No fatherly instinct kicked in. "It's not like you to be so indecisive, Cheryl. How was your weekend, by the way?" I didn't want to talk to my wife. I wanted to flirt with Cheryl. Cheryl is younger than me. She has great legs and she takes my clumsy advances in the spirit in which they are intended. Well, almost.

"You'd better take the call, Martin. I think something's wrong."

I started to say something but there was a click and then Beth was on. A version of Beth I'd never heard before.

She said my name twice. Her voice was shrill, penetrating, hysterical.

"Beth, what's…"

"She's gone, Martin. Ginny's gone." Then her voice stopped and was replaced by a long, braying, clotted sob.

I took the receiver away from my ear and looked at it. Then I put it back again. The office is open plan but my segment is surrounded by sound-proof screens and I can't actually see anyone from where I sit. I wanted to see somebody now. Anybody. I stared at the computer monitor with its mindless screen-saver and my empty coffee cup as though they might offer me some explanation. I wondered why I wasn't panicking. "Beth," I said. "Calm down. Take a breath. Tell me exactly…"

"Don't patronise me. I told you. She's gone. Come home now."

"Of course. Have you called the police?"

"OFCOURSEI'VE CALLEDTHE FUCKINGPOLICE!"

"Ok…"

Then a whisper. "Just come home."

"I'm on my way."

I didn't rush. Maybe I thought if I stayed in this normal place then everything would be fine. It was probably a mistake, anyway. By the time I got home Ginny would be back safely. We'd apologise to the police for wasting their time and they'd say, it's no problem, as long as…

Then the thought of Beth's voice and that awful elongated sob snapped me out of my reverie and for the first time I felt real fear.

I still hesitated at Robert's door, though, still knocked politely and grinned apologetically as I popped my head inside.

"Yes?" Robert said.

"I'm sorry. I've got to go. Beth called. Ginny..."

"Is she ill?"

"No. She's gone."

"Gone?"

"So Beth says. Probably nothing. But I'd better go."

"Of course."

"Actually, I need a car."

"Where's yours?"

"Being serviced."

Maybe, belatedly, he saw the fear on my face. "Look, take mine."

He started to give me the key. "Cheers, Robert."

Then he stopped. "Shit. Can't. Coleman's this afternoon, isn't it?"

His face changed. "You'd better give Tim your notes."

"Of course. Look..."

"Have you typed them up?"

"Not yet. I must go, Robert."

"Yes. Take the pool car."

I closed my eyes. "Gerry's got it. He's not back until tomorrow."

"Bollocks. Take Tim's car. Tell him I said so."

"Right. I'll see you later."

"Ring, won't you? Let me know...I hope everything's alright."

"Thanks, Robert."

The drive home took too long. And it didn't last long enough. I found myself slowing as I approached traffic lights, willing them to turn red. I thought if I could just keep driving then everything would be fine. If I arrived home then reality would intrude. The streets outside the car seemed flat, one-dimensional. The sky was a cold, marbled grey. Everything reeked of apathy, indifference. It was warm in the car. I liked it better in there, even though it was Tim's car and the little air-freshener that hung from the mirror smelled acrid and offensive and the cassette that I flicked mindlessly into the tape player contained Elton John's greatest hits. But I could handle that. I could handle anything except thinking about Ginny.

Two police cars were parked at an angle in our drive. I stopped at the curb. I expected Beth to be waiting at the door but she wasn't.

Actually, the door was locked and I had to knock. A pretty, uniformed WPC opened it and looked at me blankly.

"I'm Martin. Mr Palmer? This is my house."

"Of course," she said. Her smile was a mixture of warmth, sympathy and suspicion. I followed her into our living room. She had nice calves. I couldn't believe that I noticed that, but I did.

Beth was sitting on the sofa. Her face was the colour of paper and she had a box of tissues by her side. Most of the tissues seemed to be in crumpled heaps, surrounding her. "You took your time."

"Traffic," I said. I moved across to her and tried to hold her but she was rigid and I bounced off. I felt myself blush. I was aware of the WPC a couple of feet away and I tried to avoid her gaze. There were other people in the room as well, I realised, but I couldn't bring myself to look at them either. I sat next to my wife and rubbed her arm ineffectually. "What happened, Beth?"

"I told you," she said. She wouldn't look at me. I was thrown by her hostility. I was used to it, I suppose, but under these circumstances I expected...I don't know what I expected.

"Not really," I said. "All you..."

"She's gone. She's not coming back." Her voice was flat and distant. Not unfamiliar. The WPC moved to her other side then and took her hand and started to mutter whatever platitudes she thought were appropriate.

"Don't even think..." I started to say, but Beth's head turned towards me and the force of her gaze almost pushed me backwards in my seat.

"Look at you. Your eyes are dry. You can't even cry for her, you bastard."

I felt several pairs of eyes on me. I tried to shrink away from them. I didn't want to know what they saw.

A middle-aged man with short, greying hair took my arm and guided me into the kitchen. "I'm sorry," I said.

"For what?" the man said. Light reflected off the lenses of his glasses and I couldn't see his eyes.

"I..." I made a helpless gesture and pointed towards the living room.

"I'm Detective Inspector Yeo, by the way." He shook my hand. A much younger man with floppy blond hair and an overbite joined us in the kitchen and closed the door behind him. "This is Detective Sergeant Collins." Collins nodded and his hair bobbed irritatingly.

I'd retreated without realising it and I was leant back against the sink. I saw a miscellany of drawings that Ginny had done, fixed to the fridge door with magnetic letters. There were several of them and they spanned three or four years. The older ones looked brittle and the edges had started to turn yellow. The drawings weren't particularly good. It was hard to tell what they were exactly.

"What happened to my daughter, Inspector?" I nodded towards the living room. "Even on the phone...I have no idea what's going on."

Yeo smiled and Collins, noticing, smiled too. "I'm sure Ginny will be fine, Mr Palmer. It's very early days. She'll be at a friend's or at the shops. She'll turn up any minute, you'll see."

"I thought she was at school."

"Right," Yeo said. "Ginny has a cold, doesn't she? Your wife said you'd both agreed last night to keep her at home today."

Had we? My recollection of Sunday evening was *Midsomer Murders* on ITV, a bottle of Chianti, the routine rejection of my sexual advances. I slapped my forehead and dredged up a smile. "Of course. I forgot. I'm sorry, it's been a hell of a morning."

"I expect it has," Yeo said.

"You have checked with the school?" I said.

"Credit us with some intelligence, please," Collins said. His voice was whiny and accent-less. He was trying not to look annoyed.

"Sorry," I said.

"Your wife says she was in the kitchen, washing up, Ginny was in the living room watching cartoons. This was just after nine. Your wife says she left her for five minutes at most. When she went back into the living room, Ginny had gone. She searched the house, as have we. She knocked on the neighbour's doors and called Ginny's friend's parents. As have we. No sign of her." Yeo's voice was even. He watched me closely as he spoke, his eyes giving me nothing.

"That's..." I searched for the word.

"What, Mr Palmer?" Collins said.

"Odd?" I said weakly.

"We've got most of the local force on this. Door to door, searching gardens, spreading out. We take it very seriously, obviously. But there's no reason to believe, nothing to indicate, that your daughter has been abducted."

I looked at Yeo. Light bounced off his glasses again, throwing me. "That's good. Isn't it?"

He gave a tiny nod. "Except your wife seems to believe the opposite. She seems convinced of it, in fact."

I moved away from the sink, turned, fiddled with the kettle. I noticed something. "The washing up is still in the sink."

"Yes," Yeo said.

I stared at Ginny's half submerged cereal bowl. It had pictures of Winnie The Pooh around the outside of it. She'd had it for ages. I tried to remember where she got it from. A present, maybe. "Do you want a coffee?" I said.

Yeo shook his head. Collins waited a moment then did the same.

"Even allowing for the situation, things seem a little tense between you and Mrs Palmer," Yeo said.

"I admire your understatement," I said. Neither of the policemen spoke. "It's been a difficult year. Beth is...suffering from depression."

"Is she taking any medication?" Yeo said.

"Is the Pope Catholic?" They both stared at me in silence. "Yes. She's..."

The door opened. Beth stood with her arms folded. "I can hear, you know."

"Beth, I had to tell them. Something like this..."

"Tell them, what? That wifey's mad? And frigid? Better not forget that."

Yeo and Collins' faces betrayed no embarrassment, no concern at all. Beth's face was red, contorted. I thought she might have a stroke. She looked smaller, though. Withered.

"This isn't helping, Beth." I tried to keep some sympathy in my voice.

"Isn't it? Perhaps it's helping me. Maybe giving you a bollocking is some sort of therapy, just what I need." She flicked her head dismissively at the two policemen. The contempt on her face made me wince. "I know what those two think. You're just confirming it."

What I felt most was embarrassment. Yeo reminded me a little of Robert, who, in turn, reminded me of my father. Authority figures. I imagined speaking to any of those people the way Beth had just done and the thought made me shudder inside. "You make it sound as though she vanished into thin air."

I tensed myself for another outburst but Beth's shoulders slumped and she looked at me with defeated eyes. "I'm not lying, Martin."

"Nobody is implying..."

"I need to know where my daughter is."

I didn't miss the *my daughter*. Neither did Collins or Yeo.

"So do I."

The silence my wife left was long and telling. The WPC joined Beth in the doorway and put a hand on her shoulder. Beth nodded in the young woman's direction. "I saw you looking at her legs, Martin."

I may have caught a hint of a smirk on Collins' face. "Beth," I said, and turned towards the kitchen window. Through it I could see a knot of people, loitering. I recognised a couple of neighbours. I heard the kitchen door close behind me.

After a moment Yeo said, "It must be difficult."

I wondered if he was trained to state the bloody obvious. Then I realised he hadn't said exactly what must be difficult. I tried to think of the last time I'd read Ginny a bedtime story or sat and watched a video with her. Or the last time I hadn't humoured her and only half-listened to her telling me about her day. The last time I hadn't shoved her onto her mother at the earliest opportunity. I couldn't.

"Yes," I said.

From about eleven-thirty onwards the phone rang constantly. Beth had called pretty much everyone she knew earlier, panicking, trying to find out if anyone knew where her daughter was. Now they were calling back. Her friends, my friends, such as they were. The parents of any child that Ginny had so much as looked at. Teachers. Beth had been thorough.

People came and went. Uniformed and plain-clothed, male and female. Some of the names stuck, most didn't. After lunch Yeo's relaxed demeanour changed. I noticed him take part in a couple of fraught, impromptu meetings with an array of colleagues. A little later he and Collins again took Beth and I, first together, then separately, through the weekend and the hours leading up to Ginny's disappearance. Beth's story never wavered. Neither did mine but then Ginny hardly featured in it. Saturday morning, played golf. Saturday afternoon, went to the football. Saturday evening, went to the pub. And so on. What a dad.

A little later Yeo took me into the kitchen. "We haven't got anything," he said.

"Is that unusual?"

"It's unheard of."

"What are you saying?"

"I'm saying…we need help. I want to go to the papers, the TV. Have a press conference, some sort of appeal."

"Whatever you think is best."

Yeo hesitated. He took his glasses off and rubbed his eyes. They were blue, washed out, softer than I'd imagined. "I think we'll keep you and your wife out of it for now. I'll go in front of the cameras. I've done it before." I nodded slowly. "I don't think either of you are up to it."

"I'm ok."

"Are you?" I shrugged. "I've got a daughter," he said. "And two sons."

"How old is she?"

He had to think for a moment. "Twenty-four. If I lost her…now, I mean, let alone when she was eight…"

He let the words hang. "What? You think I'm not upset enough?"

"I didn't say that."

"You've seen the state Beth is in. I'm just trying to be strong."

"With respect, Mr Palmer, you don't seem particularly strong either."

"I love my daughter, Inspector." I winced and wondered if I'd ever before said anything as facile, as meaningless. I might as well have said, I breathe oxygen.

"It's not necessarily a given," he said, as though reading my thoughts. "Loving your kids."

"Isn't it?"

"No. The job I do, the things I've seen…" He rubbed his eyes again, then his mouth and gazed at the kitchen door. "We're going to have to search the house again. And the garden."

"You don't believe her, do you?"

"I think she believes herself. But…it makes no sense."
"Beth wouldn't hurt our daughter, Inspector."
He stared into the middle distance and said nothing.

They searched again without success. Light bled from the sky as the afternoon progressed. Beth closed the curtains in the living room an hour before she needed to. I understood why. To look into the darkness was…impossible. To imagine what lay beyond it. I didn't let my mind go to obvious places. I couldn't.

We watched the press conference that Yeo and a senior colleague gave on the local news at tea-time. They showed three different, recent photographs of Ginny. The first was taken at her birthday party. I didn't recognise the others.

I called Cheryl before the office closed, asked her to update Robert for me. I called her when Beth was busy with the WPC and I kept my voice low. I don't know why. It was good to talk to her, though. The warmth in her voice, the concern. No accusations, no edge at all. She's just a nice person, simple as that. By the time we'd finished she was close to tears and when I put the phone down I realised that I was too. I didn't let them come. I would have been crying for myself and not for Ginny.

The day slid numbly into night. But the lights stayed on and nobody slept.

Very early the next morning Beth and I found ourselves alone in the kitchen. We both headed for the kettle. "After you," I said.

"It'll be burned out soon at this rate," Beth said.

It was a very weak joke but her tone was even and although she didn't look at me I felt encouraged, somehow. She'd washed her hair and changed into a clean blouse and jeans. She looked better in some ways, worse in others. Her face was already taking on the sunken, stunned expression of permanent grief. You see it all the time, parents on the news whose kids have gone and not come back. It's worse on the mother's faces usually. They are turned inward, as are the father's, a bit, but you can almost always see the anger as well on the father's faces. I wondered how I looked. I hadn't as much as glanced in a mirror. I couldn't. I wondered how the fathers usually reacted; anger, action, I supposed. Tearing out into the world, searching with their own eyes and hands. Doing something, anything. What had I done? Left it to the police. Sat in a corner. Made tea.

"I'm sorry," Beth said. She faced the kitchen window. Her fingers strummed the edge of the unit that held the kettle. She'd painted her nails, I noticed.

"What for?"

She turned towards me, but she still didn't meet my eyes. She put her arms around my neck and leant against me. How hard that must have been, I thought. How badly she must need to be held, that even I would do.

"I'm not mad," she said.

"I know," I lied.

"She's gone."

"You don't know that."

She held me tighter. "I do. I really do. I just know." Then she laughed abruptly. It was low and hollow and as bitter as dark chocolate. "I called my mother yesterday."

"I thought that you would."

"She said I was probably making a fuss about nothing. As usual. She asked me to keep her updated."

"Her grand-daughter," I said. Beth nodded into my chest. I had no family to call. Well, there was a father, somewhere. Cornwall, Devon, last time I'd heard. Or Hell, maybe. The last time I'd seen him I was seventeen years old.

"The police don't believe me," Beth said. I just held her. "I know how it sounds. Do you think I could make something like this up?" She looked at me and, to be honest, her face was like something out of a horror movie.

"No," I said. I was no longer sure whether I was lying or not.

"It happened exactly as I said. I don't know why." Her voice grew thin and distorted as the tears came. I held her to my chest, felt her warmth against me. I tried to remember the last time she'd needed me like this, then gave up because I couldn't.

We'd met in Norwich, at the University. Same course, same classes. She was edgy then, needy and neurotic. I liked that about her. I figured that if she was damaged, close to a breakdown, then I'd have more chance of getting off with her. I didn't think anyone 'normal' would look at me twice. I let her lean on me. She needed someone. Our parents disapproved, which was a large part of the attraction. Especially for her, I think.

She told me she was pregnant towards the end of our first term. Inside I screamed 'no' over and over but in the real world of the chilly bedsit we shared I held her and told her everything would be fine, I'd stand by her, we'd get by somehow. She pushed me away and smiled and nodded. I remember the expression on her face. It said, 'this is the best I can expect.'

We quit our courses. I got a job and we moved into a council flat. When she lost the baby, halfway through the pregnancy, I was elated. I hid it, of course. At least, I tried to. I wonder now how successful I was.

As the years passed I tried to rationalise how I'd felt. I was too young, far too young, nowhere near ready to be a father. But I know that what I felt wasn't merely relief.

The next two or three years were barren, bleak and we could easily have split up. We barely touched each other, barely spoke. But on some levels things got better. Work improved. I got promoted twice in quick succession then moved to a bigger company. We bought a decent house, a car. Maybe she thought I was worth sticking with for a while longer. Physically, though, things were close to dead. Twice I went to massage parlours and left with cheeks burning, relief lost in the guilt.

But in the winter of 1994 it was as though a switch flicked inside Beth. The first time she initiated sex I didn't know how to react. I got used to it quickly, though, revelled in it, didn't question it at all, even though Beth's orgasms sometimes seemed perfunctory, a little too easily achieved.

It went on until Halloween when she told me she was pregnant.

"But you're on the pill," I said.

"I stopped taking it."

"When?"

"About six months ago."

"But...we're not ready...I'm not..."

"Not what?" A smile. A tiny smile. I hated her then.

And the switch was turned off again. We hardly touched, never kissed. She'd give me a hand job occasionally, just to shut me up.

Don't get me wrong. I still love Ginny. Love her to bits. I'm just not very good at showing it.

Mid-morning it rained. We kept the curtains half-drawn and the lights in the kitchen and living room stayed on. It was as though dawn hadn't broken at all.

Yeo was there again, and Collins, and an ever-changing cast of familiar faces, the same eyes cutting away from mine.

Ginny wasn't coming back, Beth had said. It was hard to argue. I tried to accept it, there and then. I thought it might make things easier for me in the hours and days that followed. For me. Always me. Seeking the path of least resistance. Beth had become peripheral again. I think she sought me from time to time, needed me even, but I managed to keep a distance, turn away before my eyes met hers.

I wondered who would find her. It usually seemed to be kids or somebody walking a dog. I imagined the expression on Yeo's face as he told us, Beth dissolving. Or maybe he'd delegate, leave it to Collins. I hoped that he wouldn't.

People spoke to me. I nodded, shrugged, half-smiled. I have no idea what they said. I walked from room to room. It seemed that cracks were appearing everywhere; walls, faces, mirrors, my hands. And the sky too, when I peered out of the window, seemed low and glowering and run through with a network of cracks that grew as I watched. Everything subsiding. The world collapsing into itself. Someone I didn't know – he was bald, he wore a grey suit – gave me two pills and a glass of water. I swallowed them and slept for six hours.

They found her while I slept. The couple who run the Newsagents a couple of streets down. It was early – before five, I think – and she was curled in a ball next to the rubbish bin at the side of the shop. The newspaper delivery lay next to her. The papers had been dropped there only five minutes earlier and the van driver swore that Ginny hadn't been there when he made his delivery.

They knew who she was straight away, obviously, and they thought she was dead. But she wasn't. She was sleeping, that was all. Her thumb tucked into her mouth, still wearing the pink jeans and the Pocahontas sweatshirt from the day she disappeared.

Mr Taylor carried her inside. She didn't wake. She was warm, he said, although it was close to freezing outside. She looked clean, unblemished. His wife phoned us. Beth woke me and a little later they brought her home.

Mr and Mrs Taylor had been hugged to within an inch of their lives and Ginny sat at the kitchen table, drinking milk and rubbing her eyes. I couldn't stop looking at her. Neither could Beth. The atmosphere in the kitchen, in the whole house, was extraordinary. The elation, the sheer warmth. And the disbelief.

Beth changed before my eyes. She shrugged years off. She discovered a light, easy laugh that had me looking around the room before I realised that it came from her. She kept smiling at me. She said, "I was wrong after all, isn't it wonderful!" She hugged me and kissed my cheek.

Yeo shook my hand, holding onto it a little longer than necessary. "I'm glad," he said. I nodded. He kept looking at me. I saw the questions in his eyes, in all of their eyes. I couldn't answer them. I thought it would eat them up, not knowing. It didn't bother me at all.

Ginny hopped down from the table. "I'm tired," she said. I hugged her again. "Dad," she said, in a mock-whiny voice, "you need a shave."

"Where did you go?" I whispered.

"You're all hairy," she said. She pulled back and rubbed my stubbled chin. "It doesn't suit you. It makes you look old."

I tried to make her meet my eyes. I thought there might be an answer there. But there wasn't. And there wouldn't be. Beth and I asked and asked, gently at first, then more persistently, but Ginny never answered, never even seemed to hear the question. And then we stopped asking. We both agreed. We had her back, that was all that mattered.

*

It's spring, nearly eighteen months after Ginny was taken. I'm sitting in a deck chair in our garden watching Ginny play. Beth sits beside me. We don't speak much, but her hand will slip across to mine sometimes and I'll look at her and we'll exchange a small, secret smile. It's as though I've got a new Beth too. It's hard to take in sometimes. Not that I'm complaining.

The sun is low and I have to squint against it as I watch Ginny kneel and peer hard at something lurking in the short grass. Her tongue pokes from the corner of her mouth as her eyes narrow.

"What is it, Hon?" I call. I'm aware of the anxiety in my voice and of Beth looking at me sideways. Ginny is less than a dozen steps away but she's still out of my immediate reach and I feel my chest tighten.

"It's just a worm, Daddy." Ginny looks up at me. She's smiling as usual. The dress she wears is almost diaphanous, backed by the sun.

"Leave it, Ginny. It's dirty." I put my arms out. "Come and see daddy."

Her smile widens and she runs towards me. I quit work six months ago to help Beth keep an eye on Ginny. I thought she might be a bit sick of having me around all the time, but it doesn't seem that way. Ginny jumps onto my lap with a squeal. I make an exaggerated grunting sound and Beth says, "Be careful, Ginny."

"It's fine," I say. Ginny feels warm and smells of vanilla. She always smells of vanilla. Her weight always feels exactly the same on my lap, too, has for months and months. I squeeze her waist and she turns towards me. I do the usual check: hair, teeth, nails. None have grown since the day she disappeared. Which is odd, I suppose, but Beth and I don't mention it.

"What is it?" Beth says. Perhaps she sees something in my expression.

"Nothing," I say and smile. And then we're all smiling.

"Silly daddy," Ginny says, kissing my cheek.

Beth squeezes my hand.

I look from one face to the other but the sun is low and I can't quite see their eyes.

Think of a Number

The first time I shot a man I messed up. Lenny thrust the silenced Berretta into my hand and told me to get on with it. I was just watching as usual, not taking much notice. Then the gun lay slack in my palm. Lenny pushed the barrel away from his chest.

"In that direction, please," he said mildly.

"Now?" I said.

"Now."

The fat man on the floor of the old barn was trussed and gagged. He wore only a pair of white boxers and they were wet with fresh piss. His eyes were wild, flicking between Lenny and me. He knew what was coming.

I should have got up close, pressed the barrel against his head. Instead I snapped one off from a few feet away. It took him in the right shoulder. I'm not a good shot. You don't have to be in this business. You'd think otherwise, I know, but believe me, get in close enough and it doesn't matter how bad a shot you are.

The man flopped backwards and tried to scream. He was gagged tight, though, and it came out as a mew. It reminded me of cats fighting at night-time. I fired again and this one hit him in the belly. He snapped forward as though taking a punch. I couldn't see anything at first then blood leaked through the sweat. The man spasmed, his bound feet and hands flexed, fought for purchase on the wooden floor.

I raised the gun again and tried to aim this time. But Lenny reached across and touched my arm. "Leave him."

"Why?"

"Just watch," he said.

So I did. It took a while. I didn't time it, but it seemed like ages. Probably seemed a lot longer to the man. At one point I tried to look away but Lenny wouldn't let me.

When it was over we stepped out into the bright, sweet warmth of a May afternoon. We stood for a while, getting used to the light.

"What was that all about?" I said.

"A lesson."

"Next time I'll get in close, two to the head..."

"Not that lesson."

I squinted at him. "What?"

"I wanted you to see what it can be like. Dying."

I shrugged. "It's hardly the first time..."

"The point is, it's not always quick."

"Whatever," I said.

He sighed. "Just try to remember how that man died."

"Ok," I said. But I knew that I wouldn't.

The car was parked in a nearby copse and we made our way back to it.

"Do you know who he was?" I said.

Lenny walked quickly and I had trouble keeping up. I just about caught his nod.

"And what he did?"

"Yep," Lenny said.

When we got to the car, a beat up Datsun, Lenny tossed me the keys. "You drive."

I tried not to seem too pleased. I got in and turned on the ignition and gunned the engine a little too enthusiastically.

"Easy," Lenny said.

"Sorry." I eased the handbrake down. "So, did he deserve it? To end like that?"

"Not that it matters," Lenny said, "but, yes, he did."

I nodded and steered the Datsun onto the dirt track.

*

I was eight years old when I last saw my mother. A decade ago. I stood at the front gate as dad ushered her into the back seat of a large black saloon. I remember the colours…black car, grey sky, mum's red coat. And the smell of mum's perfume and my father's breath. The taste of the ice-lolly he gave me to keep me quiet. As he slammed the car door shut I bit through the chocolate coating and my teeth ground against the wooden stick. It made me shudder.

She didn't look back as the car pulled away. It was raining. The streetlights were on. As the car grew smaller it was engulfed in golden light. That could be my memory playing tricks, of course. A lot of things could.

"Where's mum going?" I said. Melted chocolate and ice-cream dripped onto my fingers.

"Away," my dad said. "For a while."

"When will she be back?"

He ruffled my hair and said nothing.

*

When we reached the main road Lenny drove. I slept for a time and when I woke it was dark and we were still driving.

"Where are we going?"

"East," Lenny said.

"Why?"

"Why not?"

I shivered. I fiddled with the heater, but nothing happened.

"It works as well as the radio," Lenny said.

"We could have nicked something decent."

"This won't be missed. Or noticed."

I retrieved my jacket from the back seat and huddled into it.

We stopped at an all-night café for an early breakfast. I had a full English with extra fried bread, while Lenny had his usual; granary toast and orange juice.

"Don't know what you're missing," I said with my mouth full.

"You know better than that, Luke. I avoid all that rubbish. That's why I look so young for my age."

"Which is?"

He smiled and didn't answer the question. As usual. I'd put him at sixty, seventy maybe. He's tall and straight backed with thinning hair that's grey at the edges. I think his teeth are still his own but he talks and smiles in such a way that you rarely see them. His skin is smooth, coffee-coloured, unblemished. I've known him for as long as I remember. I called him 'Uncle' once, but then I've called many men 'Uncle'.

The café was empty except for us and two elderly men, who sat in a far corner and drank tea without speaking. A radio played softly and the fluorescent tube above us crackled from time to time without going off.

The girl behind the counter asked if I wanted more coffee. She was in her twenties, I supposed, peroxide hair, too much make-up, melon-like breasts that squashed against the counter as she leant against it.

"No," I said.

"Manners," she said. "Don't they teach you please and thank you at school these days?" Her voice was light, sing-song, trying to tease. I could feel her eyes on my face, willing me to look at her.

"I wouldn't know," I said. "I've never been to school."

I glanced at her and she was smiling. At first she thought I was teasing her back, starting to flirt. Then the smile faded. I don't know what she saw in my eyes, my face, and I don't care. She didn't speak again and that was good enough for me.

"I wish I had your charm," Lenny said.

"One day, maybe." I finished my breakfast and pushed the plate to one side. "Where are we off to?"

"Hemsby."

"Oh, the glamour."

"I've got a caravan there, on the front."

"How long?"

"Two, three weeks?"

"Is it for a job?"

Lenny drained his orange juice and watched the girl as she busied herself behind the counter. "I expect something will turn up."

"It usually does," I said.

*

When I was fifteen my dad told me that mum was dead. We were in his study. It smelled of leather and after-shave. I watched the rain hammer against the window. It was relentless, unyielding. I could barely make out the lawn that lay beyond the glass.

"How?" I said.

"In the asylum."

"What asylum?"

"It's very sad." He was staring at the window so I studied his face. A neat moustache, no lines to speak of. Clear, guileless eyes. He could be anyone. A normal person.

"When?" I said.

His face turned back to mine. "A year ago."

I stared at him. I tried to remember the last time my mother kissed me. I thought of her red coat and struggled to recall the smell of her perfume or the shape of her smile. If she smiled.

"But why…"

"Uncle Bernard is coming this evening."

I put a face to the name and felt something twist in my stomach. "When?"

"About six. You will…be good, won't you?"

I looked at the floor and nodded. What else would I be?

I went to my room. I had an hour to myself so I read and watched the rain. I breathed through my mouth. My room stank of semen and sweat. I flung a window open, tried to air it out a little. It made no difference. It never did.

*

We dumped the car in some woods and walked into Hemsby at first light. The caravan was smaller than I had imagined and smelled of damp.

"Wonderful," I said.

"Just needs airing out," Lenny said

"Whatever," I said, and clambered onto the narrow couch and slept for twelve hours. I think I woke once. Lenny was bending over me. His face was in shadow. He didn't touch me. He never touched me, even when I first met him, when I was still living with my dad. I asked him about that once. "People change," he said. He wouldn't elaborate. I still don't know what he meant.

When I woke Lenny handed me a mug of tea. Strong sunlight angled in brightly through a dusty window.

"I've bought us some clothes," he said. "And a new car."

"New?"

"Well, it's an '88 Metro. But the radio works." He handed me some money. "Your share of the fee."

I counted the notes. "It's more than usual."

"You earned it."

"I suppose. Just about."

I threw the blanket off and stood up. Lenny turned his back on me and drank some tea. I pulled on a fresh t-shirt and a pair of jeans.

"I'm decent."

"I somehow doubt that," Lenny said, turning. He opened the caravan's door, letting in air and light and the sound of the sea and of children playing.

"How long have you been doing this, Lenny?"

He hesitated. "Actually, you're my first apprentice…"

"I meant the job. Killing people."

"Thirty years, give or take."

"How many men have you killed?"

A pause.

"Think of a number."

"How did you meet my dad?"

He threw the dregs of his tea onto the bare grass at the front of the caravan and pulled the door shut. "In the eighteen months we've been…together, that's the first time you've mentioned your past. I've rather admired that."

"Doesn't mean I don't think about it."

"Thoughts don't count, Luke."

"My mum went to church every week. She believed in heaven and hell."

"I know."

"I've never even seen her grave, Lenny."

He buttoned his shirt to the top and slid into a linen jacket. "The day's getting away. We've got work to do."

"A job?"

Lenny nodded.

"Did it come through when I was asleep?"

He threw me the car keys. "You can drive. And watch the clutch, it sticks like a bastard."

The clutch wasn't so bad. We took the coast road for a couple of miles then headed inland. Lenny gave directions curtly and I followed them without comment. He leant forward in his seat and he drummed his fingers against the plastic dashboard. Which was pretty animated for Lenny.

"You all right?" I said.

He didn't answer so I just kept driving, taking a right by an old church. The trees in the graveyard were crammed with pink and white blossom. The road narrowed quickly, the fields either side closing in.

"I do them a favour," Lenny said. I glanced at him, but he was looking straight ahead.

"What?"

"We all die, don't we?"

"That's deep, Lenny."

"The ones I...meet, at least they go quickly. Most of them. Most of them are dead before they know what's hit them."

"Which must be a comfort."

"Don't mock me, boy." His voice was razor-edged, colder than I'd ever known.

"I'm sorry," I said, and meant it.

After a moment he said, "No, I'm sorry. I seem to be in an odd mood today."

"I noticed."

He guided me left and the road widened and we passed through a tiny village into a flat sweep of bare heath studded with clumps of trees and patches of bright purple heather. The sun was high and it was hot inside the little car. Lenny took his jacket off and slung it onto the back seat. I wound a window down. The air smelled of vanilla.

"Not that it's always quick," he said. It took me a moment to pick up the thread of his conversation.

"They have since I've been with you. Except the last one and that was my fault." I thought of the men I'd watched him kill. With a gun, mostly, close up. A couple of broken necks and cut throats. The speed of it had shocked me at first, but not for long.

"Sometimes it's in the contract. Make them suffer. And the customer's always right." I waited for him to elaborate but he didn't. He touched my arm. "Pull in here." I did as I was told. He reached into the back of the car and fished a mobile phone from a jacket pocket. He dialled a number, listened for a moment then broke the connection. He put the phone back and turned to me. "Half a mile ahead on the right hand side is a small terrace consisting of five houses. We're going to park in the drive of the first one then you'll go in through the front door, find the occupant, shoot him in the chest and head and then we'll leave again. Ok?"

"What now? In daylight?"

He passed me a gun. I didn't recognise the make. It was silenced as usual. "You take this. I'll drive."

We swapped places. "Why the rush? There could be people from the other houses about. Lenny?"

But he was already driving. Before my head had cleared the houses were in sight. The end cottage was painted pink with a shingled drive. The front gardens were small and, mercifully, empty. I winced at the noise our tyres made on the shingle. Then the car was still. "Go," Lenny said.

I went. The door was locked and I shouldered it open. Ahead of me was a flight of stairs and beyond them a kitchen and two rooms off a small hallway. I hesitated for a moment then heard movement from the second of the rooms. I kicked the door open. The man was in his fifties, short and fat. He wore a burgundy dressing gown and sandals. He was standing by a table, a newspaper in his hand. His mouth was opening and closing but no sound came out. I knew him. I waited for his features to settle and for the first hint of recognition to cross his face then I shot him in the centre of his chest and then in the head. He fell forwards and didn't move. I knelt by him. One hand was resting by his head, palm downward, fingers splayed. I held it for a moment. Then I left.

Lenny drove quickly. "I don't think anyone saw us."

"I remember his hands. He still has the calluses. I remember each one."

"He used to be a builder."

"Uncle Bernard," I said and laughed.

*

I was almost seventeen when I left home. Lenny took me. I was given two days notice and no say in the matter at all. The thing was, I didn't want to go. It was all I knew; my stinking room, an endless succession of men, a cramped, loveless excuse for a life. Leaving it scared me. Lenny was kind, but then he always was, compared to the others.

"You need to learn a trade," my father told me. He stood by the fireplace, his hands behind his back. He looked bored. "Something useful. You need to look after yourself for once."

I was by the door, a single suitcase in my hand. Lenny was next to me, his face impassive. I didn't know what he did then and it was another week before I found out.

"When will I come back?" I said.

My father looked at his watch and yawned. Actually yawned. "Lenny is a busy man."

"I'm too old," I said. "Aren't I?"

He didn't answer. Lenny said, "Come on, lad," and we left.

*

Back at the caravan Lenny said, "The next couple of days are going to be busy."

He'd made me a sandwich but I couldn't eat. "We're not getting paid for that one, are we?"

"I've got three more lined up. But we've got to be quick and then we've got to leave. Go north somewhere, maybe abroad."

"Why?"

"These men are linked. This isn't my usual way. We'd be caught."

"Why are you doing this?"

He threw my sandwich away and half-heartedly rinsed the plate in the sink. "How old were you? When it started?"

"You were there."

"No. Not at the start." He watched the water as it sluiced off the plate's surface.

"Ten. Eleven. Something like that."

"How many, in total?" He still stared at the sink as though something there fascinated him. The plate was probably cleaner than it had ever been.

I shrugged. "Think of a number." He turned towards me again, drying his hands. "How come you knew my dad?"

"It was a mistake. People change, Luke. Their...tastes change."

"Right."

"Do you want to do this? Will you help me?"

"Killing four of them? Hardly scratches the surface, does it?"

"I know. But it's a start."

I nodded slowly. "It's something. And it matters. Thank you."

He glanced at the floor. I'd never seen Lenny look embarrassed before.

We caught Eugene in the bath. Lenny held him and I cut his throat. I remembered the smell of him, the texture of his skin, the shape of his cock. In the car, as we drove away, I kept laughing and laughing until Lenny told me to shut up.

I didn't recognise Frank at all. He knew my name, though, and Lenny's. He screamed them over and over as he begged for mercy huddled in the corner of his isolated cottage. I shot him four times then handed the gun to Lenny. "I don't know him."

"You do, Luke," Lenny said. I took his word for it.

It was dark outside and the air was cold and no matter how deeply I inhaled I couldn't seem to get quite enough oxygen into my lungs.

"Are you ok?" Lenny said. He put a hand on my shoulder then let it drop away again.

"Never better."

"Nearly done. For now, at least."

"Who's next?"

"Derek."

"The name doesn't ring a bell."

He was beside me now. "I expect they all blur into one."

"Not exactly."

"Anyway, I've got a meeting with him. Tomorrow. Early."

"A meeting?"

"Derek has a wife and children."

"Ah. Your code."

"A man must have his limits."

"No women, no children."

"It's a simple rule."

"And you've always stuck to it, have you?"

"Almost always," Lenny said.

We met Derek at seven-thirty at the ruins of an old church a couple of miles from Sheringham. He stepped out of his 4x4 and frowned when he saw me. Then Lenny was next to him, smiling, slapping him on the back, driving an eight-inch kitchen knife deep into his chest. Derek fell forward and Lenny slid deftly to one side to avoid breaking his fall. Lenny knelt and rolled the dying man onto his back. I came to his side.

"Does he ring a bell now?"

"Vaguely."

"I thought he would have made more of an impression, the things he did to you."

"And how do you know what he did?"

"I watched," Lenny said. His eyes were on my face but I kept looking at the body. For the first time I felt that Lenny wanted something. Love? Forgiveness?

"Why the hell did he meet you?"

"Why do you think? He thought I had something for him. Or someone."

"Didn't he know what you do?"

"He didn't. He does now."

Then he surprised me. He kicked Derek hard in the face. He did it twice more then straightened his clothes and walked back to the car. I followed.

"Is that it, then?" I said.

Lenny gunned the engine and drove past Derek's body. "Almost," he said.

I realised where we were going long before we arrived. Not that the roads were familiar but something inside me flipped and shuddered and a flat, metallic taste settled in my mouth.

The boy who opened the door was maybe thirteen, with floppy blond hair and eyes that were too big and too bright. He could have been my brother. Perhaps he was. He held the door open and stared at the floor.

My father was in the study.

"You look like shit," I said.

His favourite leather armchair dwarfed him now. His eyes were sunken, his skin yellow-tinged and deeply lined.

I moved closer. When he spoke his breath was like a chemical spillage. "You took your time."

"Been busy," I said.

"Won't you come any closer? It's the smell, I suppose. Bowel cancer. The smell is the least of it, believe me."

I pointed the gun at his head.

"I never touched you," he said.

"Never," I agreed.

He blinked slowly. "You're doing me a favour. I've got six months. At most." He tried a smile. "I'm assured it will feel like longer."

I glanced at Lenny. He nodded. I lowered the gun. "Where is she?" A thin shaft of sunlight fell across my father's lap. He seemed to recoil from it. "Why?"

"I want to know what you did with her."

"Ask him," he said, nodding at Lenny. As the light strengthened the skin on his hands became transparent. I could see veins and bone. I had to look away. "You can go now," he said.

The boy was sitting on the stairs, his head cast down.

"What about him?" Lenny said as I slammed the door behind me.

"He's not my problem," I said.

We sat in the car for ten minutes without speaking. I kept my eyes turned away from the front door and the upstairs window. Eventually I said, "You've kept in touch, then?"

"On and off."

"Are we sitting here all night?"

I didn't think the car would start at first. It had a manual choke and Lenny was too heavy with it and almost flooded the engine. He got it going eventually and we drove towards the outskirts of the city.

It was early evening when we entered Lincolnshire. "It's even flatter than Norfolk," Lenny said.

We stopped at a service station and Lenny bought a cheap bunch of flowers. He gave them to me as he ducked back into the driver's seat.

"For me? You shouldn't have."

"You'll need them in a bit."

We bypassed Sleaford and Lenny took a couple of minor roads then stopped to wrench open the entrance to an abandoned gravel pit, closing the gate behind us. We drove across a narrow, flint-strewn road, past two small flooded pits. The road widened and we passed empty portakabins, an old weighbridge and three rusting hoppers. Ahead of us lay a lake that was bigger than both of the smaller pits combined. It was enclosed by man-made cliffs. The water was green and choppy and the low sunlight didn't penetrate it at all. Lenny parked and made no attempt to move.

"Take your time."

"Here?"

"I haven't stopped for the scenery."

"I mean, *exactly*?"

Lenny nodded.

"How do you know?"

"I just do," he said.

I took the flowers and stood by the water's edge. I had no idea what to do. I didn't know any prayers. I tried to summon up my mother's face but I couldn't. I lobbed the flowers into the dirty water and went back to the car.

"That was quick," Lenny said.

"There's something I want you to see."

"What?"

"This is difficult, Lenny. Humour me, please?"

He shrugged and got out of the car. I let him walk ahead. He stumbled on a piece of flint and dropped onto one knee. It was the only hint of clumsiness that he'd shown in all the years I'd known him. He turned his head back and upwards, towards me. "Bugger," he said, smiling. The smile froze when he saw the gun.

He wasn't heavy. I emptied his pockets then kissed his face and tipped his body into the water. He floated for a while then sank. I wiped the blood from my mouth, walked back to the car and drove north.

Dogfight

We were stood on the cliff top at Hunstanton when we first saw the Spitfire. It was a clear day and I was pointing across the Wash, telling Danny that the spit of land in front of us was the Lincolnshire coast. He shrugged and walked ahead, kicking at the gorse and heather. I bit my lip and wondered how interested I would have been at Danny's age, at fifteen. Not at all, I supposed. But I would have pretended to be.

I heard it before I saw it. Later I thought that I knew it was a Spitfire from the engine noise, but I'm not sure that's possible. I'm too young to have heard one in the flesh. There have been films, of course, and countless documentaries, and I must have watched most of them over the years. And I've read enough about the Spitfire's Rolls Royce Merlin engine to imagine that I would know exactly how it would sound. But this was different.

It began as a bass growl, grew almost instantly into an animal roar that entered not so much through the ears as the bowels and became at once all-consuming. The hairs on my arms and neck were erect before the aeroplane itself tore over us. It was unmistakeably a Spitfire; elliptical, yellow-tipped wings, duck-egg blue underside, sleek, clean lines. Beautiful and feminine and deadly. It hurled itself towards Skegness. Soon it was a speck, glinting in the low sun. Then it was gone.

"Jesus. Did you see that?"

Danny shrugged, shielded his eyes as he glanced back at me. "Some old plane."

The air still trembled. "Some old plane," I said. "It was a Spitfire, Danny."

"Whatever." He started walking again. I followed at a distance. It was my turn to sulk.

Later, back at the chalet, I cooked pasta for supper. It had darkened and the late October wind that tugged gently at the chalet's cheap curtains had the merest edge to it; winter's puppy-teeth.

I asked Danny to close the window and he did, reluctantly.

"Heat the sauce for me, mate. Make yourself useful."

He did that, too, standing next to me at the stove. He was almost my height already, gangly, growing into himself. He was good looking when he smiled, which wasn't often and, understandably, even less often since his mother died. I could smell his odour. I should have said something, but it's a hard thing to do, tell your son that he smells. A good dad would have done, without hesitation. I made a mental note to mention deodorant in the morning.

"You bought me one of those lame Airfix kits once, didn't you?" Danny said suddenly. "A Spitfire. I remember now."

"You were about ten," I said. "I had loads of those kits when I was a kid. Loved them. I hoped you would too."

"Right," Danny said. He gave me one of his rare smiles. It really did transform his face. There was something of his mother in his dimpled cheeks and clear grey eyes. "Who did you really buy it for, Dad?"

I smiled back. "I have no idea what you're talking about."

"Ok. Who built it and painted it and put it on his bedside table?"

"Well, that might have been me. Made a good job of it, too. Then mum went and chucked it away. How could she? Devastated, I was."

His smile faltered. He gave the sauce a final stir. "This is ready."

"We've got to be able to mention her," I said gently.

"I'm hungry, dad." His voice was the sullen side of neutral. He didn't look at me. It had been six months. Nothing really. And yet…you have to move on, don't you? Was it harder to lose a mother or a wife? What sort of man asks a question like that?

I served the pasta and we ate at the small table.

"I wonder where it came from?" I said.

"What?"

"The Spitfire."

Danny grunted, shrugged, and ate simultaneously.

"I mean, I don't suppose that there are many left that are still airworthy."

He kept eating. Quite noisily.

"I'm sorry," I said. "I know you're not interested."

I saw his face change as he made an effort. It was good of him, really, and more than I usually did.

"Perhaps it was being filmed," he said.

"Maybe," I said.

"Perhaps your Granddad was saying hello." The pitch of his voice had dropped a fraction and his eyes tilted towards mine from beneath his fringe.

The hairs on my neck stiffened for the second time that day. "I think not," I said. "Anyway, he flew Hurricanes, not Spitfires."

"Right. And that means so much to me," Danny said.

We ate the rest of the meal in silence.

*

It was my father's father who ignited my fascination with the Battle of Britain. Mum died when I was young and dad worked on the rigs so I lived with my grandfather for sometimes months at a time. He was different to the rest of the family. My dad and I, my uncles and cousins, were ordinary to the point of blandness. Average sized, neither ugly nor handsome, we were designed to fade into the background, to live quiet, unremarkable lives. But granddad was tall and angular with a face that would have left a cartoonist confused over which feature he should concentrate on. A prominent, hook-shaped nose jutted from beneath a vast forehead that grew alarmingly as his hairline receded. His chin was sharp and long. He wore a bushy white moustache that bristled like something struggling to declare its independence. He quivered with unfocussed energy. He kept fit and trim and walked for miles every day. He was sexually active well into his seventies, with a variety of women. I know because he told me. He had ice-blue eyes that could see straight through you and rarely settled on a single point for very long.

He fascinated and terrified me.

*

His name was Douglas Fraser. He had married into money in the mid-thirties, but his wife died in 1938, during childbirth. He told me that he joined the RAF in the summer of 1939 because he was bored and needed a challenge. After his training he was stationed in France. He found the first months of the war incredibly dull. Apart from the French women, that is. When he told me about them his eyes illuminated and his lips smacked together wetly. I was twelve. It disturbed me. It disturbs me now, thinking about it.

As Germany's air offensive became imminent he was transferred to Croydon and then to Northolt, where he spent the rest of the Battle of Britain attempting to intercept the massive waves of German bombers before they reached London.

"I was green in France," he told me, "Useless. Like most of us fresh out of training I thought I knew it all, but I didn't have a clue. Once, I chased a stricken 109 halfway to Paris. Blew all my ammo in one long burst when the bloody thing was the best part of a mile away. Just a speck. Pathetic. I panicked, got lost, limped home hours late, shitting myself, expecting any moment to be blindsided by some Nazi who knew what he was doing. But if you live, you learn. By the time I was sent back to England I was a half-decent pilot. I was ready." He leant forward in his seat. His blue eyes fixed onto mine. "28th July 1940. The first time I killed a man."

Then he told me about it. And how much he enjoyed it.

*

The next morning when I walked into town to fetch the Sunday papers and some milk the wind had swelled into something significant. It brought rain with it, too. Light rain, admittedly, but it was cold and persistent.

Danny didn't stir until around eleven. I had time to eat breakfast, read the papers. And to think. Never a good idea. Time to wonder exactly what I was doing here, alone with my son, in a tiny chalet on the Norfolk coast, as autumn bled into winter. I loved my son – words are so easy, aren't they – but we weren't close, never had been. My work took me away frequently, although with less frequency since Natalie died, and Danny was very much his mother's son. Always would be.

It was Debbie's idea, the long weekend. We met through the Internet. Just friends, that's all. I'd tried to take things further but she'd resisted. I think I liked her better for that. She thought I should make more of an effort with Danny. Stop farming him out to nannies and various distant family members. Spend some 'quality' time with him. Right. Cheers, Debs. I did it to impress her. I'm old enough to know better.

When Danny eventually surfaced he refused my offer of breakfast.

"It's raining," I said. "We'll have to stay in for a while."

"Great," he said, glancing at the Sunday Mirror then pushing it away.

"If it gets out later we'll go for a walk. Find somewhere to eat."

"Whatever," he said.

In many ways he was an easy child. Or so Natalie told me. Compliant. He never quite cared enough about anything to make a fuss. As though he was born with a very modern sense of detachment. My perfect post-ironic son.

In the middle of the afternoon the sun made a guest appearance. It was a half-hearted effort, but it was better than nothing and at least the rain had stopped.

It had become claustrophobic in the chalet. I put my book down. "Right," I said. "Shift yourself. We're going for a walk."

He unplugged the earpiece of his I-pod. "What's wrong with the car?"

"We always use the car. A walk will do us good. Fresh air, exercise. Get your coat." He sighed loudly as he roused himself. "And you can leave that behind," I said, pointing at the I-pod.

"Why?"

"It's all you've done since we got here, listen to that bloody thing. Give it a rest for a bit. We'll be able to talk."

As he threw the I-pod onto the table he said something under his breath. I nearly asked him to repeat it, but decided not to.

After half an hour I wished we had taken the car. I could have listened to a CD or the football commentary on the radio. There's a limit to the number of conversations you can attempt to instigate, to the amount of monosyllabic grunts you can absorb in return.

We made our way towards Brancaster, lingering at an old church, picking our way gingerly through the graveyard. The countryside was understated to the point of drabness, the air damp and chilly. It was as though one season, tired of resisting, was passing itself gratefully over to another.

We walked through a brief wood. Water dripped from the high branches, fell onto my face. I braced myself and tried again. "I can get us tickets to the football soon, if you want."

"I don't like football, dad. You know that."

"This is Norwich City, Danny. It hardly counts as proper football."

I searched in vain for a glimmer of a smile. We rested at a clearing. I said, "Look, we'll turn back. Get the car, try and find somewhere to eat."

Danny nodded.

We left the wood again. The church was in the distance, the sea to our left. A patchwork of fields and meadows was spread in front of us. The light, dying now as dusk fell, drizzled across them like melting butter.

"Now, that's almost beautiful," I said.

"It's better in the spring," Danny said suddenly. "When the blossom is out." I looked at him. He returned my glance, but only for a moment. "It was mum's favourite."

"You remember?"

"Of course I remember. And we used to come here when you were away."

"I had no idea."

"I know." His expression became pained. He started to say something else, but stopped. I found that I was relieved. I turned, as though to continue back towards Hunstanton, but he blurted out, "You'd be surprised what I remember." It was as though he didn't want to speak. But he had to.

"Really?" I'd spent most of the weekend trying to get my son to talk to me. Now I wanted him to shut up.

"You laughed," he said.

"I laughed?"

His face was no longer bland and soft and pleasant. His features were altogether sharper, more animated. From nowhere, I thought of my grandfather.

"In the hospital. Two days before mum..." His expression shifted. "You were with that nurse. The pretty one. I saw you by the coffee machine when I went to the loo. You laughed. Really laughed, like you meant it. She did, too. I couldn't speak to her after that."

"I don't know..."

"Did you get her number, dad? Be disappointed if you didn't. You were quite an old dog, weren't you? That's what mum said. With a smile, actually. As though she was proud. Made me sick."

I had no idea what to say.

He faced me full on. He seemed older, taller. I felt withered. He said, "By the way, dad, how's Debbie?"

"How did you know..."

"She seems nice. In a stupid kind of way."

"We're just friends."

"Right. I hope she makes you happy."

My mouth hung open.

The sound of the Merlin engine came from behind me and we both turned towards it. The noise was suddenly absurdly loud. It was the Spitfire again. This time it was too close, too low and blue smoke trailed from the engine cowling. I should have been scared, but in all honesty, I was simply grateful for the distraction.

*

"The thing about dogfights is, they're usually over before you know it." We were in his study. He was in his old leather chair. I sat on a cushion on the floor. I looked up at him, rapt. His reminiscences were a treat. It was only later that I realised that he enjoyed them every bit as much as I did.

It was winter. There was an open fire that smouldered quietly. I remember the smell of the smoke and of the whisky that my grandfather used to drink as he spoke. I sipped slowly from a glass of milk.

"At first it was just chance that you survived. And I knew plenty that didn't. Cannon fodder they were, the new fish." His voice was crisp and even and without pity. "But...you got used to it." He leant forward suddenly and his eyes glinted towards mine. I sat back with a start. "Do you play cricket, boy?"

"Sometimes. At school."

"You know how when you're batting it takes a while to get used to the pitch, the light, to see the ball properly?"

"You mean, to play yourself in?"

"Play yourself in. That's it exactly." He pointed at me and smiled and I felt an absurd stab of pride. "It was simply a matter of getting used to the speed of it all. One moment the sky is empty, the next it's full of planes, crammed with the bloody things and then you're all alone again, except for these specks circling behind you. Your face and hands are slick with sweat and you haven't even had a chance to squeeze a shot off." He shook his head, took a sip of whisky. "Bloody frustrating. I thought that would be my war. Flying around in circles until some German blew my stupid head off. I didn't think I'd ever get to shoot down a Hun. And that was all I wanted to do." He gave me another smile. In retrospect, it was horrible. "To kill a man."

"28th July. We were scrambled at dawn. Routine stuff. A formation of Dorniers heading for the docks. That was the message, anyway, but we never saw them. Instead we stumbled across a couple of 109's and a 110. You know much about the 110?"

"The Messerschmitt 110? I've got a model of it. Fighter-bomber. Big, powerful."

He nodded. "But slow. Slow to turn, at least. Compared to the Hurricane." His expression became wistful. "I saw it and I wanted it. I didn't care about the 109's, the others could take care of them."

I was leant right forward now, almost touching his legs. "But, if it got behind you..."

"With that big cannon? It would have been curtains." Another smile, slow and cruel. "All part of the game, boy. But it was never going to happen. Because suddenly, I got my eye in. It was as though time had slowed or my reactions had grown abnormally quick, because...it was all so easy. Like magic. I latched onto his tail and he couldn't shake me off. I sensed his every move a split second before he made it. Finally he made a long desperate banking turn to the right and this hulking great thing was frozen in centre of my gun sight." His voice changed. "I tilted my nose upwards and fired. He flew into my bullets. They stitched a line across the fuselage then hit the cockpit. The Perspex exploded in a spray of red. Like a boil bursting."

He drained his glass and laid it carefully on the small table next to his chair. He was quiet for a long time, his eyes fixed on the fire, his breathing slow, almost imperceptible.

"Granddad?"

"It must be time for your bath."

"But…"

"Don't argue, boy. Then it's your homework."

He stood slowly. I followed him out of the room. The house, big and sprawling, was too much for him really. But the thought of him caged in some tiny council flat was absurd.

As I ran towards the stairs he said, "I followed it down, of course. Looked around in vain for someone who could confirm my kill. Back at base I discovered that two of my colleagues were missing. They were both dead as it turned out. Nobody spoke to me. The consensus was that I had left them to it, that I was only concerned with my own glory. Poor show, they said. They were right. All I wanted to do was get back into the air so that I could do it all over again."

I waited for him to continue but he didn't. When I came downstairs after my bath he was standing on the same spot, staring at nothing.

Later that evening he beat me, as he did occasionally.

*

The Spitfire hammered over us again. I felt my hair quiver in the backwash. But it wasn't alone. Close on its tail was a Me-109. Neat and compact with squared-off wings, mottled fuselage, its engine cowling painted a vivid yellow. The large black crosses on the underside of the wings glinted in the low sun as the German fighter howled past, cannon and machine guns chattering.

"Dad?" Danny said. I had to lip read, actually. The noise was immense. My son's face was white. He looked like a child again and I found I was glad. I reached out my hand and he took it.

The air around us shifted, changed. The Spitfire banked right and climbed, the Messerschmitt followed. But everything slowed, became sepia-edged, less than real. The speed the aircraft were travelling they should have been specks already, but they remained enormous, vivid, trapped in a frame of air directly above our heads.

"What's going on, dad?" Danny's hand felt small and cold.

"It's...a film. That's all. Nothing to worry about."

Our necks craned upwards. The evening felt soft and warm. As though it was summer. The scream of engines strained beyond endurance filled our ears. The staccato clatter of machine-gun fire served as a counter-point.

"No crew. No cameras," Danny said.

The Spitfire rolled onto its back, slid sideways, exposing its belly. German cannon-fire blew a hole in it. Smoke became flame. The Spitfire peeled away. It even died elegantly. The 109 levelled out, sped away from us, then burst out of our frame of reference, emerging as a silhouette against a darkening winter sky. It became noiseless very quickly. Then it was past, gone, as though it had never been.

I was cold again. Danny shivered beside me and I put my arm around him. A bubble of summer sky still persisted, in front of us, moving right to encompass the Spitfire's final smoke-strewn glide into a distant field of barley. It dipped below a spine of trees. We heard a muffled crump, saw two thin tendrils of smoke rise above the tree line.

Danny started to walk towards the smoke. I held him back.

"What?" he said. "We can't..."

"It's over," I said.

The air was cold and normal, the light almost completely gone.

"It's been a difficult time," I said. "For both of us."

He just stared at me.

"It will all seem different in the morning," I said.

I smelled smoke and engine oil. I held my son until he became compliant again.

*

The year that passed was studded with stories of dogfights. I saw them all vividly, in black and white, like a newsreel, from my grandfather's point of view. The massive wing of a Heinkel sheared clean off, the bomber toppling sideways into the sea; getting close to a lame 109, blowing its tail off, then shooting the pilot as he parachuted towards the south coast; a Dornier exploding instantly at the merest squeeze of the fire button, its petrol tank hit; smoke, cordite, biting cold, the taste of terror and instant death, pissing yourself as another Hurricane flashes across your wingtip, missing by inches.

He made it seem so real I felt it all. He lived to kill, he said. They were the happiest days of his life.

Another winter, another evening in his study. But I was older and starting to wonder.

He made himself comfortable, filled his tumbler with whisky. Before he could start I said, "28th July, 1940."

His eyes narrowed as he looked at me. "What about it?"

"The first time you killed a man." I spoke hesitantly. I was frightened but curiosity is a powerful emotion in a thirteen year old.

"I'm hardly likely to forget," he snapped. "And?"

"The Me-110 is a two-seater." He stared at me without blinking. "Two men. Not one man."

"Semantics," he said.

"What does that mean?"

He slammed his glass down so hard whisky spilled over the rim. "Do you know how many men I killed, boy?"

"No…"

"Neither do I." He sat back heavily, looked at me in disgust. "Two men, one man, what difference does it make?"

He was lying but I was too frightened to say anything.

"Fetch my cane."

"But…"

"NOW!"

It was no more than I expected. Another beating. I was used to them and they weren't so bad. Although this one was worse than most.

There were no more stories after that. A week later my dad was home from the rigs and for once the return to our small house and his alcoholic sullenness was almost a relief.

*

It was still early when we got back to the chalet but Danny's face was wilted with exhaustion and he went straight to bed and was asleep instantly.

I sat at the table for a while, sipping beer, my hearing tuned to the wind outside, half expecting to yet again hear the roar of a Merlin engine.

A little later I watched Danny as he slept. I stood in his doorway for half an hour. He snored softly. A surge of guilt swept over me. It was almost a physical sensation, like a blow. As I said, it was Debbie's idea, this weekend. But I had my own agenda also.

"I need to talk to you," I said to his sleeping back. Then I closed the bedroom door and pressed myself against it, my eyes squeezed shut. I bit my bottom lip so hard that it bled.

I'd been summoned to Danny's school three times in the last month. Twice by his Form Tutor, once by the Headmaster. A series of unexplained fires had been started in the gym and in two sets of boy's toilets. They had no proof, they said, but Danny was always in the vicinity. He had also been implicated in the bullying of two younger boys. Again, no proof, but...

They were polite, respectful, embarrassed. They both offered their condolences for my wife's death, the older man, the younger woman, but neither of them could quite meet my eyes.

"A difficult time," they mumbled, "for you, for your son. But, if you could have a word...?"

I shook their hands, said that I would. But I hadn't.

I did, however, find time to snoop around on his computer.

In the *History* file I found reference to porn sites, which I suppose was no surprise, but also downloads of the execution of British and American hostages in Iraq, links to sites dedicated to serial killers, Nazi atrocities and a British website crammed with stills and video clips of domestic animals being tortured and killed.

I hadn't mentioned my discovery to Danny or to Debbie. I'd scarcely admitted it to myself.

Sleep, when it finally came, was deep and dreamless and it was gone ten the next morning before I woke. Danny's bed was empty and unmade. He wasn't in the chalet and his coat had gone.

I dressed quickly and headed towards Brancaster.

*

Before my dad went back to the rigs I told him that granddad beat me. He was getting ready to go out. His cheeks were flushed pink and shiny with aftershave. He smelled of whisky and Old Spice. His soft brown eyes held mine as I spoke then slid away from me as he looked for his jacket and car keys.

"I won't be late," he said. "Don't wait up." He closed the door behind him without looking back.

He didn't come home until lunchtime the next day. His face was grey and already shaded with stubble. I knew better than to speak to him.

A fortnight later he left for the rigs again. A step-aunt and uncle I barely remembered arrived shortly before his departure, to look after me. They were quiet and kind, which took me by surprise.

A week later dad was killed in a fire offshore. His funeral was the last time I saw granddad, although he didn't speak to me. Two months later he was dead as well, hit by a car as he walked to a nearby village. We were cursed, my step-uncle said. I thought he was joking, although I suppose it was an odd thing to joke about. But he wasn't.

They looked after me until I left home at eighteen. Once I asked them if granddad had fought in the Battle of Britain. They just frowned at each other and asked if I wanted another game of scrabble.

*

The wreckage of the Spitfire was in a field, hidden from the road by a row of trees. The port wing had gouged a brown furrow in the middle of the field. The aeroplane's nose was buried in a hedge, the cockpit compressed, the fuselage, its back broken, canted at an angle towards the sky. The other wing was nowhere to be seen.

Danny stood by the wreckage, hands in pockets, head down. I called to him but he ignored me. I walked closer. The air was quiet and soft and spiced with the tang of cordite and aviation fuel.

"I expect you've checked the cockpit," I said as I approached him. "Bit of a mess, isn't it? You can probably find websites that cater for that kind of thing."

I didn't understand my own anger. Danny turned towards me, his eyes wide open, his face full of fear and guilt. "What do you mean?" he said.

"What do you think?"

"I hate you," he said softly.

He faced the wreckage again, his shoulders hunched. I stood next to him. I didn't look at the Spitfire. To look at it was to admit it was real.

"It's not my fault your mother died," I said.

"It's your fault she wasn't happy while she was alive." The words came instantly and were spoken in a monotone.

I didn't have an answer.

"We'd better go. I've got to clear up before we drive home."

"We can't just leave this."

"It's not real, Danny."

"But," he gestured towards the stricken plane, exasperation overcoming his feelings for me, "Look, you can see it, it's in front of your eyes." He moved forward. "You can touch it."

"Don't," I said.

He laid a hand on the fuselage, next to the identification markings. "It reminds me of the stories you used to tell me, about granddad in the war. All the Germans he shot down. You loved them, didn't you? You so wanted me to care."

"They were lies, Danny."

"What?"

"He was a sad old man. A fantasist. He was never in the RAF, never flew. Scarcely saw any active service at all. He made it all up."

"Why?" Danny's brow wrinkled. "Why make up stuff like..." The wrinkles deepened and his eyes flicked onto mine. "And why tell them to me, if you knew they were lies?"

"I wanted them to be true."

I expected disgust, but when his face lifted to mine his eyes were curious, his expression neutral.

I thought of the smell of beer and whisky on my father's breath and of the calluses on granddad's hand as it caught my cheek again. I opened my mouth to speak. As though I had suddenly acquired wisdom enough to make everything right between us with a handful of words. Or I could restore his mother to his side and somehow magic away the memories of his father's stupidity and indifference. But I never had the chance to speak. Perhaps it's just as well.

The air was rent once more by the sound of a fighter engine. The Me-109 was back, steepling towards us, tearing through a sky that seemed old and paper-thin and impossibly blue.

"Not again," Danny said.

"It's ok," I said and he pressed against my side.

It was on us almost instantly but for some reason the 109 veered right at the last moment and its machine-gun and cannon fire smacked into field and hedge. The stump of an old oak was hacked into splinters.

"We've got to run," Danny said.

"It's not real," I said.

He pointed at the flayed hedge. "That looks pretty real to me. It will kill us, dad. We'll die." He sounded disappointed rather than scared. As though his homework had received a slightly lower mark than he expected.

"No," I said. I watched the 109 as it rose and banked right preparing for another pass. "The scale's all wrong. It's like a model. Nothing quite fits. The only things that are real here are you and me."

"Really?" he said.

"Trust me," I said. His hand slid into mine.

The howl of the engine became a scream. The horizon was all Messerschmitt. When it was almost on us I said, "It can't hurt us, Danny."

He moved closer still. Flank to flank, we faced it together.

Mimic

The man who could be my identical twin sits on the edge of a metal-framed bed in an isolation cell that's deep in the recesses of a secret bunker, which itself is buried beneath an abandoned Second World War airfield, somewhere in Norfolk.

He smiles at me. He has a thick black beard, as do I. He has long dark hair that badly needs a wash. As do I. His skin is putty grey as though, like me, he'd spent God knows how many years underground breathing in dead air and other men's sweat. His clothes are the same as mine. Crumpled white cotton shirt and faded jeans.

"So what the fuck have they brought us this time?" Kelly says.

The carpets in our bunker are thick and I hadn't heard him come up alongside me. We stand together and look into the cell. My double gazes back impassively through the strengthened glass. I wonder if in fact I am looking into a mirror and that I can't see Kelly because, perhaps, he's a vampire. Stranger things have happened.

I realise that Kelly is waiting for an answer. I shrug. How am I supposed to know? Kelly wears a stained yellow polo shirt and black shorts. I try to remember his rank. I think he was/is a Major. It scarcely matters. Rank has become redundant in our accidentally egalitarian underground world. Kelly is tall and thin and somehow retains enough motivation to shave almost every week.

"They found him on Dartmoor," Brady says. He sits at a low table in the corner. I think he was a Private back in the days when anyone gave a shit. "Reports of UFO sightings just prior to his discovery. A couple of witnesses reckon they saw something crash on the moor. No sign of any wreckage, though. Just him." Brady frowns. "Weird, though. He was bald and naked when they dropped him in."

Kelly looks at his watch. "That was two hours ago. You didn't think it was worth mentioning?"

Brady shrugs. "Nobody asked."

"But you took photos when you logged him in?"

"Forgot."

"How about the video surveillance?" I say. "Were the cameras running?"

Brady shrugs again. "Doubt it. Unless they turned themselves on." He is picking his nose and reading the same thin paperback that has kept him occupied since...since God knows when.

"I suppose they'll e-mail us a report sooner or later," Kelly says, pretty much to himself. "Take some pictures will you, Mills? Write something down."

"Yes," I say, frowning.

"I thought you'd be a little more interested," Kelly says, "given that he could be you."

"Interested?" I say; "it hadn't occurred to me. It's a little strange, I suppose. Has he spoken?"

Brady marks his place on the page with a dirty finger, looks up, shrugs. "Don't think so."

My double lies on his back with his hands linked behind his head and stares up at the shadows on the low ceiling. "What's the point," I say, "he'll go the same way as all the rest."

"Hope so," Brady says, "might calm Pearce down a bit."

"Will it, fuck," Kelly says, "It's my turn." I notice that his fists clench as he glances at his Browning 9mm lying on the table.

Brady shrugs and turns back to his book.

*

'You are our front line against the alien invasion.' So said the Private Secretary for the Minister of fuck knows what when they sealed us in this tomb Christ knows how many years ago. We swallowed his bullshit as though it was a pint of cold lager on a summer's afternoon. All I can remember of him is the smell of his expensive aftershave and the way his pink fat jowls gleamed in the artificial light.

There were six of us; two scientists, three Army regulars of varying rank and sanity, and me, a low rank civil servant who'd skirted around the edges of the secret service without having the ability or contacts to make any impact. I was a patriot and an idealist. In other words, a really sad bastard.

One of the scientists – I think his name was Hunt – shot himself in the mouth years ago. He even messed that up. Pearce had to finish him off. Which made his day, as I remember.

*

I sit in my sparse living quarters typing a report on a laptop that's perched on the small wooden table. I've been writing the report for years. I'll take two or three months over a draft then read it and decide it makes no sense at all, delete it and start all over again.

Kelly opens the door without knocking. "He still hasn't spoken. Or eaten anything. Just lies there doing his Mills impression, staring at the ceiling."

I shrug. "They'll send our instructions through soon enough."

He rubs his chin with his hand. His eyes seem small and unfocused. "Yeah, well it's my turn, Mills. You tell that bastard Pearce."

"Whatever," I say.

He peers over my shoulder. "Are you still doing that? Why do you delete it every time? You haven't quite got the hang of word processing, have you?"

"I know what I'm doing. I can't get it right. I need to start again."

"It was years ago. Who gives a shit?"

I did.

*

It was meant to be our Roswell. A slow trickle of so called subversives and anarchists had been funnelled down to us in the first decade. It was not what we expected. We followed our instructions anyway and they never varied. None of our prisoners saw daylight again.

Then, during Brady's shift, we had a delivery that was not a political oddball or potential embarrassment. Brady woke us all and dragged us to the holding cell.

"We've got a live one," he said, eyes wide open.

We stood in a semi-circle around the cell.

"Sweet Jesus," Kelly said.

The thing we stared at stirred slightly. It was in the corner of the cell, partly in shadow. It was not human.

"They found it near Wicken Fen," Brady said. He seemed more alive than he had in years. We all did. "They thought it was dead at first."

"Instructions?" Kelly said.

"Just observation for now. Further orders will follow."

"It's a fucking piss take," Pearce said. "Must be April the first. It's a bloke in a suit. Might as well shoot the bastard now, save us the trouble later."

"We're not shooting this one," I said, and surprised myself with the fervour in my voice. "This is different. This is what it's all about."

"Grow up, Mills," Strachen said, "Pearce is right. It's some twat dressed up."

"Funny shaped bloke," Kelly said as peered into the shadow. The creature's sleek black flank turned slightly and gleamed where it caught the light.

"It's not human," Brady said, his eyes still bright with excitement. "I touched it. It felt...I don't know how it felt, but it's not human."

Strachen sneered and said, "You've probably caught something, Brady. The suits are just waiting to see if we all drop dead."

"Bollocks," Brady said uncertainly.

For the first time in years time mattered and we counted the days until our orders came through. Our visitor remained almost motionless in the cell's shadow. We tried to coax it from the darkness as one would a puppy or a kitten, but with no effect.

"I think it's dying," Kelly said. "You've got to feel sorry for the poor bastard."

"My heart bleeds," Pearce said.

"Is that right?" I said. "I couldn't sleep last night. I saw you trying to feed it bread and milk."

Pearce's face flushed, but he said nothing.

"Bunch of soppy wankers," Strachen said. "Why not stick a collar on it and call it Tiddles?"

Two days later I pulled a message off the fax machine. There were seven words on the sheet of green paper.

IF IT'S STILL ALIVE, KILL IT.

I stared at the message for a moment then crumpled it into a ball and stuffed it into the pocket of my jeans.

"Give me that," Strachen said.

I turned. He and Kelly stood in the doorway.

"It's nothing," I said. "Junk fax, that's all."

"Come on, John," Kelly said gently. "Hand it over."

The use of my Christian name made my bowels contract.

"Useless fucker," Strachen said, and lunged at me. He caught me off balance and I tumbled backwards. I tried to fight back, but he was taller and heavier than I was and he pinned me down and fished the paper from my pocket.

He trapped my arms under his knees and unravelled the fax. I could smell his sweat and his foul breath. He read it out.

"You can't kill it," I tried to shout. My words came out high and strangled. I realised I was close to tears.

"We have to, you twat," Strachen snarled. "If we disobey orders they'll pump the gas in and seal us up for good."

I tried to appeal to Kelly but Strachen locked his arm around my throat and I couldn't speak.

Kelly looked at me then looked away. "Pearce, Brady," he snapped, "You know what to do."

I struggled against Strachen's weight, but he held firm.

I heard Pearce and Brady's footsteps fading down the corridor. I heard them cock their semi-automatics.

The gunfire sounded distant and seemed to go on and on. I lay beneath Strachen's flexed muscles and wept.

They spent days swabbing the cell and corridor with hot water and disinfectant, but they never removed the stink of cordite and death.

*

Pearce sits eating corned beef and cold baked beans as my double gazes
equably back at me from his cell.

"I'm looking forward to shooting this ugly bastard," Pearce says.
"Be just like blowing your head off, Mills. That'll be a laugh."

"It's Kelly's turn," I say.

"We'll see."

I turn towards Pearce. "I cut my hair last night, trimmed my beard,
did you notice?"

He glances up from his food. "Yeah, you look great Mills. Lovelier
than ever."

"But look at him, Pearce," I say, pointing at our prisoner, "he's still
my twin. His hair and beard, it matches mine."

"Fascinating."

"Doesn't it interest you at all?"

Pearce wipes tomato sauce from his moustache. "What's the point?
He's dead meat. What's the point in giving a shit?"

He grins up at me and I'm trying to think of an answer when the
lights go out.

"Fuck, fuck, fuck," Kelly says, "it's all down. Back up supply,
everything."

Torchlight scissors the darkness. "Why can't you fix it? You're the
electrical engineer," Brady says.

"Because I can't find anything wrong. It's all perfect, except that it
doesn't work. Phone lines are fucked. That means no e-mail, no
Internet." He pauses. "I take it you all remember what else it means."

"What?" Strachen says.

"It means we've got two hours," I say.

"What do you mean?" Strachen says. My torch picks out his face. I
quite enjoy the fear in his eyes.

"Come on, shit for brains," Pearce says, "you remember. If they lose
contact with us up top for more than two hours they assume we're
compromised. Cyanide time. We'll be gassed and concreted up." He
smiles. "I don't fancy cyanide. I've read that it's not particularly quick.
A bullet in the head will do me. I'll do you lot first for a fee."

"Shut up, Pearce," Strachen sobs and runs into the darkness.

"You think he'd remember something like that," Pearce says.

An hour later Kelly has given up and we sit in candlelight waiting for the end.

"Anyone seen Strachen?" Brady says, and we all shrug.

I take my torch to the holding cell and shine it inside. For a moment I think our prisoner has disappeared, then I see him standing at the back of the cell. He moves forward and smiles. I'm not surprised to see that his navy T-shirt and trousers are identical to mine.

"I can help you," he says.

I hesitate then say, "I thought you were mute."

"No, I just prefer to listen." His voice is my voice, down to the faint interrogative at the end of each sentence, whether it's a question or a statement.

"I should ask who you are, where you're from."

"It's a long story and time is short, I believe."

It's strange sitting in the torchlight with my twin. I can't quite shake the feeling that he's taking the piss. "How can you help," I ask, "can you get the power back on?"

"Of course." I don't attempt to hide my scepticism. "It doesn't matter what you think. I've been weak, but I'm getting stronger." He leans forward on the bed. "I can have the power on in the blink of an eye, but you must understand that everything will change."

His hairline, like mine, is slick with sweat. The air in the cell is fetid.

"What are you talking about?"

"They'll close this place down. You'll have to start a new life, on the outside."

"The outside? We all volunteered for this. We all knew we'd never see the outside again."

"Times change. It'll be difficult, adjusting. But I know you've dreamt of it."

I looked into the darkness, away from his eyes. My eyes. "Rubbish. There's nothing for me out there. Never was."

"She's still alive, you know. Divorced a couple of years ago. Lives alone in a big house. Quite wealthy, apparently."

"Where d'you get all this shit? And what the fuck are you trying to do to me?"

"I'm trying to help you."

"Assuming for a moment that this is not all bullshit, what happens to you?"

He smiles. "What was always going to happen. A bullet. Several bullets. It doesn't matter."

"Doesn't matter?"

"I'm older than you'd think. Too old. It's meant to be this way. I'm giving you another chance."

I stand, shaking my head. "I don't get any of this."

"You don't have to," he says, "just go back to your friends. By the time you get there the power will be back on."

Kelly, Pearce and Brady are sitting around the candlelit table. Pearce is praying, which is a bit of a surprise.

I open my mouth to speak when the lights come on.

Pearce opens his eyes, winces against the brightness of the light then looks down at his hands, which are still clasped together. "Shit, I'll have to try that again," he says.

The air conditioning hums fitfully, a telephone rings and Kelly and Brady sit with their mouths hanging open.

It takes Kelly almost fifteen minutes to download the backlog of e-mails. He and Brady collate them and read them over and over, scratching their heads and laughing occasionally.

Pearce, who wandered off a little while ago, comes back and nods towards the others. "What's up with them?" he asks.

"They're coming to terms with our orders," I say. "We're being closed down. In forty-eight hours we'll all be free."

"Fuck off," Pearce says.

"It's true. Back pay, full pension, rent free accommodation. New identity if you want. Which I'd recommend in your case, Pearce."

He blinks. His face is white. "But this is my home. They can't make me leave."

"I think you'll find they can. Did you find Strachen?"

"What?" Pearce says. His eyes seem wet. "Yeah. He's in his room."

"Better give him the news."

"I wouldn't bother. He hanged himself with his belt."

*

Kelly and Brady wash and shave and change their clothes. Pearce and I cut Strachen down and lay him on his bed. Pearce's face is still bloodless and he doesn't speak.

Later, Kelly takes me to one side. He wears a freshly pressed white shirt and a tie and his face is pink and clean and the stink of deodorant is almost overpowering.

"You know what we've got to do, don't you?" he says. "We've got to shoot him."

"I know."

"Would it be easier for you if you did it yourself?"

"No. Anyway, how do you know bullets will kill it?"

"Don't start that again. He's just a bloke who happened to be in the wrong place at the wrong time. It's sad, but shit happens."

"How do explain his appearance? Whatever I do, whatever I wear, he copies me."

"Coincidence," he says, looking away. "Anyway, we're all stir crazy, perhaps we imagined it."

"You know that's not true, Kelly."

"Do I? Well perhaps I just don't give a fuck. We're getting out of here, whatever the consequences." He closes his eyes and breathes in deeply. "I'm going to do it now."

"Just give me a minute with him then."

Kelly nods reluctantly.

By the cell Brady chats animatedly to Pearce who ignores him and stares at the floor.

I open the cell door and walk in. He sits on the bed and smiles at me.

"Will you speak to me? It makes no difference now."

He shakes his head slowly. His eyes are a little too bright and I assume mine are too. I want to understand, but I can't find the words. He extends his right hand towards me. Like me he has a callus on his first finger. His grip is firm and dry. He puts his other hand on my shoulder and pulls me into a rough embrace. Close to tears I pat his back.

He may look like me, but at least he smells different, I think. His scent is acrid, faintly chemical, nothing I recognise at all. I close my eyes and try to remember how the wind feels and how cut grass smells in the summer.

Then a warning flares somewhere distant, but it is far, far too late. Something twists deep inside. There's no pain; in fact a deceptive, pleasant, warmth seeps upwards. I feel my perspective change. When my eyes open I'm lying on the bed, propped up on my elbows and my double is pulling away from me. He is smiling slightly and seems close to tears.

I try to sit up further, to push myself off the bed, but I can't move. I can't speak either; my mouth seems frozen in a half smile. Kelly waits at the door of the cell, his Browning in his hand. My double joins him. "Let's get this over with," he says.

Kelly puts his hand on his shoulder. I rage briefly against my immobility, try to scream a warning, but can't do it. The thing that resembles me turns to observe my impotence. I see something shimmer beneath the mask he has chosen, something dark and gleeful. "I can't watch," he says and turns away. I see something glitter and caper even through the white shirt and the pale flesh.

"Fuck this," Kelly says, and points the pistol at my face.

Tilt

On the first day of March a vicious northerly wind and acres of low, snow-stuffed cloud swept across the East of England. Brisk and business-like, it dumped its load and disappeared across the Wash. For a day-and-a-half Norwich was snowed to a stand still. Monday, wiped out. *White-Out*, as the Eastern Evening News called it. Every school in the county closed. And most of the shops and businesses in the city centre. For once, most people took police advice and didn't attempt to drive. A few did, of course, and the days eerily muffled quiet was fractured by the mew of sirens and the sudden scream of brakes.

Our house is close to Thorpe Road and the growl of traffic is a constant. Drew and I found the lack of it a source of wonder as we listened to the local news on the radio and drank cup after cup of tea and ate biscuits and pretended it was exciting. It was a bonus, us having the day off together. She couldn't admit she'd rather be at work. Neither could I.

I stood by the bay window at the front of the house, tense for no obvious reason, the smell of Drew's perfume and the sense of her behind me. The snow had stopped, but the wind had a shrill, hysterical edge and it seemed to be hurling itself directly at us, battering glass and bricks, resenting them for standing in its way.

I took a step back and felt Drew's hand on my shoulder. "Sorry," I said.

She took her hand away. "It *is* scary, isn't it?"

"Yes," I said.

I don't think I was talking about the weather. I don't think she was either.

*

Thirty-six hours later the temperature was nudging double figures and the roads were awash with snowmelt. The wind had gone and a low sun kept the streets sleek, slick, shimmering. When the traffic eased the air was full of the sound of water fleeing drain-ward.

Work resumed. Drew gave a little sigh when her boss called early on Tuesday morning. "Back to normal," she said. Her voice was sing-song, hiding the relief.

"Me too, I expect."

"Let me know?" Drew said. "Leave a message on my mobile?"

I nodded. I wouldn't bother and she knew that I wouldn't. But she asked anyway.

I watched her dress from the bed. "Anyway, perhaps you'll be lucky, get another day off. You know what the Council's like."

"Can't see them leaving the loons another day."

"I wish you wouldn't call them that." She fastened her bra, quickly, expertly, her back to me.

She was gone within ten minutes. No coffee, no breakfast. A whiff of perfume as she kissed my cheek. "You're in a hurry," I said.

"Busy, busy. Insurance waits for no girl. We've got a day's backlog to tackle and Barry says that Janice is off sick."

She said something else but I tuned it out. I waved at her as she backed towards the door.

It turned out she was right about my job. The entrance of the Adult Education Centre where I work was flooded so I had another day's leave.

The next day was Wednesday and that afternoon the first bomb went off.

I was in the garden when it happened. I went to work in the morning then said I had a stomach bug at lunchtime and went home. I should have been in a hotel room across the other side of the city. It was much closer to the blast. Maybe the windows of our room would have been shattered and Sam and I would have been added to the long list of those suffering minor injuries.

I was thinking about Sam, I suppose. Vaguely, at least. It wasn't the first time she'd called off at the last minute. A pattern was starting to form. I was wondering if I should take the hint. I don't know why I was in the garden. There's not much to see, even in the summer. Now it was dead, dun-coloured, a brief lawn and narrow, unadorned borders. I'd pave the whole lot over if I could be bothered.

The noise was sudden and shocking. It didn't last long. The earth beneath my feet trembled and the walls of my house and the air surrounding them seemed to shudder for a moment. The whole city heard it, felt it. Norwich is a small city and it was a big explosion.

I took a step backwards. I looked up and down the long row of back gardens but there was no one else to be seen. In the stunned, vacuum-like silence that immediately followed the blast I wondered if I'd imagined it. Then the car alarms kicked in, and the screams. I wondered if the distance made them worse. They seemed disembodied, spectral. Soon they were drowned by the sirens.

I went inside, turned on the TV and the radio. After a couple of minutes of excruciating normality both the local and national stations reported news of an explosion in Norwich city centre. I thought of Drew's office, at the city end of King Street. I thought...I don't know quite what I thought.

I switched between TV and radio and between the various stations but it was half an hour before the reports had any sort of coherence. By that time Drew was home. Her face was milk-white, expressionless.

"Thank god," I said. I tried to hold her but she pushed me away. "I called your office," I lied.

"Did you?"

"The line was busy."

She nodded. "I saw...some of it. On the way home. They were cordoning it off, but..." She put a hand to her mouth.

I held her again and this time she let me.

The news was a blur of speculation, updates, corrections. Casualty figures eddied, peaked at fifty, dropped to twenty, settled at twenty-four. Give or take. Deaths, that is. An aerial shot of the bombsite played over and over. The targets seemed arbitrary, odd. A row of small business units just to the east of St Andrew's Hall had gone. Ceased to exist. A loan company, an estate agent, a software specialist, a beauty consultant. Most of the dead were employees, apparently. Some customers, a handful of passers-by. Many more injured and shocked scattered throughout a two-mile radius.

Drew sat in an armchair, trembling, drinking wine, mouthing 'why?' over and over again.

It got on my tits eventually.

"Can we turn this off now?" I said. It was close to midnight. I stood by the TV. "They're just repeating themselves."

"No." She sat forward, hugged herself. "Trust you to be so calm. Detached. Can't have you feeling anything, can we?"

"What do want me to do?"

"Just look as though you care."

I pointed at the screen. "It's words, that's all. They don't know anything. It's knee jerk stuff. I mean, al-Qaeda, the IRA. Please."

"Who, then?"

"I don't know. They don't know. All will be revealed, I'm sure."

Drew poured herself some more wine. "It's like 9/11."

"Is it, bollocks," I said. "This is Norwich, Drew. It'll be a mistake. Perhaps it's not a bomb. Maybe a gas main fractured..."

"They said..."

"They're guessing. Just like we are."

Then she was crying again, silently. "Those poor people. I saw..." She closed her eyes and shuddered.

"You saw what?"

"I saw enough," she said. "I saw..."

Then the phone rang.

I answered it. I covered the mouthpiece and said to Drew, "It's your mother. Again."

Drew had already fielded several calls from family and friends across the country making sure she was ok. But then Drew was popular. A sweetheart. Nobody had enquired after my health. I was almost hurt. She stood with her back to me as she took the call. I was on my way out of the room when I heard her say, "What about Sam?" Then, "She'll be fine. You know, Sam. She gets in touch when she's ready." A pause. "I'm not going round there now. I don't care if she is my sister." Then she hung up.

"What?" I said. I was by her side.

"Sam's not answering her phone. And her mobile is dead. Mum wants me to go and check on her. Bloody pointless. She'll be with her latest..." She searched for a word.

"Victim?" I said.

"Mum and dad are blind to her promiscuity. Always were."

"You're a bloody prude, Drew."

"She's my sister and I love her." Her voice had all the animation of the speaking clock.

Something nagged at me. "Aren't you worried? She *could* have been..."

"Not Sam. She's probably not even in the country. She'll have swanned off somewhere on holiday without telling anyone." She wouldn't look at me.

I tried to remember what Sam had said when she'd phoned me that lunchtime to cancel our arrangement. Something about an appointment. I'd stopped listening once it was obvious I wouldn't get my end away. I never bloody listened.

"What?" Drew said.

"Nothing. I'm going to bed."

In the morning the weather changed again. It was milder still and the wind rose suddenly and shrieked across the city, flattening dying trees, shredding nerves and the low, grey cloud that had gathered at roof level. I was up early, but Drew was already dressed, hunched in front of the TV, drinking coffee.

Without looking at me she said, "The weather's not helping. They worked through the night but they don't think there are any more survivors."

"How many dead, then?"

"Twenty-three, they think. They've started naming them."

"Anyone we know?"

"Are you taking the piss?"

I put my hands up. "Bloody hell, Drew. It's a small city. I just wondered…"

"I'm sorry, Tom." She stood slowly and stretched. "I didn't sleep well. I'll get you some coffee."

I watched the TV as she rummaged in the kitchen. When she came back she handed me a mug and I said, "They've changed their tune, haven't they?"

"What do you mean?"

"Back tracking. Last night it was a bomb, no doubt about it. Five hundred pounds of Semtex they reckoned. Now…nothing official at all. And the speculation has stopped. Nobody dare say anything. Someone's had a word."

"It's too early, that's all. Last night was a reflex, hysteria. Media instincts and all that."

I looked at her, saw for the first time the dark pools under her eyes and the fresh lines next to her mouth when she tried to smile. "How long have you been up?"

"Long enough."

"Have you heard from Sam?"

"It's barely seven, Tom. She'll still be in bed. If not actually asleep."

"Drew. She's not that…" I hesitated.

"Not that bad?" Drew snorted. "Why the concern?"

"She's your sister."

She held my gaze for a long moment. "Anyway," she pointed at the screen, "I'm going there today."

"What? Ground Zero?"

"Now you are taking the piss."

"Yes. What do you hope to achieve?"

"I want to help." She tried to look defiant, failed.

"Help? How, exactly? You won't even get near it. I'm not sure there's an urgent need for insurance brokers on site at the moment." She seemed to shrink as I spoke. Her face became small and pinched and I thought she was going to cry but she didn't. "I'm sorry. I don't know…look, you do what you need to do."

"I don't need your blessing."

"Of course not." I caught her expression. Haunted. She looked haunted. "What exactly did you see yesterday?"

Then she was animated suddenly. She gave a huge shrug as she grabbed her coat. "Oh, you know, Tom, body parts, that's all. No big deal. Just something to sneer at and dismiss."

"Drew…" I said, but she was already in the hallway, at the door, slamming it behind her.

I watched the wind bully her to the car then went to the phone and tried Sam's mobile number but it was still dead.

*

Three weeks earlier Sam and I had spent the afternoon in a shabby room in a small hotel on Queens Road. She was dressing slowly, I was watching her from the bed. "Why here, Sam?" I wrinkled my nose. "Bloody room stinks of curry. Could have gone to your place. Or to a nice hotel."

She buttoned her blouse. "You know I like slumming it."

"You talking about me or this place?"

"Take your pick." I threw my shirt at her. She caught it and dropped it on the floor. She was short, stocky, the opposite of her sister. Drew was languid, laid back, but Sam emitted a curious restless energy that made her hard to ignore. She looked out of the window at the main road. It was awash with rain. "Bloody weather. Wish it would make its mind up. It was like summer yesterday."

"Chatting about the weather? What have we come to?"

"It's odd, though, don't you think?"

"Not really."

"You've got no imagination."

"You weren't saying that a minute ago."

"Get over yourself, Tom." She zipped her jeans up and sat on the bed. "Seriously. Can't you feel it? There's something in the air. And the seasons are fucked."

"You sound like Drew."

Sam stood quickly and cuffed my head. "God forbid."

She slid her shoes on and searched for her bag. "In a hurry?" I said.

"Things to do."

"Like what? Scrounge some more money off daddy?"

She tilted her head towards me. "Why are you trying to wind me up?"

It was a good question. "Just trying to make you laugh. I like it when you laugh. Gives me a hard on."

"Tom, everything gives you a hard on."

"Not quite," I said.

"You mean my blessed sister? Poor you. Shouldn't have married her, should you?"

I reached for her but she pulled away from me. "You wouldn't have me. What was I supposed to do?"

"I have you once a month, sometimes more." She gave a half smile that I didn't return.

"Not quite what I meant."

She glanced at her watch. "I prefer to keep my options open."

"Along with other things."

"It's not working, Tom. I've got to go."

She went. I lay back and stared at the rain.

*

I didn't go to work. I didn't phone in sick. I turned the TV off and slumped onto the sofa, stared at the blank screen. The silence wore me down eventually. I listened to Elliott Smith's *Figure 8* and *Either/Or*. Didn't exactly cheer me up. I tried to read a book, but, as good as Graham Swift's prose is, it couldn't compete with the enormity of what was happening outside.

I turned the TV on again. The names of the dead ran on a loop across the bottom of the screen. Ten bodies had yet to be identified. A local reporter interviewed people in the city centre, to 'get their reaction'. What exactly did she expect? It was pointless, of course. What could they say, besides the obvious platitudes? The white, shocked faces had impact, though. I looked at them and thought of Drew.

She came home just before noon.

"Was it worth it?" I said.

"It's amazing, actually." She ran both hands through her hair. Her eyes were brighter and there was colour in her cheeks. "The atmosphere…it's hard to explain." Her expression changed. "What are you doing here?"

"Skiving, like you." She didn't say anything. "I couldn't face going outside. I suppose I don't want to accept the reality of it."

"It might do you good."

"I'm fine. What do you mean about the atmosphere?"

She sat and leant forward. She seemed younger, energised. "People are talking. Connecting. It's as though all sorts of barriers have been stripped away." She pulled a handful of paper scraps from her coat pocket and dumped them on the coffee table. "Names, phone numbers."

"Lucky you. It won't last."

"Just trying to make sense of it, I suppose," she said it as though I hadn't spoken.

"And did they? Make sense of it?"

"Not really. How can they? We?"

"I don't know," I said. "Someone will, though. I expect. Did you get close to the site?"

"Close enough." She snorted indignantly. "Did you see those vultures on the telly?"

"What?"

"Bloody Pepsi, McDonalds, Cadbury's. Handing out burgers and drinks, free samples for the crowds and the rescue workers. With their bloody logos and stupid hats. Advertising now, for Christ's sake."

"I didn't notice them."

"Well, that will piss them off. Bloody drug dealers."

"That's a bit harsh, isn't it?"

"Is it?" Her eyes met mine. "Let's go upstairs," she said.

"What?"

"Nothing." She stood suddenly, flustered.

"Ok."

"Forget it. I'm sorry…" She was mumbling, her head down.

I stood as well, extended my hand. "No, come on. Why the hell not?"

"I'm sorry," I said, twenty minutes later.

We were naked on the bed. Drew had her hand on my chest. She was on her side, next to me. Her hair fell across her face. "Well, it's been a while, hasn't it? With me, at least."

"Drew."

"And I'm not Sam, am I?" She didn't sound angry, or particularly disappointed. Which was something. I think.

I turned towards her and rested my hand on her stomach. "I can still…"

"Still what?" She slapped my hand away. "I've got something in the drawer that will take care of that."

She kissed me with surprising tenderness on the mouth then stood and dressed quickly. I wondered idly if we would ever kiss again. She stood by the window. "This weather," she said.

I thought of Sam, how she'd said something similar in a different bedroom three weeks earlier. "You too," I said.

"What?"

"Nothing."

She pulled the net curtain to one side and pressed her face against the glass. "It's bloody snowing again."

"You're joking."

"Come and have a look."

I joined her at the window. I felt her dress rub against my bare hip. I made a hole in the condensation and peered through it. The light was the colour of paper. The air was still and crammed with snowflakes the size of dinner plates.

"This morning it was blowing a gale," I said.

"The wind died at about ten. As though someone flicked a switch. Now this. It's changing every hour or two."

"This is England," I said. "The weather's meant to be changeable."

"But this?" she said, gesturing at the window.

"How should I know? Global warming?" Drew looked at me in disgust. "Well, what do you think? Signs and portents? The first glimpse of the apocalypse?"

"You shouldn't joke about it."

"Who says I'm joking?"

We were facing each other. Suddenly, absurdly, I got an erection. Drew glanced downwards then said laconically, "It's a bit late for that."

"Years too late," I said.

I'd just got downstairs when the phone rang. It was Mike, my boss. Drew gave me a quizzical look from the sofa and I mouthed his name at her.

"Are you ok?" Mike said.

"Fine. Look, I should have called, but…"

"Don't worry about it," Mike said, "the place is deserted. Hardly any inmates, hardly any staff. I'm buggering off myself in a minute."

"The thing is, Drew's sister is missing. Drew's beside herself. We all are."

"Missing? Shit."

"I'm sure it will be fine, but..." I could feel Drew's eyes on my back. She hissed my name but I ignored her.

"You must be worried sick. Are the police any help?"

"Trying not to worry them at the moment."

"Right. Look, take all the time you need." I heard him sigh and when he spoke again his voice had thickened. "It's a terrible thing. All those people. I can't get my head around it."

He obviously wanted to talk. He lived alone. His wife had left him a year ago. "I know. It's a fucker. You've been great, Mike, but I've got to go. Keep the line open, in case there's any news about Sam."

"Of course. Take care."

I mumbled something and was already putting the phone down. When I turned I saw that Drew had turned an interesting colour.

"How dare you? I'm beside myself, am I?"

"Perhaps you should be. Her phone's still dead. No answer on her landline."

"You've been trying, then?"

"Someone's got to."

"I think my mum and dad can handle it."

She was close to me now, rigid with anger. I couldn't hold back. "I've never seen you like this. I don't get it. Even if I have been fucking her, don't pretend you give a shit. I know very well you've been banging your boss for the past eighteen months." I shrugged. "Whatever. He's married so this is probably easier for both of you. Works for me, too. Nice little front..."

"SHUT UP!" She had her eyes closed tight and her fingers stuffed in her ears. As though if she couldn't see me, hear what I was saying, then none of this was real. None of it counted at all.

The storm came from nowhere. The first crack of thunder was directly above our house and it was so loud that for a moment I thought another bomb had gone off. Then the lightning came and the room was a brilliant, frozen white for too many seconds.

Drew said, "Jesus Christ Almighty," and started crying.

I ran to the back door, stepped into the garden. The sky was like bruised velvet. The snow that Drew and I had watched only a few minutes earlier had completely gone. The air was so thick I thought I could see it settle in front of me. Thunder punched through it, like an artillery barrage. All the hairs on my body stiffened. Then the rain came, massive drops hitting the window behind me like gunshots. The water that drenched my face and hair was as warm as blood.

*

The next day Drew went back to work. I didn't. I kept the curtains drawn and sat and watched television until Drew came home. I liked not being able to see the weather. I could hear it, though. Hail for a while in the morning, peppering the windowpane. A sudden, hysterically sharp, shower later, and then the wind again, whimpering. On the national news the weather conditions had taken over from the explosion in Norwich as the main story. I must have heard the expression 'experts are baffled' a thousand times. The freakish weather was nationwide now and showing signs of creeping across the channel. Meteorologists did their best to sound reassuring. The current patterns could not, would not continue. They didn't dwell on the fact that they had no idea what was causing them in the first place. But they all agreed. It wouldn't last. A Christian fundamentalist disagreed. He thought it was all down to God's wrath and it would get much worse before it got better. He seemed quite pleased about the prospect. A disproportionately high number of suicide attempts had been reported across the country over the past couple of days. Again, experts were baffled. The weather was confusing, admittedly, but not life threatening. There was no need to panic.

Of course there wasn't.

The local news was still understandably obsessed with the explosion, although the word 'bomb' was being used less and less. Yet there was no indication at all that it had been an accident. Nobody was quite sure what that left. They dwelt instead on details of those who had died. Two bodies had yet to be identified.

*

We didn't mention Sam for three days. I tried her numbers when Drew wasn't around. I didn't mention her boss, Barry, either. We slipped back into our old routine. Except that I no longer left the house. Drew brought me food and news of the outside world. In some ways we got along better than we had for years.

It was Saturday, I think. We ate soup at the kitchen table. The portable TV played with the sound down. Pictures of storms in the Balkans. It was midday but I had the curtains shut tight. Drew tutted, but humoured me.

"It's lovely out, actually," she said.

"For now."

"I think people are getting used to it."

"Apart from the ones who are topping themselves."

Drew wiped soup from her lip. "That's all exaggerated."

"Three more found hanging in Mousehold woods. Twelve in Norwich in two days."

"It's a cull," she said.

I paused with a piece of bread halfway to my mouth. "A what?"

"A cull. Across the country, the world, perhaps. Getting rid of the weak."

I looked for a sign that she was joking, but found none. "What happened to Miss Compassion?"

"Things are changing, that's all." Her eyes were flat.

I dropped my spoon into the bowl, my appetite gone. "I suppose they are," I said.

She went to church on Sunday. She wore a smart trouser suit I hadn't seen in years and just a hint of make up.

"You should come," she said.

"No thanks."

"You think I'm a hypocrite?" She was examining her face in the bathroom mirror, adjusting her make up, paring it down. She looked pretty, desirable even. Coldly assured. A Drew I'd never seen before.

"Just trying to recall your last visit. Do you think God will remember you?"

"Funny," she said. She gave a little twirl. "How do I look?"

"Good enough to eat."

She smiled and touched my face. This surprised me so much I stumbled backwards and collided with the bathroom door. "Are you planning to shave any time soon?" she said. "You look like a tramp."

"Does it matter?"

"It might," she said. Her smile was crooked. There was a light in her eyes that scared and aroused me.

While Drew was on her knees praying to a God she'd just discovered a church in a tiny village in the Lake District exploded. It was a small church but it was packed – church attendances had been expected to rise by 500% – and early estimates put the number of dead at around a hundred. No survivors, that was for sure. They played shots of the church as it was and the site now. It was as though a giant hand had plucked it from the earth and tossed it into the Windermere.

When Drew arrived home she shone with an evangelical light. "You should have come, Tom. Standing room only. It was won…"

I pointed at the screen. She peered at it for a moment, bewildered. Then she sat heavily.

"It's ok," I said. "I expect they deserved it, had it coming."

She looked up at me and for a moment she seemed lost, feral. The lipstick, the smart suit, merely a disguise.

Before she could speak the news bulletin was interrupted. The white-faced presenter said they had breaking news of another explosion, this one in the centre of Edinburgh. He started to say something about casualties then he halted in mid-sentence and absorbed more information. His face went slack, years of professionalism dropping away in seconds. He tried to gather himself, but the eyes that met ours through the TV screen were glazed with shock. "Reports are coming in of multiple explosions across the whole of the country." He paused again and took in more information through his earpiece. "It seems that it is not just the UK that is affected. News of explosions across Europe and parts of Asia and the Middle East are also filtering through. Details are sketchy at the moment but we will keep you updated as more information becomes available."

In the middle of his next sentence the electricity cut out. The TV and the lamp on the coffee table died. The curtains were closed so the room was almost dark. Drew stifled a scream. I pulled her towards me. She fought briefly then let me hold her. After a moment we sat on the sofa together, hand in hand.

"Do you still think it's a cull? God's will?" I said.

"Maybe," she said.

"But he took out one of his own churches. At least one. What's that, then? Friendly fire?"

She rested her head on my shoulder. "Don't try and score points off me now, Tom. Please."

"I'm sorry."

"It's all unravelling, isn't it? It's as though the world is tilting, shifting on its axis."

"Perhaps it is."

"It could be us next, couldn't it? Any moment."

"I suppose it could. I suppose it always could."

She moved closer to me and I put an arm around her. "Barry and I..." She hesitated. "I mean, we no longer..." Her voice tailed off.

"Since when?"

"Recently. Very recently. But still."

"Is this for the Lord's benefit or mine?"

"Does it matter?"

I thought for a moment. Thunder rumbled somewhere distant. I suppose it was thunder. "Do you want me to say something about Sam?"

"Sam's dead."

"Possibly," I said.

"It was an accident." She sat upright suddenly and threw a cushion across the darkened room. "Actually, I stabbed her in the throat. That's hardly an accident, is it?"

"What are you talking about?"

Her face was in shadow. "It was the Friday before the explosion. I took the day off work and we met at Ringland, went for a walk. I said we needed to talk about dad's sixtieth. She never believed that for a moment. She started telling me about you before I even asked. What you did together, how often. She was so damned smug." Her head moved but I couldn't see the expression on her face. "It wasn't that I wanted you. Not then. I just didn't want her to have you. She always took my stuff, always." Her voice slid into a whine. "Never asked. Just took. With mum and dad's blessing, of course."

"Drew," I said as gently as I could. "I spoke to her on the Wednesday. She cancelled..."

"Yes, she told me about your little rendezvous. That was me, darling. Cancelling on her behalf."

"Rubbish," I said. "I know Sam's voice. You couldn't..."

"Like this, you mean?" In the darkness it could have been Sam sitting there. I felt the hairs rise on my neck. "Not bad, is it?"

"Jesus Christ."

"She didn't expect the knife. And then she didn't expect me to use it."

"What did you do with her?"

"I put her in the boot. Bit of a struggle, but I could hardly ask for help, could I?"

"Where is she now, Drew?"

"She's still in the boot," she said.

It turned out lightning had struck the electricity works and most of the city was cut off for several hours. We fell asleep on the sofa. The sound of the TV woke me. My eyelids were gummed shut and it was several seconds before I could see anything. It was just after six. The TV news was like a disaster movie on a continual loop. Drew had gone.

Early reports said that there had been at least a thousand explosions worldwide. The last one – a primary school near Munich – had occurred five hours ago. Which was considered a good sign. The death toll was estimated at twenty, possibly thirty thousand, maybe as many as...well, nobody knew. Quite a cull, I thought. The government had declared a state of emergency. Already there were reports of looters being shot in Brixton and Toxteth. In Surbiton a group of vigilantes – men and women – cornered two youths and kicked them to death. Nobody knew why.

I heard the car pull into the drive at about ten thirty. I opened the front door and shielded my eyes against the natural light. The weather had been calm since I'd awoke and now it was misty and still. No wind, no snow, no hail. It took some getting used to.

Drew had changed into a sweatshirt and jeans. She slammed the car door, locked it. "Nice to see you outside," she said.

"Where have you been?"

"For a drive. To clear my head."

"Is it safe?"

"More or less." She was next to me now. She took a deep breath. "It's calmer, isn't it? I think it's over."

Another volley of sirens screamed in the distance. "Or just beginning."

"Whatever." Her grey eyes were guileless. She brushed my fingertips with hers. "I'm taking a shower. Join me?"

She squirmed past me. I glanced at our old Volvo. The mist was clearing now and the bodywork glinted in the new sunlight. I turned away from it, closed the door behind me.

"Why not?" I said.

Holding Pattern

Douglas had just finished shaving when it first happened. It was a Tuesday morning. Early. Ordinary. Gayle was stumbling around in the semi-darkness behind him. He was a morning person, she wasn't. He caught her reflection in the mirror. She wore only a beige slip. She was in her early fifties, her face puffy and naked, her hair spectacularly unregulated, and yet his heart quickened at the sight of her. He smiled, revealing a last dot of foam hiding in a dimple. He smoothed it off with a finger. A fraction of a second later his reflection did the same. He frowned and again it took a heartbeat, maybe two, for the face in the mirror to catch up.

"Gayle," he said.

"Where are my tights?"

"Did you see that?"

She was behind him, her hand cool on his shoulder. "I can't see anything without my glasses."

"My face."

"Oh, it's not so bad. All things considered."

"I mean, my reflection…"

She moved away from him. "I have no idea what you are talking about. I can't find my tights. Have you cut yourself shaving?"

"What? No…"

"Are you wearing your contacts?"

"Yes."

"Perhaps you need new ones. You should make an appointment. No, I'll make you an appointment. You'll only forget." She was halfway down the stairs. "Do you want toast or cereal?"

"Toast," Douglas said. His reflection said the same thing at the same time, which he found reassuring.

On Saturday morning he played squash with Richard. He was on the point of losing the second game and was chasing down an evil lob to his backhand when the ball and Richard, who had claimed the "T" in textbook fashion and was waiting for the kill, both stuttered then froze for a second, maybe two. Douglas was momentarily aware of his heartbeat and the exaggerated sound of his breathing as his shoes squeaked on the wooden flooring. His racquet continued its movement towards where he believed the ball to be heading before it become becalmed in still air. Naturally he completed his shot too soon and when the laws of physics kicked in again the ball dropped lamely over his racquet, rebounded off the back wall and hit him on the left thigh.

"Jesus, Douglas. That was poor, even for you."

"Didn't you see that, Richard? Didn't you feel anything?"

Richard regarded him quizzically. "I think the expression you are looking for is, four-love. My serve."

He held his hand out. Douglas tossed him the ball, watching its flight carefully. He saw that Richard wasn't even sweating. The bastard.

"Seriously…"

"No excuses. I want to get this whitewash completed before our time runs out."

He was serving already. Douglas' forehand reply limped into the tin.

"You could at least try," Richard said, turning and preparing to serve again.

Douglas didn't win another point. After the game they drank orange juice in the club bar. Richard looked slim and tanned and younger than he had any right to, Douglas thought. Gayle once said that he resembled his namesake, Mr Gere. She had a dreamy, faraway look on her face at the time that Douglas didn't appreciate.

Richard talked. Douglas was usually good at pretending to listen but today he was distracted and he felt his façade of interest crumble.

Richard finally stopped in mid-flow, leant forward and said, "Douglas? Are you all right, man?"

"You're asking about me? My goodness."

"What?"

"I'm fine."

"You're as white as a sheet."

Douglas hesitated. Who else could he tell? Nominally, Richard was his best friend. In reality this meant nothing. The only person he loved, needed, would ever need, was Gayle. Which meant that sometimes she was the last person he could talk to. Richard on the other hand...he didn't care at all what Richard thought of him.

He told him about the incident in front of the shaving mirror and what had happened on court a little earlier.

Richard nodded and tried to look thoughtful. "It could be a tumour," he said.

"Well, thanks."

"That or The Matrix was, in fact, a documentary."

"The Matrix?"

Richard sighed and adopted a heavily patronising tone that he thought Douglas found amusing. He was wrong. "It was a popular motion picture, Douglas. I'm astonished it escaped your notice."

"I'm only four years older than you."

"Hard to believe, isn't it? I take it you've heard of Keanu Reeves?"

Douglas said nothing. The only reason he'd heard of Richard Gere was because Gayle tended to dribble over him.

Richard sighed again then précised the plot of The Matrix and its sequels.

"I must be missing the point," Douglas said.

"No shit," Richard said. Douglas looked blank. Richard said, "Don't worry about it. I think we can safely assume that reality isn't fracturing. Something up with your eyes, old boy, that's all. You're at that age, aren't you? It's not a big deal. I don't know what you're making such a fuss about."

"Hardly a fuss, Richard. I just thought I'd mention it."

"I suppose in a world as serene and perfect as yours you notice the tiny flaws. How is Gayle?"

"Still beautiful. Have you heard from the twins?"

Richard angled his face towards the bar. His voice was dry. "Since last week? No. It's been six years, after all."

Douglas nodded. He and Richard had worked for the same engineering firm for the best past of a decade. Richard left to form a new company with a senior colleague. The venture bombed after eighteen months, leaving Richard at the brink of bankruptcy. His wife, with the money, the lifestyle gone, no longer tolerated his affairs and left taking their twin daughters with her. Contact was fitful, then non-existent. Richard's tendency towards being an arrogant prick meant that none of his former colleagues kept in touch. Except Douglas. They had remained friends in spite of Richard's bitterness and jealousy and the fact that they didn't actually like each other.

But Richard preferred not be reminded of his failure as a father and husband. Douglas asked after his ex-family every time they met; solicitously, as a friend would.

Douglas said, "She's a cold one, that Serena."

"Yes," Richard said. Something in his voice made Douglas look at him more closely. Richard's expression was almost comically bereft. Douglas realised that his friend was close to tears. "Douglas, I've got to tell you something."

Douglas stood. Richard was displaying genuine emotion. Was on the point of unloading it onto Douglas. Who was appalled. This wasn't part of the contract. "Richard, look…the time. I've got to go. Now. I'm sorry."

Richard stood as well. Douglas stiffened. People were watching. Richard said, "Please…"

Douglas thought, shit, shit, shit. He said, "The time. God, didn't realise." He shot Richard a stupid, sideways grin. "It's Gayle." He said her name twice more in a sing-song voice, all the time backing towards the door.

Richard watched him, his hands tucked into the waistband of his shorts, his expression bewildered and hurt.

As Douglas drove home a thunderhead formed with alarming speed in the east. It had been a benign April day but by the time he pulled into the drive of his detached house the sky was pewter-coloured and swollen. Thunder was rumbling like the hunger pangs of a wild animal.

Rain snapped out of the low sky and instantly became all embracing. Douglas stepped out his BMW and the force of the water hitting his scalp and shoulders cowed him, held his breath in abeyance as he scuttled crab-like to the door. He flung it open, shouted, "Jesus Christ," as he crossed the threshold.

"What?" Gayle said, the living room door banging behind her, her face creased with impatience, or concern, or both.

Douglas was still hunched, his hands bunched over his head. He realised suddenly that his hair was dry, as was his shirt, his face. He glanced through the open front door. The sun was shining. The air was still and blue.

"What on earth is wrong, Douglas?" Impatience was winning now. Understandably, perhaps.

He straightened. "Nothing. Just a pain, that's all. I'm fine now."

Her voice softened. "What sort of pain?"

He leant towards her, let her arms take him, pressed a smile into her hair and skin. "Old war wound, I reckon. Sorry I shouted."

"Silly old bear," she said. "Is it your head? Did you get your eyes checked?"

As long as she was squeezed against him everything was fine. "Too old for squash, that's all."

She stepped back from him. "Did Richard beat you again?"

"Narrowly."

"How is he?"

"Fantastic. You know Richard."

Gayle wandered towards the kitchen. Douglas followed. "I haven't seen him for ages."

"He's such a busy man. It's a shame."

"Did you give him my love?"

"As always."

Gayle made him a cup of strong tea. He looked out of the window. "Had any rain?"

"What?" Gayle said.

"I thought it clouded over earlier."

"Hardly. It's as clear as a bell. Thought we could get out into the garden later." She put a hand on his brow. "If you're up to it."

"I'm fine."

"Do you want me to cancel tonight?"

Tonight, Douglas thought. Shit. Dinner party. Four of Gayle's old teacher friends. She'd retired four years earlier. Missed it every day, she said. "Cancel? God, no. Can't wait."

Gayle rewarded the lie with a sweet smile that made his heart skip.

The evening passed without incident. The last of the guests left a little before one.

"You look tired," Douglas said. "Go to bed. I'll clear up."

"You are a sweetheart," Gayle said, kissing his cheek. "Clarissa is always telling me how lucky I am."

"Such a perceptive woman."

Gayle hesitated in the doorway, appraising him. She wore a raspberry-coloured woollen dress and her hair was down. She looked so beautiful Douglas ached. "Did you have a good time? You seemed distracted."

No more than usual, Douglas thought. The irony was that he was popular with Gayle's friends. They considered him a thoughtful host and an excellent listener. They found him reflective and intelligent. In reality he barely heard a word they spoke. He had no interest in their lives or opinions. He had trained himself to smile or chuckle at the appropriate time. If he spoke at all it was merely to encourage or flatter. It was enough. It kept Gayle happy and that was the point of it all. For over thirty years every ounce of his charm and charisma and talent had been focussed on her happiness. On being the husband she wanted, needed. He had worked hard at a job he didn't particularly enjoy, genuflected to men he despised, to provide for her materially. He was no longer aware of his own needs. They were there somewhere, he supposed, circling deep and distant. It didn't matter.

"It was, as ever, a triumph. Your cooking just gets better and better, I swear it does."

Gayle's smile deepened. Then her eyes left his and fixed on a spot above his head. The smile shrank, her expression emptied.

"Gayle?"

Her face was white and waxy. Her mouth fell open, shaped as though to scream, although no sound came out.

"Gayle?" he said again. His voice was shrill, bird-like. He tried to move towards her but a hand, several hands, pinned him in place. They were made of metal, it seemed, and invisible.

Now her face was deeply lined, aging visibly, shrinking in on itself. Douglas watched it implode. The raspberry dress emptied, fluttered to the floor. Dust settled on it.

The hands released him. He fell to his knees. The knowledge that this couldn't be real didn't help at all. His screams were as thin and reedy as a child's. He longed for unconsciousness. Then something huge struck him in the small of the back and the floor rushed up to meet him, granting his wish.

Douglas woke to the sound of music. The radio was on. Classic FM. It wasn't tuned properly but he was pretty sure it was something by Bach. His face was gummed to the floor. He freed it, straightened, wincing at the shaft of pain between his shoulder blades. He turned the radio off and glanced at the clock on the wall. Ten past three. He walked to the doorway. No dress lay on the floor, no dust, no body parts. No trace of Gayle at all, apart from her scent and Douglas could smell that anywhere, at any time.

It seemed to take an eternity to reach the top of the stairs. Gayle was asleep in bed, lying on her side, snoring quietly, prettily. Douglas nearly wept with relief.

He went to the bathroom, tried to urinate, but couldn't. He drank some water from the tap then braced his arms on the wash-basin and stared at his reflection in the shaving mirror.

"You started it," he said in a whisper.

He gazed back at himself implacably. He half-expected things to change again; for his face to melt, perhaps, or for something large to emerge from the shadows behind him. But the night ticked on, silent, without comment. A tumour, Richard had said. Maybe he was right.

Douglas briefly considered consulting his GP. He didn't even remember the man's name, it had been so long since he'd seen him. But he rejected the idea immediately. To do so would mean facing things, taking action. Illness meant weakness. If was weak he might lose Gayle.

To Douglas, truth was an interesting concept. The previous evening – it already seemed years distant - Clarissa had said something about valuing the truth above all else. He couldn't remember the context. He'd smiled and nodded. He thought it was the stupidest thing he had ever heard.

Richard finally caught up with him ten days later. Douglas had cancelled their squash game at the weekend, leaving a message on Richard's mobile. For Douglas the days had passed slowly, but without incident. It seemed that normality was reasserting itself. He was wary, though. He moved with an odd sense of deliberation that puzzled and irritated Gayle. He believed that if he braced himself for the unexpected it was less likely to happen. He couldn't explain this to Gayle though, as that would mean dwelling on the previous incidents. To her he simply appeared to be acting strangely. He also phoned in sick for two days, something he hadn't done for twenty-five years. This irritated Gayle further. Douglas was hurt. He thought she might like having him around, but she seemed disproportionately put out and he ended up driving to the park and walking away an afternoon.

The day he cancelled the squash game was the first Saturday of the month and that evening he and Gayle made love as usual. Except it wasn't as usual. He was tense, as he thought this was an obvious time for reality to distort again. He found it difficult to get an erection and when he did he was reluctant to let himself ejaculate. Finally, fifteen minutes after Gayle had come, or at least pretended to, he grunted and rolled off her, onto his back.

"Have you finished?"

"Yeah."

"Are you sure?"

"I think I know…"

She put her hand on him. His head fell back onto the pillow. "Why lie about it, Douglas?"

"It's just…"

"Is it me?"

She sat up in bed. Her voice had a quality to it, a brittleness that he'd worked all his life to avoid hearing.

"Of course not. I'm just tired."

He didn't like the silence that followed. He thought he could hear her thinking.

Finally she said, "It's just…"

He waited but she didn't go on. Her voice had changed again, though. It was thicker, clotted. It scared Douglas. He didn't want her to continue speaking. It would only be of regrets, recriminations. If they were never voiced he could believe they didn't exist.

To his relief she just lay back in the darkness and said, "Go to sleep."

Eventually, he did.

On Wednesday evening he found Richard waiting for him outside his office.

"They seek him here, they seek him there," he said.

"I've been meaning to call," Douglas said. He kept walking towards his car. Richard fell into step beside him.

"Really?"

"I've not been well."

"I didn't think you'd been ill a day in your life."

They reached the BMW. Douglas opened the door. "I must go. I've got an appointment."

"I've got to talk to you. It's about Gayle."

Douglas stopped, stood in silence for a moment. "What could you possibly have to tell me about Gayle?"

Richard turned his head away. A breeze was getting up and it flicked a strand of Richard's hair across his face. "This is so hard. I could hardly believe it myself."

"What are you talking about?"

"Not here."

Douglas gestured at the passenger door. "Get in."

They found a pub nearby. It was a new place, or at least Douglas had never noticed it before. It was horribly trendy, all blond wood and muted lighting. It was almost empty. They got their drinks and found a corner seat. Douglas hadn't spoken since Richard had got in the car.

"You mustn't shoot the messenger, Douglas," Richard said. He kept his eyes cast down. Douglas said nothing. "You've heard of Internet dating?" Douglas looked at him. "I mean, you know what the Internet is, right? I know what an old Luddite you are." The grin was off-centre and brief.

"Just tell me," Douglas said.

"About the Internet?"

Douglas closed his eyes. "About Gayle." He almost left then. Just walked away. He didn't have to listen to this. But, actually, he did.

"I've been on a few singles sites since Serena left. They're quite respectable these days. Nothing to be ashamed off…"

"I'm not interested in judging you. Just tell me if you've slept with my wife."

"What?" His eyes were wide with indignation. "Of course not. What kind of man do you take me for?"

Douglas didn't want to answer that. Didn't want to do anything. "What, then?"

Richard visibly braced himself. "Gayle's on one of the sites."

"A singles site?"

Richard squirmed. "Not exactly. It's a little more adult than some of the others." He hesitated, turned his head away. "To quote her profile, she's seeking younger men for daytime meetings. No strings. She says that she's married."

"How do you know it's her?"

"Her photo, Douglas."

Douglas longed for reality to change again. Wondered if it already had. "What sort of photo?"

"Not what you're thinking. She's wearing a red dress, she's got her hair down. She looks…"

"I know how she looks."

"I couldn't believe it. She's been a member for over a year."

"This is ridiculous. Her photo? Anyone could see it. She must have known that someone would…"

As Douglas faltered Richard said, "I'm sorry."

"I don't believe you."

"Look, I know this is hard, but…"

"I don't believe any of it. Is this what that charade at the squash club was about?"

"Charade?"

"You were almost in tears. I didn't know you could act."

"You're my oldest friend. I knew how you'd take it. Of course I was upset."

"You've always been jealous of us, haven't you? Especially since Serena saw sense and left."

"Why would I lie? I can show you the site..."

"I don't need to see it. I don't need anything from you. We don't all screw around behind each other's backs."

"You're deluded," Richard said.

Douglas stood and made his way to the door.

"She's making a fool of you," Richard said, following him.

Douglas walked to his car without looking back.

Richard stood at the pub entrance and shouted, "Nothing ever touches you, does it? You're a fucking iceman."

Douglas got into the car and drove away.

He drove towards London. He didn't want to go to London particularly, he didn't like the place. It was too big, too crowded. He'd only ever been there to humour Gayle. But he didn't want to go home, either. Not yet, at least.

Nothing ever touches you, Richard said, and he was right. For once he had cut straight to the heart of things. When Douglas was nine years old his baby sister died of meningitis. It happened with appalling speed, over a weekend. He remembered that suddenly no longer having a baby around meant that the house was quieter and it was easier to sleep. He remembered also being bewildered by the intensity of his parent's grief. It scorched them, left them shredded, empty, useless to him, to each other, to anyone else as far as Douglas could see. His sister had been a tiny blob of a thing. She ate, cried, slept. It was sad when she died, a shock. But...

Within a year both of his parent's were dead as well. His father had a heart attack. His mother took an overdose. Douglas found her body. He never forgot the look of relief on her face.

As he approached Thetford his mind was clear and empty. Dusk was falling. Something by Bach played on the radio. The windscreen blurred suddenly, then cleared and Douglas saw the dual carriageway in front of him distort. It was rippling, forming languid waves of tarmac. The car in front of him, a silver Lexus, was flicked aside as though it was a toy. Douglas braked sharply, to no effect. He rode the waves, found he didn't need to steer. Ahead an articulated lorry jack-knifed and he passed it on the inside as the cab toppled sideways and ploughed into a transit travelling in the opposite direction. Douglas felt the heat of the vehicles as they exploded. He travelled faster and faster although his foot had left the accelerator. He felt no fear, no exhilaration. Debris passed him like a meteor storm, a chunk of masonry clunked off his windscreen, leaving no mark at all. He was no longer breathing. It didn't matter. He closed his eyes.

When he opened them again he was parked on the hard shoulder, bent double, dry-heaving onto cold tarmac.

When he straightened a coach screamed past, horn blaring, missing him by inches.

"You're late," Gayle said.

Her voice came from the kitchen. It seemed higher than usual. Douglas hesitated in the hallway. He felt wiped out, insubstantial. He wasn't sure he could face Gayle. He no longer knew what to say, what to think. Everything was slipping away from him.

"I'm sorry," he said.

She was standing by the sink, her back to him. Her shoulders were taut, her arms cradled at her front. He thought she was angry with him for being late. He knew he had an anger of his own somewhere, but he wasn't sure how to retrieve it. He expected the kitchen to smell of cooking, of the meal he had missed, but all the surfaces were clean and empty and the only scent was that of Gayle's perfume.

"Richard was here," she said.

"What? When?" He was wrong-footed again. It was becoming a habit.

"An hour. A little less. I know what he said to you. I know why."

He thought suddenly that he should rush to her side, hold her, make sure she was real. But he couldn't.

"What are you talking about?"

Gayle turned. Her face was cast down briefly then she tilted it upwards into the light. There was a bruise under one eye and a crust of dried blood stained her upper lip. She had been crying, was close to crying again.

"I rejected him once, years ago." She was propped against the sink.

Douglas was yards away. Neither moved to reduce the distance between them. She looked at the floor. "I've always found him attractive. But I love you, Douglas."

He pointed at her face. "He did this?" She nodded. "Did he..."

"No. He was angry. He lashed out."

"But why now?" Douglas felt numbed by the stupidity of it all. It made no sense. Then a thought occurred to him and he cursed his own stupidity. His life had been built around absolute control but that was fading now, becoming useless. Something white and pure was swelling within him and it felt good.

"I've got to go," he said.

Gayle's eyes held his, noted the expression on his face. He expected her to protest, to plead with him to stay with her and not to do anything rash. But she didn't.

Richard answered his door promptly. Douglas pushed him firmly in the chest and he staggered backwards, falling onto his side as his leg caught the edge of a decorative table.

"We haven't got a computer," Douglas said.

Richard hauled himself upright. "What are you doing?"

"We haven't got a fucking computer."

The fact that Douglas swore seemed to shock Richard more than the physical attack. A flicker of fear crossed his face that Douglas relished. "Look, I'm younger than you, and fitter, so don't..."

Then Douglas was on him, driving him into the lounge, bouncing him off one wall, then another, then pinning him to the thickly carpeted floor. Before Richard could speak he punched him in the face. It felt good so he did it twice more then his hand hurt so he stood and kicked at Richard's torso and groin until the prone man squealed and pulled himself into a ball. Douglas was breathing heavily. He rested on his haunches for a moment then kicked Richard in the back and buttocks with his left foot until he felt his big toe break. Richard was whimpering softly and barely moving. Douglas hobbled into the kitchen, found a bread knife, then went back into the lounge. He knelt on the floor, forced Richard onto his back then stabbed him in the chest until his arm felt numb and the knife blade broke and the air was rich and thick with blood.

*

Gayle was out when he got home. It was just after eight, the time Douglas had thought it was when he had first arrived home and found Gayle in the kitchen. It had been a long day, though. Longer than it had any right to be. He slumped in an armchair, staining it with blood. Gayle won't be happy about that, he thought distantly. Then he slept.

Gayle's voice woke him. She was in the kitchen again. She's always in the bloody kitchen, he thought, then looked at his hands.

"I'm sorry I'm late," she called. "Did you get my message? Clarissa is hopeless with that computer. It was hardly an emergency; I had it fixed in no time. But we had a couple of glasses of wine, you know how it is. I don't like not being here when you get home from work, but I didn't think you'd mind. Why didn't you answer your mobile? You had me worried. Didn't you get yourself anything to eat? We can get a takeaway, I suppose, in a minute."

Her voice carried on as she rattled around in the kitchen. Douglas was still looking at his hands. Then the living room door burst open and there she was, her face unblemished. When she saw him she stopped talking. She stood completely still.

Douglas looked at her and tried to think of something to say. He waited for reality to reassert itself. Waited and waited.

Last Kiss

We were halfway around the Crome Gallery when Becky started crying again. I didn't notice at first. I was reading a poem by Andrew Motion that was printed on Perspex and mounted on the gallery wall. It was his tribute to the Norwich School of Artists. It was all right, I thought, what I understood of it.

Becky had her back to me as she studied a self-portrait by John Crome. I glanced at her casually. My first thought was that she still looked good in jeans. Then I saw that her head was trembling and that she held her right hand against her face.

"Becky," I said.

She raised her hand suddenly, fingers splayed. It was a little melodramatic, I thought. "I'm ok."

"You're obviously not." Mr Perceptive. I moved to her side, touched her waist, then, for some reason, her head. Her hair, although long, black and beautiful, was greasier than it looked. I let my hand drop, wiped my fingers surreptitiously on the bottom of my sweater. "How long have you been crying?"

"About six months." Her voice was small and stiff. A child's voice. It didn't sit well on a woman of forty. I stifled a sigh. "I can see your face in the reflection," she said.

So she could. I tried to look sympathetic, failed.

"People will see," I said.

"The place is empty, John." As though that, too, was my fault.

*

The trip to the art gallery in Norwich's Castle Museum was for her benefit. Becky had studied art years ago. In her twenties she produced a string of competent watercolours and held a joint exhibition with a friend in one of Norwich's smaller galleries. I never saw her work. She burnt them all a year before she met me. She started sketching again after the second miscarriage. There was a folder full of drawings in our bedroom; small, intense, bitter things that I couldn't bear to look at. They were good, but awful, if you know what I mean.

I barely knew an oil painting from a watercolour. I could think of better things to do on a Sunday afternoon. Liverpool versus Chelsea was on Sky for a start.

We drank coffee on a wooden bench outside the Castle's café as Becky's eyes dried. It was grey and cold. The low sky was stiff with cloud. A small but persistently frigid breeze reminded me why I hate January.

"We could go inside," I said. "A bit radical, I know, what with it being winter and all."

"I like it out here." Her nose and cheeks were red with cold. She hunched into her jacket.

"You're a strange little woman, aren't you?"

"Don't patronise me."

"And what would you have me do?" I lent forward, touched her nose with mine, kissed her mouth and waited for her to kiss me back. She did. She always did.

"I'm sorry I cried."

"No you're not," I said. "You just wanted some attention."

"Bastard," she said.

I shrugged. "By the way, I'm out tonight."

"With Charlie, I suppose."

"If the wind changes you'll stay like that."

"You know what I think of Charlie."

"Well, we're all bastards, aren't we?" She didn't smile. "You're welcome to join us. It's just a couple of drinks, nothing special."

"I don't think so."

"You'll stay in on your own. As usual."

"You could keep me company."

"I could. I'm not going to."

She sulked for the rest of the afternoon. I ignored her. Which was why she loved me.

I met Charlie at the Walnut Tree Shades in the city centre.

"You're late," he said.

"As usual."

"And yet I was still early. What does that say about me?"

"That you're a pillock?"

He bought me a drink. We stood at the bar although there were tables free. Charlie dumped a whisky into what was left of his lager. He drained the glass and smacked his lips. "That's better," he said. He was tallish, about my height, but slimmer, with dark hair that was long enough and just the right side of lank. He was sporting the beginnings of a goatee. It suited him but I wasn't going to tell him that. The barmaid kept glancing at him. He didn't even notice. Becky fancied him. Hated him but fancied him. Which was ok. I didn't like him much but I enjoyed his company.

"I suppose Becky is languishing on her own."

"Just to buck a trend."

"What a waste."

"Her choice."

"I meant, her being married to you."

"So did I."

We drank quickly. I don't know why. I'd told Becky the truth. It was meant to be a quiet night. It seemed Charlie had other ideas.

"I know somewhere we can go. When the pubs are shut."

"A party?"

"Something like that."

"On a Sunday night?"

He tapped the side of his nose. His eyes were beginning to glaze but he was steady enough on his feet and his speech was clear. "As I always say, it's who you know."

Charlie. By day humble insurance clerk, by night bass player in a Pink Floyd tribute band. Very rock and roll. He got invited to some good parties, though.

"But it's a Sunday night."

"You're getting old, John."

This was true. "You have work tomorrow?"

"Yep. Don't care. I'm hardcore."

"So I'm told. I've got a day off. Jealous?"

"A bit. And so you have no excuse."

"Dunno. I've still got to get up early." Charlie looked blank. "Becky thinks I'm going to work."

"You bastard."

"I just need a day on my own."

"On your own? Not planning a little trip to Cromer, then?"

I fixed my gaze onto the stamped tin ceiling. The pub was now full and the air was thick with cigarette smoke and mingled conversations. Something bluesy played in the background. "Don't know yet."

"That's bollocks."

"You should try living with Becky."

"Anytime."

I think he meant it. But as I'd told him many times before, words are easy.

I drank some more. So did Charlie.

"The thing is, you'll fuck it up. And then you'll regret it." His voice was softer, reflective.

"And you'd be there to pick up the pieces?"

"I know what she thinks of me."

"She'd fuck you, at a pinch."

"Well, who wouldn't?" he said. But something in his face changed.

"Ten years and counting, Charlie. She needs me."

"My point exactly."

"She needs me how I am."

He raised his eyebrows. "Really?"

"She's been indulged all her life. By her parents, by an army of therapists. By that useless wanker of a first husband. All pandering to poor little Becky."

Charlie looked uncomfortable. "But..."

"What? The miscarriages? Sad," I said. "But shit happens. And she was like this anyway. Self-indulgent. Depressive." I was angry and wasn't sure why. "It's just another excuse."

"Excuse? Do you realise how cold you sound?"

"Yes. I do. You know, she never wanted kids. Not really. And she would have been a crap mother."

"Jesus."

I'd drunk too much. That didn't make what I was saying any less true. "To be honest, when she told me...about the first one? I was relieved. I didn't want kids, either. Not with her."

"You bastard," Charlie said softly.

"That word again," I said.

All expression dropped from his face. He didn't look at me or speak to me for fifteen minutes.

Eventually I said, "Well, am I still invited to this party?"

"Fuck it, yeah," Charlie said. "I'm not going on my own."

It was a waste of time. We arrived at a large Victorian terrace house on the outskirts of Thorpe just after eleven to find a handful of men and precisely three women, all older than me, scattered throughout a number of cold, cavernous rooms. I didn't recognise the music, but it was awful. Some bastard soft-country-rock hybrid. There was little to drink and the buffet had long since been picked clean. The bright spark who'd invited Charlie wasn't even present.

"Hardcore," I said.

"It's not quite what I expected," Charlie said.

"You astonish me."

We lasted until midnight.

"Another taxi?" I said, as we stood on the front path, hunched into our jackets, breath billowing in the cold air.

"I think I'll walk," Charlie said.

"But it's miles. And it's freezing."

"I'm wide awake and as sober as a judge."

"Nothing like a crap party to sober you up."

"Precisely. And I fancy a walk."

"I suppose I'd better keep you company."

"I'm a big boy. I think I can manage."

"If something happened to you I'd never forgive myself."

"Right. That and you're too tight to pay for a taxi on your own."

"How well you know me."

We took a shortcut, through a field, past a disused children's playground, into a clearing that led to an old bridge that led across the railway tracks. I think I was teasing Charlie about his band as we approached the bridge. He had a couple of gigs later in the week.

"So what will you be playing? Don't tell me – *Money. The Wall. Dark Side of the Moon*. Just for a change."

"Funny man."

"Don't you get sick of it?"

"Most bands play the same stuff over and over." His voice was flat. I was getting to him.

"Yeah, but most bands aren't pretending to be somebody else. What's that all about?"

"Fuck you, John."

It was familiar ground. I suppose it irritated me, Charlie playing in a tribute band. He was a talented musician and I couldn't understand why he wasn't writing and performing his own material. He simply wasn't interested. Which I suppose was his business. Perhaps I was just jealous because he had a talent and I didn't.

Irritated, Charlie took the lead as we approached the steep metal steps that led to the bridge's walkway. He clattered up them briskly then stopped when he reached the top. I almost bumped into him.

"Wait," Charlie said.

I peered over his shoulder. "Shit," I said.

Halfway along the bridge, on the wrong side of the safety rail, stood on the narrow stone parapet was the figure of a man. He was silhouetted against the moonlight, slender and unmoving. His arms were angled out behind him, hands grasping the safety rail.

After a moment Charlie walked towards him. "You all right, mate?" His voice was bright and normal.

"Easy," I said as I scuttled up behind him.

"What are you up to?" Charlie said.

"What do you think?" the man said. His voice was conversational, amused. He was in his twenties, I supposed, with a smooth, cherubic face and thinning, sandy hair.

Charlie slapped me on the back. "You heard the man. Let's go."

"What?"

"I've got work tomorrow. I don't want to fuck about."

"You can't be serious."

Charlie glanced at the man, who gazed into the distance, his face expressionless. "This is none of our business." I just looked at him. He shrugged. "It's not even that much of a drop."

I peered over the edge of the parapet. It looked far enough to me. The railway tracks, cut deep into the embankment, seemed a long way below.

"Perhaps he'll just break a leg or something," Charlie said. "Or he could end up a vegetable. If he takes my advice, he'll trot into the city centre. Try the car park at St Stephens. It's a dead cert. If you'll excuse the expression."

"Thanks," the man said. "But I think this will do."

"Your funeral," Charlie said.

"What the hell is the matter with you?" I said.

"What?" he said, all innocence, arms open wide. "I'm off. You coming?"

"No," I said.

His arms dropped slowly to his sides. "Found your conscience, John?"

"I've always had a conscience," I said quickly. Perhaps a little too quickly.

"Do you think Becky would agree?"

He held a half smile as I looked at him. "This is different."

"Sure. You don't even know this guy." I started to say something else but Charlie turned and flung an arm up and said, "I'm gone. You do what you want."

I watched as he walked into the darkness.

"You can go too," the man said. I turned back towards him. His head was twisted in my direction. He wore only a thin sweater and a pair of jeans but if he was cold he didn't show it. "No-one will know. Your friend is right. This is nothing to do with you. It's not your fault."

"I can't just walk away."

"Actually, you can." The truth is I wanted to. I was cold and tired. He gave a thin smile. "And it might get messy."

But some of Charlie's comments had struck a nerve. "What's your name?"

"Luke. Not that it matters."

"I'm John."

"Well, that's two of the Disciples sorted."

There was a silence. It dragged on. I didn't have a clue what to say next. Luke was calm and still. He didn't appear to be in a hurry. I don't think I ever believed he would actually jump. Not while I was there.

Belatedly I remembered my mobile. I pulled it out of my jacket, flicked it open.

"Don't," Luke said mildly. "If you make a call, I'll jump."

I put the phone away. "There's no-one you want to contact?"

"No."

I moved closer to the rail. "Why are you doing this?"

"That's my business."

"It's just...you seem so calm."

"Why wouldn't I be? I'm in control for once."

"Is that what this is about? Control?"

Luke sighed. "I know you mean well, John, but please, spare me the cod psychology."

I felt my cheeks flush. I was glad he wasn't looking at me. "Sorry," I said.

"No problem."

I shifted position. My feet ached. I wondered if anyone else would come past. I hoped that they would. Someone who knew what they were doing.

"Have you been here long?" I said.

"Long enough. Hours, I suppose. But that's nothing, is it? Not in the scheme of things."

"And no-one else has tried to help?"

"Nope. Just you. Aren't you special." His voice was flat and colourless and although it sounded as though he was taking the piss it was hard to be sure.

"I'm surprised, that's all."

Luke grunted.

And I thought maybe Charlie had been right. He'd be halfway home by now. I was being mocked by somebody I'd never met before. If he jumped it would be...unpleasant. Inconvenient. But would I actually care? No. Of course I wouldn't. But at least I had tried to help. That was something. Wasn't it?

"You're right," Luke said.

"What?"

"Just fuck off. I'll be fine." His voice had changed. It was lower, gruffer.

"What are you talking about?"

"I didn't ask for an audience."

I nearly left. I wish now that I had. "Well, you've got one. And how come you've been here hours? What's that all about?"

"You think I'm having second thoughts?"

"Yep. Don't blame you. Lets face it, it's going to hurt, isn't it?"

"Fuck you," he said. He took his hands off the safety rail, leant forward a fraction.

"You selfish bastard," I said.

And he jumped. Actually, he didn't. But in my mind he did, and with such clarity that for a moment I thought it was real. In my mind he didn't jump as much as lean forward and let gravity take over. I heard the soft, muffled thump of his body hitting the tracks. I moved forward, intending to peer over the edge of the bridge, in order to satisfy a morbid curiosity.

In reality Luke still stood on the ledge, tensed slightly, eyes closed. Then he leant back and his hands found the safety rail again.

"Have I struck a chord?" I said.

After a moment he nodded.

"So there is someone?"

He said nothing. He stood for a while, without moving at all, as condensation formed on the metal bridge and the cold settled and deepened around us.

Finally I was about to speak, just to break the silence and the stillness of the night when Luke turned to me and said, "So, what do you do, John?"

As though we'd just met in a pub and I'd bought him a drink.

"What?"

"You're right. I'm selfish. It's all me, me, me. Tell me about yourself."

His voice seemed easy, more relaxed than it had been since I'd stumbled across him. But there was something behind it, a tension that also showed in his eyes as they met mine.

"I'm in IT. How boring is that?"

"But the money's good."

"Too good, really. For what I do, what I know. Money for old rope. Not that I'm complaining."

"And Becky?"

"Becky?"

"Your friend mentioned her. Your wife, I assume. What does she do?"

"Why?"

"Just making conversation. Humour me."

"She does nothing. Sometimes she stacks shelves at Sainsbury's."

"Why say it like that? As though you're ashamed? Are you a snob, John?"

He turned as he spoke so that he had his back to the drop. He leant his elbows on the safety rail and stared at me. Full on, his features were wide and bland. And he looked older, I thought, than my initial impressions.

"No. I'm not clever enough to be a snob. I'm a lager and football man, me. Becky's got the brains, the education. But it's me that's on 25k. It annoys me, that's all."

"No children, then?"

"Is it that obvious?"

"From what you've just said, yes."

I shrugged and didn't speak.

"Am I being intrusive?" he said.

"A little."

"I'm sorry."

He levered himself over the safety rail and clambered onto the bridge. He walked up to me so that we were face to face, inches apart. I caught a hint of cologne. Something old-fashioned, that maybe my father would have worn. Sandalwood, perhaps. I was taller and heavier than he was but, for no reason that I can think of, I felt physically threatened. I took a half step backwards.

"Will you make a call for me?" he said.

I grabbed my phone, handed it to him. "Help yourself."

He held up his hands. They were red and swollen from grasping the safety rail. "I don't think I could manage at the moment."

I nodded as I turned the phone on. "No signal," I said.
"Let's get off the bridge. Lead on," he said. He laid a hand on my
shoulder and I hurried forward so that he was no longer touching me.
When I reached the far bank I checked my phone again.
"It's fine now," I said, turning. But Luke had gone.

When I got home I took a long shower and went to bed. Becky was there
already, fully dressed, huddled beneath the covers, asleep. I pressed
against her for warmth. She didn't stir. After a moment I realised that
she smelled and I moved so that my back was to her. Becky can go days
without changing her clothes and sometimes she forgets to wash herself
or brush her teeth. In contrast to her personal hygiene she kept the house
almost pathologically clean. And before she could leave a room every
piece of furniture, every ornament had to be in exactly the right place.
It drove me nuts sometimes.

It was a long while before I slept. The events on the bridge already
seemed distant, unreal. I knew that in the morning I would doubt that
they had actually happened at all.

But when I finally slept I dreamt of Luke. I saw him fall; from a
bridge, a car park, from the top of the office where I work. His body
tumbling through cold air. I saw him broken on concrete and stone,
smeared across a live rail. His bland face, backlit, loomed above mine.
For a brief, terrifying moment when I woke I was certain that Luke was
beside me, twisted, wrecked, the bedclothes heavy and sodden with his
blood. Then Becky belched quietly and stirred and the smell of her
drifted over me. I lay on my back and felt my heart hammering in my
chest.

I was out of the house by seven-thirty. Becky was asleep. When she
was taking her medication she could sleep twelve hours a day, barely
moving, and still need a nap in the afternoon.

It well before nine when I reached Cromer, too early to visit Helen.
I parked in the town centre and found a café, where I took my time over
a full English and a mug of weak coffee. I read the Eastern Daily Press
from cover to cover. Riveting. The place was filling up and the waitress
was shooting me dirty looks when I finally left.

The mist had thickened into fog. I tensed myself against the cold but
the air was milder than it looked. Helen lived in a terraced house in a
side road, parallel to the sea front. It took me fifteen minutes to reach it.

*

We'd had an affair five years earlier, Helen and I, when she'd briefly temped in my office. Our fling burnt itself out quickly but we kept in touch and slept together every now and then.

She answered the door in a cream towelling dressing gown that I remembered well. Her blond hair was tousled and she wore no make up. She looked great, though.

"I was hoping you still had Monday's off."

"It's been nine months."

I was surprised. I didn't think it was as long as that, but I did the math quickly and she was right. "I suppose it has."

"I didn't think..." She ran a hand through her hair. "You should have called."

I shrugged. She didn't move. "I'm cold," I lied.

"Tell me something I don't know," she said.

"What?"

"You'd better come in."

I followed her through the hallway. "You've redecorated," I said. "Terracotta. Nice."

"I'm glad you approve."

In the kitchen she lit a cigarette and made us coffee. I watched her from the table, as I'd done many times before.

"Nine months," I said. "I didn't realise."

"Time just rushes by when you're having fun, doesn't it?"

"I meant to keep in touch."

"A Christmas card would have been nice."

"You didn't send me one."

"It's a bit tricky, what with you being married."

I nodded. The kettle boiled. Helen stood for a moment, staring into the steam. There were tiny purple flowers embroidered along the hem of the dressing gown. I'd counted them once, while she fellated me.

"What is it?" I said.

"My dad died."

"I'm sorry."

"You never even met him."

"Still..."

"Heart attack. Last October. Two days before my birthday."

I didn't say anything. She made our coffee, dumped the spoon in the sink with a clatter and sat heavily opposite me.

"I nearly called you then."

"You should have."

She looked into my face. Her smile was so bleak I had to look away.

"You'd have expected a fuck."

"Might have done you good," I said. I closed my eyes. "Shit. I'm sorry…"

She stood carefully and retrieved an ashtray from the worktop. "That was low, John. Even for you."

"I know. I'm sorry. It's just…Becky…"

She sat again, blew smoke angrily past my shoulder. "Spare me, please. I tell you my dad died and you want to have a bleat about the Basket Case."

I was quiet for a moment. "I think that's fifteen-all, don't you?"

She stubbed out her cigarette in three precise movements. "I'm seeing someone."

This wasn't unusual. The expression on her face was.

"So?"

"It's serious."

"And?"

She pushed the ashtray to one side and blew on her coffee. "I mean, moving in serious. Getting engaged serious. Not fucking around serious."

Even I knew that I had no right to feel hurt. But I did. And stupid and betrayed. But mostly hurt.

"Where did you meet this prince?"

"At a support group."

"A support group?"

"After dad died. His name's Dominic."

"Dominic? Jesus."

"Don't sneer, John."

"But it's my default setting. I thought you knew that."

She got up from the table and went to the sink where she stood with her back to me, her shoulders stiff and hunched. Hair colour aside, she could have been Becky; tallish, willowy, slender waist. For a moment I thought she was crying, but I was wrong. Because she wasn't Becky.

Not at all. Which was most of the attraction. I think.

"Why are you here?" she said.

It was a good question but that didn't mean I had to answer it. Not honestly, at least.

"I would have thought it was obvious. Just the usual, that's all."

She turned and leant her back against the edge of the sink. Her arms were angled behind her, hands gripping the worktop. For a moment I thought of Luke. I looked at Helen's breasts, pushed upwards by the position of her shoulders, and shoved the thought aside.

"Really?" she said.

I adjusted my line of vision so that I met her eyes. "What else?" I stood. "I mean, you just caught me checking out your tits. That's me, isn't it? Typical bloke. Led by my dick."

"You sound angry, John."

"Angry? Really?" Actually I was almost shouting. I don't know why.

"I'm going to take a shower, get dressed. If you're still here we can walk into town, get a late breakfast."

"I've already eaten."

"Ok. Some more coffee, then."

"Are you going to counsel me?"

She was by the door now. She sighed. "You can wait here for me or you can fuck off. I'm not too fussed either way."

I waited.

When she came down again she wore grey tracksuit bottoms and a shapeless beige sweater that was too big for her. She shrugged an old anorak over her shoulders to complete the ensemble. I assume she was trying to make herself as unattractive as possible, trying to make things easier for me. It didn't work.

We walked down some concrete steps onto the beach and made our way towards the town. The fog had lifted a little. The sea was vast and still and gormless and the air smelled of brine, which was understandable under the circumstances. The beach was as empty as you'd expect it to be on a Monday morning in late January.

"We've been here before," I said.

"Are you speaking metaphorically?" Helen said.

"You'll just confuse me, using big words like that."

A gull screamed nearby and we both turned towards the sound.

"How rude," I said.

Helen tucked a stray hair behind an ear. She kept herself a couple of paces away from me. We *had* been here before and she knew it. The previous spring. It had been hot and we'd walked hand in hand, barely speaking. Thinking about it that was probably the last time I'd seen her.

"I don't think you're just after a shag," Helen said.

We paused for a moment, turned towards the sea.

"Wouldn't be the first time," I said. "After all, I am that shallow."

"Well, we agree on that." She tipped her head towards me, offered me a ghost of a smile.

"So?" I said.

She played with her hair again. She did that a lot. "You're different, that's all. Somehow." I waited. She shrugged. "I don't know. You're...sadder."

"Sadder?"

"Yeah. Something like that. Beneath all the bullshit."

She was right, but I wasn't going to admit it. It was Becky, I suppose. Living with her wasn't getting any easier, wasn't likely to in the foreseeable future. I don't know what I expected Helen to do about it. We just screwed each other now and then. It wasn't as though I loved her or anything.

But I found it hard to look at her.

When we reached the town we got coffee to go and sat on a wooden bench next to an ice-cream parlour and looked out at the sea. Helen told me a little about Dominic and I nodded in the right places and tried to look interested. She was happy and I should have been glad and of course I wasn't. I'd wanted her to be miserable, alone, glad to see me. What exactly we could have done for each other I don't know. I hadn't looked that far ahead. I never do.

I asked some questions, forced a brightness into my voice that was entirely false. I realised I was dragging it out. Once she was gone that was it. We'd never been friends, exactly. We had nothing in common except an occasional mutual desire. Which now wasn't mutual any more. And I'd been kidding myself that what I felt was something more than simple desire.

No fool like an old fool. Except that I'm not that old.

I stood and tossed my empty cardboard cup into the bin that was by the bench. Helen stood as well. She was halfway through a sentence and I waited for her to go on but she didn't.

"Good luck with the whole Dominic thing," I said.

She nodded and shivered a little although it wasn't particularly cold. "Will you leave her, then?" she said. Her gaze was out to sea.

"I've lasted this long."

"Becky might say the same."

"And she'd have a point."

"But something's changed, hasn't it? That's why you're here."

I made a face. "Perhaps something hasn't changed. Maybe that's the problem." Helen waited for me to go on. "I don't think I ever believed Becky was ill. Not really. I thought it was all her parents' fault. That she was a spoiled brat that just needed to grow up."

"And now?"

"I think I was right. Up to a point."

"But?"

I shrugged. "I suppose there's a bit more to it than that."

"It's taken you ten years to find that out?"

"The miscarriages didn't help."

"I don't suppose they would."

"They are still a smokescreen, though. Really."

"You have a way with words, John."

"I know how I sound sometimes."

"I'm not sure that you do." She sighed and let her shoulders relax. "But it's your choice, isn't it? If you leave or not."

"That would depend on how much of a bastard I am, wouldn't it?" She looked at me quizzically. "What sort of man leaves his wife because he realises that she's mentally ill?"

"For you, John, it shouldn't be a problem." If the smile was meant to soften her words it failed miserably.

She walked me to my car. Just as she was about to leave I said, "Oh, I almost forgot. I saved a man's life last night."

She tipped her head to one side. "That's such bullshit."

"Seriously."

I told her about the incident with Luke, leaving out any bits that made me sound bad. When I finished I looked into her face.

"You don't believe me."

She nodded slowly. "I don't think you've got the imagination to make it up."

I couldn't read her expression. "It's not as though I did much. I don't think he was going to jump anyway."

"You stopped, though. You could have walked on. Like Charlie, like the others. That means something."

"I suppose." I realised I was blushing. As I stared at the pavement Helen leaned forward and kissed my cheek.

"You did a good thing, John."

Then she left.

I drove back to Norwich and after lunch killed most of the afternoon in the Ladbrokes on Ber Street. I lost the best part of two hundred pounds backing favourites then won most of it back on a long shot in the last from Lingfield. It's always good to end on a winner. I finished the afternoon a few quid down but I felt as though I'd won.

I got home at the same time as I would if I'd been to work. Becky was on the sofa, drinking tea. Luke was sitting next to her.

When he saw me he jumped up and flung his arms open wide. "Here's the guy!"

Becky smiled at me. Her hair glistened as though freshly washed. "You should have told me, John."

I thought Luke was going to hug me but he settled for a handshake. "You're so modest," he gushed. "I've just been telling your lovely wife what a hero you are."

It was hard to believe it was the same man. He wore a mauve cord shirt that hung over the top of a pair of too-tight jeans. His features, so bland and immobile the previous night, were now absurdly animated. His voice was knowing and arch.

"What are you doing here?"

"Why, saying thank you, of course." His face was all innocent incredulity. But something else glimmered underneath. "I rushed off last night. It was thoughtless."

"How did you find me?"

"Don't be so rude, John." Becky was by my side. Her voice was soft, her eyes mild as she looked at me. She linked an arm through mine. She smelled faintly of peaches. "You did a wonderful thing. He just wants to thank you, that's all."

"It was nothing," I said.

Luke snorted, "Nothing. Right."

"He told me, John. You risked your life. Reached over the edge of the bridge and pulled him off."

"So to speak," Luke said. He shot an awful, hammy wink in Becky's direction. She giggled. I couldn't remember the last time I heard her giggle. I wanted to hit her.

I said, "That's not quite..."

"And he told me about Charlie."

"Not that I'm blaming him," Luke said. "In his place, I'd have done the same thing."

Becky tutted. "I doubt it, Luke," she said.

I looked at them both and wondered what planet they were on.

"Look, this is great and thanks for coming, but I'm hungry and..."

Luke held up a hand. "Of course. I'm sorry. It's just I'm going to tell the local paper about you. I wanted to make sure you don't mind."

"What?"

He gave a little smile. I didn't like it much. "The Evening News loves stuff..."

"No."

He looked hurt, or pretended to. "John," Becky said.

"I mean, you do whatever you need to do, but leave me out of it. I'm no hero."

"Your call," Luke said. "Shame, though."

We stood for a moment, the three of us. Becky looked crestfallen.

I said, "So what's your story, Luke?" He looked at me quizzically, didn't say anything. "Why were you there last night? What changed your mind, besides my heroics? I'm curious. I really am."

"I've intruded enough." The campness had gone from his voice.

"Dinner can wait. I'll make some more tea and you can tell us all about it."

"John," Becky said again, less indulgently this time.

Luke kissed Becky's hand. "I must go."

I followed him towards the hallway. Becky started after us but I raised a hand, stopping her. She went back into the living room and fussed with the furniture.

At the door Luke said, "How was the coast today? Did the fog clear?"

I was closing the door after him but now I hesitated.

"I just wondered," he said.

I felt Becky behind me. "Coast?" she said.

"I was at work," I said.

I looked back at Luke and he was at the gate. He shot me a wink. "Be seeing you."

I closed the door.

"I told you to wait in the living room."

"I wanted to say goodbye to Luke." Her eyes were trembling and wet at the edges.

In the kitchen I said, "You haven't even started dinner."

"I've had company. I've got to wash the tea things up. Put them away. You know that, John." She was whining. She came up to me, pawed at my chest.

"How long was he here?"

"An hour or so. He phoned just after lunch and…"

"Phoned? How did he get our number?"

She locked her hands behind my neck and squirmed against me. "I don't know. Does it matter?"

"And you let him in? He could have been anyone."

"But he was lovely, John. And the things he said about you…"

I touched her blouse, her hair, her face. "You're wearing make up. You've washed your hair. Is that for Luke's benefit or for mine?"

She tried to hold me. "Yours, of course. I'm so proud of you."

I pushed her away and searched the fridge and cupboards for food.

"I'll fix us something," Becky said.

"Forget it," I grabbed a beer from the fridge, opened it and stomped into the living room.

Becky followed me. "Why are you so angry? You can't be jealous. Luke's gay. I thought even you might have noticed that."

I turned on her. "And did the lovely Luke really strike you as a man on the brink of suicide?"

"He said that he's a manic depressive. I know about this stuff. The mood swings…"

"You know about what? You're not a manic depressive."

"No, but I've read…"

"You've read? Bloody wonderful." Her hand flew to her face and the first tears spilled onto her cheeks. "I wondered how long it would take."

She sat carefully on the edge of the sofa, leant forward with her knees together and composed herself. "I don't understand this, John. You did a wonderful thing. You saved a man's life. The thought of it made me feel…I don't know…warm, grateful. I couldn't wait for you to get home. To be honest, I didn't think you were capable of something like that."

She looked up at me and her eyes were dry again. I forced myself to breathe evenly, made my voice gentler, normal. "I didn't save anybodies life, Becky. I stopped. I talked to him. But he never had any intention of jumping. I'm not a hero."

"He said you grabbed him."

"He's lying. I don't know why. Perhaps this is a game to him. I don't understand. I don't want to understand." She looked at me blankly. "The Luke you met today was nothing like the Luke on the bridge last night."

"What the hell are you talking about?"

"I know how it sounds…"

"I thought I was the loon."

I let out a long breath, ran a hand through my hair. "You're not to see him or talk to him again. Do you understand?"

She looked at me for a long time without speaking.

I woke in the middle of the night to find Becky straddling me. She was leant over me, a hand planted either side of my head. Strands of her hair brushed against my cheek.

I breathed slowly and looked up at her, waiting for my eyes to become used to the darkness. There was something feral in the way she was tensed over me and in her expression, as her features became clear, the curl of her lips exposing the tips of her incisors. Her eyes were hooded, mostly hidden by her hair.

Her breath was shocking. I thought of how clean she'd seemed the previous day, of the sweetness of her scent. It was as though she had decayed from the inside out in a matter of hours.

Eventually I said, "I'm a bit tired, love. And it's not even the first Saturday of the month."

She was wearing pyjamas, but even if she'd been naked the situation would have been less than erotic. We had made love in the position we were frozen in often enough in the past. It was one of my favourites. But that was then; a mythical, nebulous time. Possibly years ago. Or months. Or never.

"Would you have saved me, John?" Becky said. I turned my head to one side so that her breath slid past my cheek.

"What are you talking about?"

"Would you have stopped for me? Would you have pulled me away from the edge?"

"I didn't pull…"

"You showed more compassion towards a man you'd never met before than you have ever shown to me."

Her voice was flat and calm and matter of fact. What she said was wrong on several levels. She also had a point.

I put my hand on the back of her head and pulled her face towards me. Her lips parted and I slid my tongue into her mouth. The taste was indescribably bad. But I didn't stop kissing her.

In the morning I assumed that it was a dream. Becky got up at the same time as I did and pottered around in the kitchen. She smelled fine and her breath was normal. I ate my breakfast, drank some coffee then stood under a hot shower for half an hour and tried to wash all thoughts of the previous night away.

As I was about to leave for work Becky kissed my cheek and said, "You know we didn't use any protection last night, don't you? And it's my fertile time."

I looked into her face but her expression was impossible to read.

That night I went to bed late, Becky was waiting for me with the bedside lamp on, reading. When I got into bed she curled against me. She was naked and her small breasts squeezed against my chest. She smelled of apples. When I kissed her I tasted Aquafresh and nothing else.

On Saturday evening I met Charlie at the Playhouse Bar. Neither of us mentioned the previous Sunday. Charlie's band had played a gig on Friday night and we chatted about that. After a while Charlie said, "What's up with you?"

"What?"

"We've been talking about the band for ten minutes and you haven't taken the piss."

I tried to shrug, but it was difficult in the crowded bar. "I would have got around to it."

"Really?" He squinted through the smoke. "I'm not so sure. You seem distinctly mellow. You're either stoned or you've been getting your end away for a change."

"You have such an elegant way with words."

"And you're not stoned, are you?" I shook my head. "So who's the lucky lady?"

"What the hell is that supposed to mean?"

"Easy," Charlie said. "I thought with your trip to the coast on Monday…"

I realised I'd pretty much forgotten about Helen. "That didn't quite work out."

"So we're talking about Becky?"

"*You* are talking about Becky. I'm not sure this is any of your business."

"What the fuck has that got to do with anything?" He looked so indignant I almost smiled.

"Things are different. Better."

"What, in less than a week?" I could understand his incredulity. I had only ever moaned about my marriage in all the years I'd known him.

The music and the level of conversation were so loud we had to shout to make ourselves heard. I pointed in the vague direction of the door. "Shall we move on?"

Charlie nodded and we squeezed our way to the exit.

The Playhouse is set on the bank of the Wensum and we stood on the small bridge that crosses the river and looked out at the water. It was perfectly still and as dark as ink. The night was unseasonably warm. The air was heavy with a scent I couldn't quite place.

"So what happened?" Charlie said. "Have you found God? Has Becky found God?"

"Now who's taking the piss?"

"I'm sorry. It's just…"

"I know." I considered mentioning Luke then, but decided not to. I wasn't sure if he had anything to do with the change in Becky, in me, with the improvement in our relationship. But I didn't want to admit the possibility. Not to Charlie. Not to myself. "She's a bit better, that's all. She's off the medication. And she's looking after herself. You know, eating properly, washing, stuff like that."

"And you?"

"Dunno. I'm a bit more patient, I suppose. I try to listen to her, not just dismiss what she says out of hand."

"Big of you." His voice flattened and I remembered how he felt about Becky. I looked at him but he kept his eyes fixed on the river.

"I know it doesn't sound much…"

"Actually, it does." He gave a tight smile. "Good for you." I think he meant it.

"As you say, it's less than a week."

"But it's a start."

"It's a start," I agreed.

We walked past the Art College, some flats, a deli.

"What changed?" he said, as we turned right at a pub called Armstrong's, skirting a pair of bouncers in the process. The state of Armstrong's I thought they probably needed them to keep people in. "Why now?"

"Shall we go to the Ten Bell's?"

"Anything to do with that dude on the bridge?"

I stopped. "Why should it be?"

"I just wondered…"

"Don't."

He hesitated then said, "Did he jump? I didn't see anything in the papers, but…"

"No," I said. "He didn't jump."

Charlie nodded. We stood for a moment. Then he said, "Hey, you should have seen this chick last night. She so wanted me, man…"

We walked to the pub.

*

We found a corner table in the Ten Bells. I told Charlie about Helen and he shrugged and said he thought it was for the best. He was lying, of course. I think part of him always imagined Helen and I getting together, leaving him to save Becky. I'd probably had similar thoughts myself. Neither of us bothered to find out what Becky thought.

We spent half an hour discussing Charlie's love life. It was as complex and sordid as usual. Entertaining, though. Then we ticked the usual boxes; football, music, films. This led, as it always did, to Uma Thurman, who Charlie, inexplicably in my opinion, found irresistible.

By ten, though, I was getting restless. I realised I wanted to get home to Becky. Which was something of a first.

"You're turning into a lightweight," Charlie said. We stood on the pavement outside the Ten Bells.

I started to button my coat, decided against it. The night was milder still, far too warm for January.

"Could be," I said. I was pleasantly sober. Charlie had drunk considerably more than me and seemed vague and unfocused. I felt bad for him suddenly. "I'm sorry. I've buggered up your evening."

"Hey, the night's young," he said.

"That's right. Maybe you can scare up one of those women of yours. The list is long enough, after all."

"Always an option," he said. But his heart didn't appear to be in it. For a moment he looked lost, alone.

Then someone tapped me on the shoulder. I caught a whiff of sandalwood as I turned. Luke said, "Hi guys."

Charlie squinted at him. Then he pointed and started to say something, but instead Luke said to him, "Hey, no hard feelings. In your place I'd have done the same thing. We can't all be hero's like John here."

He was different again. All trace of campness had gone. His voice was loud and coarse. On the surface he appeared drunk, but I doubted that he was.

"We're just off," I said.

Luke clapped me on the shoulder and took a deep breath. "Odd weather, isn't it? And that smell. A bit like spunk. Like maybe God just had a wank."

A couple across the street turned to look and a big, bearded guy slowed as he passed and sneered into Luke's face.

"What is wrong with you?" I said.

"What?" Luke's eyes were wide open. "Don't act all offended, John. It's not as though you even believe in God."

"How the…"

"Don't bother denying it. How about you, Charlie? Do you believe in the Big Guy?"

"I believe you're a nut," Charlie said.

"But not a hypocrite, right? Not like you two." He was smiling. His voice was loud, but playful. "Lighten up. It's no big deal."

"What the fuck are you doing here?" I said.

"You're a hard man to find, John."

"Why are you…"

"I mean, Becky's a sweetheart, but…"

Before I could speak Charlie stepped past me and planted a hand on Luke's chest. "What about Becky?"

"Whoa," Luke said. He took a step back, his arms held wide. Everything about him seemed exaggerated, cartoon-like. Except the small, hard thing that glittered behind his eyes. "Easy, tiger. Becky's his wife. Am I right?"

Charlie drew back.

"What about Becky?" I said.

"We've had a couple of chats, that's all. Like I say; a sweetheart. By the look on your face you didn't get my messages?"

"Just say what you've got to say and fuck off."

He was close to me. He leant forward quickly and kissed me softly on the mouth. I was appalled but I didn't move. For a moment I thought I tasted something dark and foul. That may have been my imagination. Luke took a couple of steps backwards. His eyes shone with a lunatic light. He grinned enormously, as though he'd told a fantastic joke and I was the punch line.

Charlie tried to go for him but I held him back. Luke laughed once then turned and ran.

I wiped my mouth again and again.

Charlie said, "Jesus Christ."

I said nothing.

Charlie said, "Is he fucking around with Becky?"

"I don't know. I'll find out. I'll sort it."

Before he left me Charlie said, "Last Sunday? Still glad you stopped?"

"Sure," I said. "I'm glad I stopped. It's not giving the fucker a push that I regret."

I found Becky in the living room. She stood by an armchair, manoeuvring it a millimetre at a time.

"It's fine," I said.

"It isn't," she said. Her voice was small and intense. Her eyes were fixed on the chair as she tried to get it into exactly the right position.

"Sit down," I said.

"Not yet." She wore her black silk kimono and her hair was wet. Her face was rapt with concentration. She hadn't looked at me since I'd walked through the door.

"I know he called." I tried to keep my voice light, conversational. My mouth burned where Luke kissed me.

It was as though she hadn't heard me. She stood upright, backed away from the chair, squinting at it through her hands, like an artist getting a scene into perspective. "That's better."

"Becky," I said.

Her eyes flicked around the room, seeking out other inconsistencies. "I didn't speak to him. I just put the phone down."

"Why didn't you tell me?"

"I thought you'd be angry. You said I mustn't talk to him. But I didn't talk to him. I put the phone down." Her voice was flatter than the Fens. The words chopped up, laid out in a line.

"He said something about a message."

Her eyes were as large as a child's as they found mine. "No."

"You mean…"

"He didn't leave a message."

"Ok."

"You believe me, don't you?"

"Of course."

"Don't you?" Again, as though I hadn't spoken. She stood with her hands clenched together in front of her. Her whole body quivered.

I wondered where the real Becky had gone; the Becky I'd held the night before and who'd held me back. The one I'd looked forward to coming home to. Perhaps this was the real Becky. It's not as though I've ever really known.

I stepped forward, held her shoulders gently. "Of course I believe you, Becky."

She started crying.

I held her for as long as she'd let me, which wasn't long, and then we sat at opposite ends of the sofa.

"You should go to bed," I said. "You look exhausted."

"Can't. My hair's still wet." She ran a hand through it absently.

"Why did you wash it so late?"

"You like it clean, you said. When it smells nice. I washed it five times today, just to be sure."

I stood. "I'll get us some hot chocolate, then. While we wait for it to dry."

I must have moved the sofa slightly because when I brought our drinks into the living room she was still trying to get it back into position.

I woke late. My head felt thick and woolly, as though I'd drunk heavily or been drugged. Becky sat on the edge of the bed, watching me. She was dressed. There was something in the calculated emptiness of her expression that frightened me a little.

"What time is it?" I said.

"Just after ten."

After a moment I said, "What is it?"

"Luke was here."

I sat up. "When?"

"A little while ago."

I slid out of bed and started to dress. Becky's gaze remained on my pillow, as though I hadn't moved at all. "Why didn't you wake me?"

"He told me not to." Her voice was matter of fact. I felt old and slow and stupid. I tried to think but found that it hurt so I stopped. Easier to accept that nothing made sense anymore. I started to look for a clean shirt, then realised I didn't give a shit so I slipped on the one I'd worn the day before.

"He kissed me," Becky said.

"What?" I stopped buttoning my shirt. I put my hand on her chin and tilted her head until she faced me.

Her eyes widened as she saw the expression on my face. "I couldn't stop him. It was just a peck. That's all." She wrinkled her nose. "It tasted...bad."

I thought of how quick he'd been the previous night. I let my hand drop from her face. "What else did he do?"

"Nothing. Honestly. I thought he was going to, for a moment, at least. I suppose he could have done. He had me backed against the wall in the hallway."

"Why didn't you shout?"

"He told me not to. I was scared, John."

The spaced-out vagueness that had enveloped her the night before seemed to have gone. I supposed that was a good thing. I was no longer sure.

"I've been sat on the bed for the last hour, waiting for you to wake up."

"Why did you wait, Becky?"

Her head dipped and I stroked her hair. "I'm scared of you too, John."

I sat on the bed and held her.

We went downstairs. I put my coat on.

"Where are you going?" Becky said.

"I'd better try and find him. Or go to the police. I can't just leave..."

She grabbed my sleeve. "It's ok. I think we've seen the last of him."

"Why?"

"After...after he kissed me he said that he was sorry. That was why he came round. To apologise. To both of us."

"Right. So why didn't he let you wake me?"

"He couldn't face you, he said."

I grunted.

"I believe him, John. Really. He said that someone he loved had died suddenly, violently. He couldn't get over it. He wasn't himself, he said. He thought we'd both like the real Luke."

"I somehow doubt it. Was that it?"

She shrugged and smiled. "Pretty much. He ran on a bit about this girl, about how they used to go for walks along Cromer beach, drink coffee on the front. I mean, winter beaches, how original. I don't know..."

Her smile froze when she saw my face. "This girl. Did he mention a name?"

"Yeah. She was called Helen. Why?"

It was raining hard when I parked on a double yellow line a few doors down from Helen's house. I'd tried her mobile every five minutes during the drive to Cromer but could only reach her voicemail. Becky had let me go without a word. I kissed her cold cheek and said I'd explain when I got home. She didn't look as though she believed me. I didn't blame her.

I was half-soaked by the time I got to Helen's door. I knocked hard ten or twelve times but got no reply. I stood on the step and stared at the bright red door as if it might give me some sort of clue what to do next. Something caught my peripheral vision and I turned my head to the right to see two figures, blurred by the rain, approaching hesitantly. They stopped as they reached the gate and I turned to face them.

"John?" Helen said as she pulled the hood of her anorak down. Her blond hair was immediately drenched and flattened against her scalp.

It was an immense relief to see her. I also felt utterly, exquisitely stupid.

It was Dominic she was with, obviously. I didn't hang around long enough to even get a look at him. I just mumbled an apology, ignored the look of concerned bemusement on Helen's face and got the fuck out of there.

It was uncomfortable driving home. My clothes were soaked and, consequently, so was the driver's seat. The inside of the windscreen kept fogging up. All I could seem to find on the radio was a political debate or something about gardening or music by some bloody boy band or other.

When my mobile rang I thought it would be a welcome distraction. I was wrong.

"Did you really think I'd hurt her?" Luke said.

After a moment I said, "What am I supposed to think?"

"That's cold, John."

"Can we stop this now? You told Becky it was over…"

"Sweet Becky. She'll believe anything, won't she? Quite endearing, really. There's a bit of chemistry there, believe me. Between Becky and I. No offence, of course."

"There's something missing, isn't there, Luke? Maybe you were dropped on the head as a baby, maybe…well, whatever. We'll just agree you need help. But that's not my problem. But I promise you, bother us again and I'll find you and I'll shove your head so far up your fucking arse…"

"I'm trembling, John. I'm all a quiver." His voice dropped to a whisper. "She doesn't know about Helen, does she?"

I said nothing. I wanted to ask if he'd told her. I wanted to beg him not to. I did neither. The rain was so hard now I could hardly see where I was going. I pulled over to the side of the road and turned the engine off.

"That's pretty poor, John. What's a relationship without trust, without honesty?"

"Why are you doing this? I…saved your life. I stopped, at least." I heard my own voice, judged how pathetic it sounded and mentally shot myself in the head.

"I know." He sounded different again. I thought I heard something in the background. "It's nearly over." His voice flat-lined and I felt the hairs on my neck stiffen. "We're getting to the vinegar strokes now, John."

Again I thought I heard something. A voice maybe, muffled.

"Where are you?" I said.

The line hissed for a moment then he broke the connection.

I started the car again and pulled onto the road without checking for oncoming traffic.

When I got home Becky had gone. I flailed around the empty house looking for her. As though she might be hiding in a cupboard. Upstairs I found that most of her clothes were missing along with all of her underwear. But her medication was still in the bathroom cabinet and, in the tumbler on the hand basin, her pink toothbrush leant against mine.

There was a note on the coffee table on the living room. It said simply, 'I know'. Becky had signed her name with an 'i'.

The room smelled faintly of sandalwood. The sofa and one of the armchairs were at least six inches out of position.

My adult mind spoke to me in a quiet, sane voice. It told me that everything could be easily explained. It reminded me gently of the things I had to do. Practical things; like calling the police and speaking to Becky's parents. That was where she'd be, the voice told me. Almost certainly.

As these thoughts continued, mannered and reasonable, I ran out of the front door into the indifferent rain. I stopped at the gate. I grabbed hold of the cold metal and called her name again and again.

More quality fiction from Elastic Press

The Virtual Menagerie	Andrew Hook	SOLD OUT
Open The Box	Andrew Humphrey	SOLD OUT
Second Contact	Gary Couzens	SOLD OUT
Sleepwalkers	Marion Arnott	SOLD OUT
Milo & I	Antony Mann	SOLD OUT
The Alsiso Project	Edited by Andrew Hook	SOLD OUT
Jung's People	Kay Green	SOLD OUT
The Sound of White Ants	Brian Howell	SOLD OUT
Somnambulists	Allen Ashley	SOLD OUT
Angel Road	Steven Savile	SOLD OUT
Visits to the Flea Circus	Nick Jackson	SOLD OUT
The Elastic Book of Numbers	Edited by Allen Ashley	SOLD OUT
The Life To Come	Tim Lees	SOLD OUT
Trailer Park Fairy Tales	Matt Dinniman	SOLD OUT
The English Soil Society	Tim Nickels	£5.99
The Last Days of Johnny North	David Swann	SOLD OUT
The Ephemera	Neil Williamson	SOLD OUT
Unbecoming	Mike O'Driscoll	£6.99
Photocopies of Heaven	Maurice Suckling	SOLD OUT
Extended Play	Edited by Gary Couzens	£6.99
So Far, So Near	Mat Coward	£5.99
Going Back	Tony Richards	£5.99
That's Entertainment	Robert Neilson	£5.99
The Cusp of Something	Jai Clare	£5.99
Other Voices	Andrew Humphrey	£5.99

All these books are available at your local bookshop or can be ordered direct from the publisher. Indicate the number of copies required and fill in the form below.

Name_____

(Block letters please)

Address_____

Send to Elastic Press, 85 Gertrude Road, Norwich, Norfolk, NR3 4SG.
Please enclose remittance to the value of the cover price plus: £1.50 for the first book plus 50p per copy for each additional book ordered to cover postage and packing. Applicable in the UK only.

While every effort is made to keep prices low, it is sometimes necessary to increase prices at short notice. Elastic Press reserve the right to show on covers and charge new retail prices which may differ from those advertised in the text or elsewhere.

Want to be kept informed? Keep up to date with Elastic Press titles by writing to the above address, or by visiting www.elasticpress.com and adding your email details to our online mailing list.

Elastic Press: Winner of the British Fantasy Society Best Small Press award 2005

Previously from Elastic Press

That's Entertainment by Robert Neilson

What if John Lennon had been kicked out of the Beatles? What if Elvis' twin brother had survived? What if we could go back in time to give reality TV a historical perspective? What if the Pope was Irish, a gambler, and needed to bet on a dead cert? In Neilson's science fiction, fantasy lives just around the corner from reality.

A great new talent in storytelling – Anne McCaffrey

Previously from Elastic Press

The Cusp of Something by Jai Clare

Jai Clare's stories are filled with the disaffected, those who kick against their everyday lives, who crave the mystic when seeking their spirituality, and who are desperate to be alone as much as they are desperate to be with someone. Finding meaning in the universal and the personal, through transient sex or emotional depth, her characters stand on the brink of discovery, laid bare to misfortune and fortune.

A courageously inventive writer – Jim Crace

For further information visit:
www.elasticpress.com

Forthcoming from Elastic Press

Another Santana Morning by Mike Dolan

This is a book about magic. It is also about love...and other emotions. But mainly it concerns those moments when suddenly we become aware of the magical aspects of the world, when we catch a glimpse of reality's other side, peering through ordinary barriers, past a split in the sky, into somewhere else, where we might find something wondrous.

> *...fresh and untried and interrogative...* – Chaz Brenchley

Forthcoming from Elastic Press

Binding Energy by Daniel Marcus

Marcus maps out possible futures and theoretical pasts, crisscrossing reality with fantasy, and weaving intricate storylines in the process. His characters are frightened and fragile, facing brave new worlds whilst retaining their humanity. If you want to know what the future really looks like, then look here.

This is Science Fiction of the highest level. The stores ring with authenticity. The language is sharp and funny and unflinching. The science crackles – Michael Blumlein, World Fantasy Award finalist

For further information visit:
www.elasticpress.com

Extended Play:
The Elastic Book of Music

What does music do for you? Is it an art form, mood enhancer, or just something to jump around to? From the orchestra pit to the mosh pit music inspires our lives, is universal and personal, futuristic yet primordial. As the soundtrack trigger to a thousand memories it can be seductive yet soulful, energetic and prophetic. But the immediacy of music has rarely been exploited within literature. Until now...

With fiction from Marion Arnott, Becky Done, Andrew Humphrey, Emma Lee, Tim Nickels, Rosanne Rabinowitz, Philip Raines, Tony Richards, Nels Stanley, and Harvey Welles.

Accompanying the stories, songwriters comment on how fiction has influenced their music, with contributions from JJ Burnel, Gary Lightbody, Chris Stein, Sean "Grasshopper Mackowiak, Lene Lovich, Chris T-T, Rebekah Delgado, Tall Poppies, jof owen, and Iain Ross.

www.elasticpress.com

We Want Your Stories!

Elastic Press is currently open for submissions to "Subtle Edens: The Elastic Book of Slipstream" to be edited by Allen Ashley, the award-winning editor of our previous anthology, "The Elastic Book of Numbers".

Full guidelines can be viewed on our website.

"Subtle Edens - The Elastic Book of Slipstream" - anthology.
Allen Ashley requires:
Original Slipstream stories up to 5000 words.
Payment: via Contributor copy / copies.
Response Time: 8 weeks.
Opening date: 1st June 2007.
Closing date: 29 February 2008.
Send "Disposable" hard copy manuscripts to:
Allen Ashley, Editor - "Subtle Edens", 110 Marlborough Road, Bounds Green, London N22 8NN, England.

All email enqiuries to Allen at:

editorsubtleedens@hotmail.co.uk

The British Fantasy Society exists to promote and enjoy the genres of fantasy, science fiction and horror in all its forms. We are well supported by the publishing industry and have many well known authors among our members, not least our president, Ramsey Campbell, who says: "This is an invitation to you to join the community of the fantastic. Many years ago, when I was a struggling writer and a vociferous fan, I tried to convince people that we admirers of fantasy needed a society to bring us together for fun and for sharing our ideas, and I don't know of a better such organisation than the British Fantasy Society..."

We hold regular Open Nights which are open to all, not just our members, and these are listed on our website, http://www.britishfantasysociety.org.uk, as well as in our bi-monthly news magazine, *Prism*. We also publish a bi-annual fiction magazine, *Dark Horizons*. Once a year, we hold our main convention, FantasyCon, an event that is always well attended by known and unknown alike. Recent Guests of Honour include Clive Barker, Neil Gaiman, Raymond E. Feist, Juliet E. McKenna, Robert Holdstock, Steven Erikson, not to mention our president, Ramsey Campbell.

Subscriptions: £25 (UK), £30 (Europe), £45 (Rest of World)p.a. Membership entitles you to six free issues of Prism, two of Dark Horizons, and free copies of all BFS Special Publications, also discounted attendance at BFS events. Cheques should be made payable to: British Fantasy Society, The British Fantasy Society, 36 Town End, Cheadle, STAFFS, ST10 1PF England. Or you can join online at the BFS Cyberstore: http://www.britishfantasysociety.org.uk/shop/info.htm.